CREEP

MONSTERS IN US DUET BOOK ONE

MARIE ANN

TRIGGER WARNING

This book is a dark romance and has dark themes. As such it is only recommended for those 18 and older. There will be swearing, mentions of drug use, and sexual situations that could be hard for some to read. There are triggering topics so if you have many triggers this book may not be for you.

Copyright © 2021 by Marie Ann
All rights reserved.
No part of this book may be reproduced in any form or by any electronic or mechanical means, including information storage and retrieval systems, without written permission from the author, except for the use of brief quotations in a book review.

Formatting and Cover by Studio Four Twelve
Edited by Briggs Consulting, LLC
Proof Read by OnBrand Author Services

PLAYLIST

CREEP — RADIOHEAD
CREEP - ELDEST !!
GHOST — BADFLOWER
NEVER SATISFIED - CORPSE
NAILS — CALL ME KARIZMA
PRISON - PR0LMS
CHOP SUEY! — SYSTEM OF A DOWN
LUNA - SHINIGAMI
I FEEL LIKE I'M DROWNING — TWO FEET
NO WAY OUT - THE WORD ALIVE

"Words have no power to **impress** *the mind without the* **exquisite horror** *of their* **reality**"

—Edgar Allen Poe

*To those who have had to grow up around **addiction** and **abuse**. Know that it **does get better**. You are **not alone**. There **is hope**.*
*And to my **sister**.*
We fucking survived.

Twinkle, Twinkle, little star.
How I wonder what you are.
Up above the world so high,
Like a diamond in the sky.
Twinkle, Twinkle, little star,
How I wonder what you are.

PROLOGUE

ESSA

EIGHT YEARS OLD

I sit outside, staring at the sky, like I have been for the last two years. It is a nice night out, no breeze or clouds in sight, but I still have a blanket wrapped around my arms for comfort. It is my mother's, a purple, ratty looking thing, but she refuses to throw it away. These nights are my favorite because I can see every star, and the more stars I can see, the more could hear my wishes. I don't know why my wishes aren't coming true, but I have to keep trying. I have to do whatever I can to save Holley and me.

Mom and Dad are always acting so strange. They are never home, but when they are, they are so mean to us. We never have enough food to keep our bellies full so my stomach always hurts. Thinking about not eating today makes me rub my belly to ease the ache. I am so hungry. *So, so hungry.*

I lie down on the grass, continuing to stare at the stars and repeating the same words over and over. *Twinkle, twinkle, little star. Save us. Someone please come save us.*

MARIE ANN

Sometimes I will even whisper out loud to the sky, in hopes they can hear me better that way. That's what I had done again tonight. Except I think my father heard me, because out of nowhere, I see him stalking towards me. From the direction he is ambling from, it means he is coming from the neighbor's house down the road. That's where my parents are always at because those neighbors do bad things too.

"Hey sweetheart. What are you doing out here? Aren't you supposed to be in bed?" He sits down next to me on the grass, putting his hand on my leg, which is right next to his. I sit up and glance over at him while twisting my fingers together nervously. I don't want to get into trouble for being outside this late at night because when I do something he doesn't like, he always spanks me, really *really* hard. Sometimes he even leaves bruises, so him catching me scares me a lot.

"I'm sorry, Daddy. I couldn't sleep, so I came out to look at the stars." I can't tell him I was wishing on them to get us out of here 'cause I know it would make him very angry. Daddy is really scary when he's angry.

"You can't be outside by yourself at night, Essa Jaymes. Bad things happen to little girls who are outside by themselves at night." He looks over at me and smiles. But something's wrong. Daddy never smiles at me. *Never.* I feel goosebumps on my arms, making me shiver. I don't like this.

"I'm really sorry. I'll go to bed now." I start to get up when he squeezes my leg hard, forcing me to stay sitting down.

"You're going to stay right here, Essa. I'm not done with you yet." He shoves me down and I make an *oomph* sound as my body hits the ground, my head hitting hard against the earth below. I attempt to sit

CREEP

up, but he shoves me down again, keeping his hand on my chest.

"Daddy, what are you doing? Please let me up, this hurts. My head hurts, Daddy." I plead with him as I struggle to keep the tears from my eyes, attempting to be strong, but it's impossible. He squeezes my leg even harder as he shoves them apart. I try to pull them back together, but he moves his hand from my chest to my face, pushing down.

"Quit fucking moving, child," he growls at me. He stares into my eyes and I freeze. They are so black. He looks like a demon. My heart starts to race, and fear coats my entire body.

Oh no. Oh no. Please stars, please stop my daddy. He's hurting me so bad. I wish to the stars with all my might.

His hands move to my sleep shorts, shoving them to the side as his fingers rub against my underwear. I wriggle away from his touch but he slaps me across my face, causing me to scream out in pain. He then yanks the blanket out from underneath me and shoves part of it into my mouth to stifle any noise I might make.

"You need to shut the fuck up, you little fucking tease. You make any more noise and this will be so much fucking worse for you. I've been waiting for you for years and tonight's the night. Walking around in your little shorts and tank tops, tempting me to touch you. You knew what you were doing, didn't you? Well, I'm done listening to your fucking mother and I'm done waiting."

Wait, mother? What does he mean my mother? And what does he mean waiting?

I'm so confused, all these thoughts swirling in my head, but I soon forget them when I feel his fingers in my underwear and then a sudden, ripping fire between my legs. I scream at the intrusion, more tears

MARIE ANN

flooding my eyes and running down my face. I struggle to fight my father off, but with his large palm covering most of my face, he easily shoves my head to the side and into the dirt.

I continue to scream through the blanket in my mouth while flailing my body in a futile attempt to stop him; to stop the agonizing pain he's bringing me, but it's no use. The next thing I know, he's hovering over me and ripping my shorts off. *No. No. No!*

I scream with everything in me, not knowing what else to do when he can overpower me so easily, but I have to try something. He slaps me, hard. My head jars and black dots jump into my vision. My head feels like it's underwater. Everything is fuzzy and sounds are muffled. I feel as my body grows limp, my eyelids drooping shut. I plead with myself to stay awake, to keep fighting him, but it's impossible.

I'm not strong enough.

I can't help the blood curdling scream that tears from my throat, the sound loud enough to make more than a muffled noise through the blanket in my mouth.

The pain.

So. Much. Pain.

My head feels light and I'm being pulled under a blanket of darkness, and he must notice because he grabs my throat and squeezes, stopping any noise from leaving me and also keeping me from being able to breathe. The loss of air into my lungs makes me snap my eyes open. The panic of dying sets in and the darkness retreats.

"Stay the fuck awake. I want you to feel this because this is what you fucking get for teasing me all these years." I can sense him moving over me, his breath crawling across the skin of my neck like

CREEP

a cockroach. I turn my head and look up at the stars, disconnecting myself from my body and the pain.

Save me please, stars. Please send someone to save me. Please. I'm begging you. I repeat in my head over and over again while I struggle to breathe. Pleading to the stars to save me. This can't be happening. I don't want to be here. It hurts so much. Why would my daddy hurt me like this? What did I do wrong? What's wrong with me?

After lying underneath him for what feels like forever, more pieces of me dying by the second, I hear my father grunt and then the absence of his body over mine. He stands up, zips his pants, then reaches down to touch me. I flinch and cower away when I feel his fingertips graze my cheek in an endearing manner.

"You were so fucking perfect sweetheart, just like I knew you'd be. You're such a little spitfire. It's going to make our time together much more fun." I can't help the vomit that shoots up my throat at his words. I manage to spit the blanket out of my mouth and roll my head to the side just as I throw up everything in my stomach, which isn't much, so I end up puking stomach bile. My throat now burns even more than it already did. Disgusted, my father yanks himself away and stands, hovering over me.

"Get the fuck up and get inside. I don't want anyone finding you out here." He turns and walks back toward the neighbors as if nothing happened, without a care in the world.

Not wanting to be outside alone ever again, I barely manage to shift to my knees before crying out, but I bite my lip to stifle the noise. Everything hurts. My body, my heart, my soul. A crushing weight refuses to let me up. Pain radiates throughout my entire body, making

5

it impossible for me to move. I stare at the stars, wondering why. Why me?

    And that's when I realize the truth.

    The stars aren't going to save me.

    No one will save me.

    I'm all alone.

    My body finally succumbs to everything I have endured and everything goes black.

CHAPTER ONE
ESSA

"Get the fuck out of my house, you piece of shit! I hate you!"

I can hear my mom and dad screaming back and forth, like they have been for the past twenty minutes. Actually, it's probably been longer, but I'm used to it by now so I lose track of how long it goes on.

Their screams echo through the thin walls surrounding me. Same shit, different day. *Happy birthday to me, I guess.* You'd think since it was my birthday, my eighteenth to be exact, my parents would get their heads out of their asses and actually be parents for a day, but I don't have those parents. Well, I would never expect it from Ben. I was pathetically hopeful my mother would, but that day will never come. She's never been a mother to me before, so why would she start now?

It's been this way all my life, but it still hurts, nonetheless. My parents prefer their little magic baggie full of dope. For as long as I can remember they have always been high out of their fucking minds. Or when they're not high, they're sleeping it off until they regain the energy to go out again. What else is there to do when you run out of drugs?

Whenever Holley and I get frustrated with them, they always feel it's appropriate to throw it in our faces that at least we have a roof over our heads and water to drink and bathe in. Saying we should be grateful because there are kids out there who have it far worse than we do, as if their struggle somehow makes ours okay.

Like, gee, thanks Mom and Dad. We have the bare minimum of basic necessities—not including fucking food—and you want to try and make it appear okay by saying we should be grateful we're not on the streets?

But what can I do to fix it? Absolutely nothing because my "father" makes sure I can't. He knows just the trick to keep my mouth shut, so we're fucking stuck here, and it makes me feel more and more useless every single day that goes by living in this hell on earth.

Sinking further into the deepest pits of my depression, I sit here contemplating my shitty life and the lack of options I have to change any of it. I hear the front door slam and my mom starts crying. I don't particularly care she's crying, but I should go see if she's doing anything stupid. I'll take every opportunity I get to make sure she doesn't get high, even though it never works in my favor. She just happens to be the lesser of two evils, though not by much. Ninety percent of the time, she's the one starting the damn fights between them and blames everyone but herself, especially me. I swear she thrives on the drama of it.

I creak open my bedroom door, which I made myself out of plywood. It was that—so I could have some semblance of privacy—or nothing at all. I chose the plywood even though my room is the size of a large closet. I can't complain too much about the size though, because at least I have my own space—space away from everyone and everything. A space where I can drop the mask I wear every day and finally be my fucking self.

I step out into the hallway and quietly make my way toward my parents' bedroom. I know my mom is in there without having to look anywhere else because she's always in her room. We rarely ever see her outside of it when she decides she wants to be home for a change. The door is cracked so I decide to peek through the gap and be nosey because I have the right to be. I need to be aware of everything going on in this house so I can take the necessary measures to protect Holley.

My nose scrunches in disgust but I already knew she'd be getting high. *What a shocker.* She's sitting on the side of her bed halfway covered up with her ratty ass pale purple blanket. *That fucking blanket.* The all too familiar feeling of panic begins to set in. My ears begin to ring and blood rushes to my head, causing me to sway on my feet.

I rest my hand against the wall to steady myself and take a deep breath, over and over.

Fight it. Fight through it. You're not there, you're here—inside. You're okay.

I scoff, but manage to bring myself back to the now. I'm most definitely not okay, but that's beside the point. I'm alive and I'm no longer there. That's what matters in this moment.

I'm going to light the fucking blanket on fire. Preferably with it wrapped around her body as the flames devour them both.

Steeling my spine and taking another deep breath, I peer back through the door. She grips a glass pipe in her right hand while holding

MARIE ANN

a silver mini blow torch in the other. She sits with her eyes fixated on the objects in her hands. I look over to her fixated gaze and for a second, I imagine I can see regret in them. Maybe even indecision. It gives me hope, but that hope lasts only for a split second, because in the next, it shatters into a million fucking pieces when she brings the fucking pipe to her lips and lights it, seemingly, without a care in the world. She takes a massive hit, then slowly sets the pipe back down and closes her eyes with a big, fat fucking smile on her face.

Disgusting, pathetic excuse of a fucking mother.

An immense pressure radiates throughout my torso and I bring the palm of my hand to the center of my chest, attempting to rub the pain away. After all of the years of hell I have endured, I didn't think I had any pieces of my heart left to break, but I still find myself standing in her doorway, watching my mother choose drugs yet again.

No matter how many times I witness it, which is more than I'd ever admit, it always hurts the same. I tell myself every single time she lets me down, this will be the last time I will cry over her—over them—and what they put us through. Yet, I stand here, at the cusp of another break down. My eyes burn with unshed tears, but I refuse to release them over her. Fuck her and fuck them both for choosing their addiction over us. I don't know how much longer I can deal with their problems. I'm losing my mind.

Unable to stomach being in the same vicinity as her any longer, I retreat to my bedroom, or literally any fucking where else as long as it's away from her, but I halt my movements when I hear the front door slam so hard against the wall, it shakes the fucking house. *This night just got even more entertaining—and not in a good way.*

CREEP

I have a feeling tonight's going to be downright grim—but it's not just a feeling—it's a fucking fact. My parents fought, Ben left, and now he's back in an even worse mood than he left in.

It's moments like these I miss wishing on the stars. They gave me the hope I needed to stay strong, but no. They got ripped from me just like everything else did.

I take a much needed deep breath, making the effort to prepare myself to deal with my father—if I can even call him that. He's not biologically my father, which I found out a few days after the first time.

I had been lying in bed for days, not eating, not drinking, just lying there, broken. He came into my room and I can still remember the instant terror I felt deep in my soul. He fucking terrified me, but I stayed silent. He sat next to me and began rubbing my leg, from thigh to knee, inching higher on each swipe of his hand. Too frozen to move, I just scrunched my eyes shut, struggling to block out his touch.

He brought his hand to my face and pulled it towards him. "Essa, I need to talk to you." I didn't answer, hoping if I didn't, he would just leave. "The other night was one of the best nights of my life, sweetheart. You are so fucking sweet, but I need you to know something. I am not your biological father. I'm not sure if you know what that means, but you've always been pretty smart, so maybe you do. Anyway, it means I'm not your real father.

"Your whore of a mother fucked some guy for drugs shortly after Holley was born and she got pregnant with you. You were never wanted, but I just wanted to tell you, for the first time since you were born, I'm happy you're here 'cause now you can finally be mine."

Everything he told me caused my head to spin. He wasn't my real

MARIE ANN

father? Who was then? Why did he hurt me? Why did he say "I'm his" now?

I was so confused and his hand on me was not helping. It made me feel dirty all over again. The tears welled, then fell down my cheeks. I couldn't help them from falling, it was all too much.

I frantically shake my head in hopes of distorting my thoughts and make my way to the kitchen to make sure it's actually Ben who is here and not some druggie my mom invited over to fuck—which actually happens a lot believe it or not.

My father walks into the kitchen and my feet stutter in their tracks when I spot the look on his face. A look telling me he wants to fucking kill someone—that someone being my mother or probably even me at this point. My life is a whole ass fucking party.

I muster up every ounce of strength I have left and look Benjamin in the eyes, trying to decipher his mood. I don't know why I try, because he leers at me with eyes so cold and dark, they see right through me. Goosebumps run up my arms to my neck.

Fear.

It's my constant companion and has been for the past ten years. It has decided it's not leaving me tonight, or anytime soon for that matter. Ben doesn't speak a word to me as he shoves his way past me, making his way to his room. I suck a deep breath into my lungs as I try to calm the tension radiating over my entire body. I fucking hate being afraid, because it makes me feel like a coward.

I know as soon as he sees my mom in their room getting high he's going to lose his shit and surprise surprise, I'm right. I walk behind him, ever the mediator, ready to jump in and stop their fight from becoming a catastrophe Holley will become involved in. I hate being the one to deal with this shit, but it's my job. Holley may be older than me—only by a year—but ever since that night, I have felt the burden of our family has fallen on my shoulders.

Still to this day, she has no idea what happened to me, or what continues to happen, and I do everything in my power to keep it that way. It's not something she should ever feel laden with when there is nothing that can be done about it. What's done is done. My one goal for the night is to keep Ben and Sierra's fighting to a minimum, and to keep Holley from waking up. I don't want her to end up in the middle of their drama. I love my sister more than anything, but she can't cope or deal with the bullshit our parents spew. She's too damn positive and too damn forgiving. Which means it all ends up falling to me.

When he gets to their door, he kicks it open. The door smacks against the drywall and the handle leaves a dent in the wall. Once I'm close enough, I take in my mom flying around the room. Shit is strewn everywhere and she's mumbling to herself saying some shit like she's looking for the wires she knows the Feds planted in their room. *Always on the bullshit about the Feds. As if they give a shit about a couple of lowlife drug addicts.*

Even across the room I can tell her pupils are blown, showing nothing but black. *Jesus fucking Christ, how much did she smoke?* When I saw her not even five minutes ago, she wasn't high yet. But then again, she was left alone with a full baggie and no Ben around to help smoke it.

Benjamin takes one look around the room with pure disdain in his eyes before he begins screaming and flailing his arms around the room as he storms toward her. "You stupid fucking bitch! Did you smoke all my shit?"

"What the hell are you talking about, Benny? I haven't done a single damn thing but wait for you to get back! You left me, you piece of shit!" My mother screams right back at him. *The screaming match has begun.*

"Ohhh. You don't know what I'm talking about, huh, Sierra? Always running your goddamn mouth. Why don't you just shut the fuck up and give me my shit you better still have. Can't deal with you fuckin' sober." He storms over to their bed where the pipe lays and picks it up, checking to see if it's still loaded. Without a care in the world, he brings the torch to the rounded end and starts smoking it right in front of me. Usually, they try to avoid doing anything around Holley and I, thank fuck, but apparently he doesn't give a shit tonight.

"Are y'all fucking kidding me right now? You're screaming at each other at the top of your lungs about getting high when Holley is right down the hall? We all already know you don't give a shit about me, but Holley doesn't need to hear this bullshit and you fucking know it.

"I get you don't give a fuck about anything but putting that glass dick in your mouths. But, you should at least respect Holley. We are all aware her knowing what's going on will just make our lives far more complicated than they need to be!" I shoot my eyes over to Ben as the last of the words leave my mouth. I want him to know I'm talking about him, but I know he already does.

My chest is heaving as if I ran a marathon, my anger consuming me, but my anger is quickly replaced with the ever loved feeling of fear. It seeps back into my pores full force because I just did something so fucking stupid and I know I'm going to pay for it later.

My father flings his demon eyes over to mine, squints, and cocks his head to the side. All I can see is the rage in them. Rage somehow strong enough to override the high he just gave himself.

"What was that, Essa? What the fuck did you say, *sweetheart?*" He sneers that nickname, his lip turning up in disgust at the same time.

Oh fuck. Fuck, fuck, fuck. I royally fucked up by losing my temper and running my mouth. I've always struggled with keeping my mouth shut and I'm regretting it right about now.

The only time that nickname leaves his mouth in reference to me is when he wants to hurt me. He stalks forward, advancing on me. Every step forward of his, is one step backwards for me. I don't know where to move to because there is nowhere I can hide where he won't find me.

Still advancing towards me, I push myself up against the wall in a pathetic effort to get as far away from him as possible. He takes one last step, stopping right in front of me. His chest brushes against mine, more so with every heaving breath leaving me. A sick smirk appears on his face when he notices. He leans his head closer to look at me right in my pale green eyes. His are surprisingly focused despite the drugs coursing through him at the moment.

"Oh, *sweetheart*. You never fucking learn to keep your mouth shut about shit not concerning you. So guess who's gonna pay you a little visit tonight? It's been way too long since daddy has gotten to stick his dick in your sweet little pussy and it's missing you." He chuckles in my face, his rancid breath fanning me. I dry heave at his words and my stomach churns with the need to vomit, but it doesn't deter him. My vomit never fucking does.

"Tonight is going to be a fun one." He licks the shell of my ear as he pulls away. My face burns as bile rises up my throat and I throw my head to the side just in time to throw up all over the hallway floor. I dry heave when my stomach completely empties. A cold sweat breaks out across my forehead and my entire body feels clammy.

When he sees, he smiles wider. *Fucking disgusting pig.*

Keeping the creepy ass smile on his sunken in cheeks, he trails his grimy finger down my cheek, to my chin, and down my throat.

"Tonight, I'll be paying you a well-deserved visit because I've fucking *missed* you, sweetheart. So, make sure you wait up for me." He kisses my cheek and pushes off of the wall at my back to spin back around to his bed. He picks the pipe up again, staring at me with a smirk on his face as he lifts it to his mouth and flicks the torch on.

I swivel around and slam the door behind me, completely terrified and crawling out of my skin in disgust. An everlasting feeling which resides deep in my bones. Every time he puts his hands on me, I feel his disgusting touch linger, imbedding itself inside of me. I desperately need a shower and to scrub my skin raw. No, better yet, I need pain. *Yes, I need to feel the pain.*

But first I clean up the vomit in the hallway—I can't leave a fucking mess.

When I get to Holley's room, which is thankfully at the other end of the hallway from our parents' room, I crack the door open to check on her. She's curled up in a ball on her twin bed, lightly snoring.

There are only two beds in this house, Holley's and my parents. I mainly sleep in my room, but I'll occasionally crash in Holl's bed with her when my parents have their druggie friends over. I don't trust them not to go into her room and fuck with her, so I always make an excuse to sleep with her when it happens. She never questions my intentions.

When we found her twin mattress at a garage sale for ten bucks a few months ago, Holl tried to argue with me to get me to take the bed, but I vehemently refused. She deserves it and I made her take it, not giving her a choice in the matter.

It took me three months to save up the ten dollars from loose change I scrounged up from around the house or the occasional dollar my dumbass high parents left around, but I did it. I don't regret it either. Holl is the good one and she's always happy and blissfully unaware. I don't *think* she's ignorant about what's going on with them, but I do believe she wants to pretend she is, so I let her. It makes both of our lives a little easier that way.

Not wanting to wake her up, I slowly pull her door shut and make my way to my room. It's small and cramped, but it's the only place I have any alone time, so I cherish it. It's the only place Benjamin doesn't come to bother me, surprisingly, which is the main reason I'm always in my room.

I plop my ass down on the lumpy comforter I have lying on the floor, which makes up my bed. I grab my old school iPod and pop the earbuds in. I stole the iPod from some rich kid at school a couple years ago because it's not like he'd miss it. Besides, the dude was a fucking asshole and he deserved it.

MARIE ANN

I spin my finger around a few times on the circle of buttons in the middle, searching for my favorite song. I hit play on "Creep" by Radiohead and turn it on repeat. I close my eyes and lean my head against the wall, resisting the urge to cut even though I really don't want to.

Everything about this song speaks to my soul. How often do people find a song, one fucking song, that is one hundred percent them? It's about someone who feels a massive amount of self-loathing—someone who hates the person they have become. We spend so much time trying to appear as the brightest light in the room, when in reality, we all have our shadows. We *are* the fucking shadows, and we have our own demons fighting and crawling their way to the surface, changing us and who we used to be into someone unrecognizable.

This song sums up all of my self-loathing to a T and my heart physically hurts because of it. I hate feeling like this, wanting to die, needing to hurt myself to stay barely alive. Guilt wracks me daily because of Holley. She doesn't deserve a sister who thinks about death and dying as much as I do. She deserves someone strong enough to conquer all of this for her.

I'm battling this shit in my head more than anyone could ever know. I fight tooth and nail to stay strong, but sometimes we give in to the temptation of our weaknesses. I just happen to be someone who gives in on a daily basis.

The pressure of today's bullshit boils over the precipice and I *need* the fucking pain to survive the rest of the night because I know it's far from over. I crave it more than anything else.

I peel my eyes open and peer down at my arm, seeing all of my

CREEP

previous cuts. Some new and raw, others healed with silvery scars remaining as a reminder of how fucking weak I am. Guilt consumes me. I'm a fucking failure of a sister, of a daughter, of a fucking human being. There are millions of people with shitty lives and shitty situations who deal with it the right way, without harming themselves. Then there's me, Essa Jaymes fucking Monroe, eighteen years old and cutting herself every single day just to stay sane. It's not right, but I never said I wasn't fucked up. I know there is something wrong with me—how could there not be with the shit I've been through?

We all go through shit and we all choose to deal with it the only way we know how. This just happens to be the way I figured out works for me. It's unconventional, but so am I. The pain centers me; I need it.

I reach over to the little brown table beside me and grab my knife. It's small, black and silver in color, with a blade that flips open. The top half of the blade is sleek and sharp, making clean, deep cuts. The bottom half of the blade is serrated and that's why it's my favorite. The jagged edge rips my skin open in a way which makes the pain so intense, it's all I can think about. It also leaves the worst scars, and scars are reminders of what we've been through—reminding us we fucking survived—and I need them along with the pain to make it through the days.

Living in that pain is what I need at this moment. I flick open the knife and bring the blade to my forearm. I can see a sliver of skin not angry and red with healing, which is where I put my blade. Without a second thought, I push down as hard as I can with the serrated edge and drag the blade harshly across my skin. Over and over and over again because in moments like these, I lose myself to the feeling and lose count. In my haste, I end up going over cuts which were beginning to scab over, but it makes the pain even more intense. I choose to revel in it rather than care.

Fuck. I drop the knife and lean my head back against the wall, my mind in blissful agony. I can feel the red hot of my blood dripping down my arm and onto the floor but giving a fuck isn't even an option at this point. My arm feels like it's on fire and fuck if it's not the best feeling I've ever experienced. Every feeling and thought I have running rampant through me becomes *nothing*. It's gone and a complete euphoria washes over me.

Pain.

Pain.

Nothing but pain.

Closing my eyes, I let myself get lost in the agony and music because although my entire life is full of pain, *this pain* I can fucking control. It's mine and mine alone.

Exhaustion hits me hard. This day has taken its toll and my thoughts slowly start drifting. With a life like mine, there is no peace—even when you're unconscious.

I'm jerked awake by my earbuds being ripped from my ears. My eyes fly open and I see Ben sitting next to me on the floor.

"Still doing stupid shit, I see," he says, rolling his eyes at me in mockery. My anger flares as I yank my sleeve back down, not concerned about the blood covering my arm and hand which has long

CREEP

since dried. I scooch up and move farther away from him.

"What I do is none of your fucking business. What do you want?" When I manage to force my eyes to his, I can see his pupils are completely blown. Exactly the same as my mother's were earlier.

"I told you I'd be coming to pay you a visit tonight, so get undressed." What? I start to panic, the bliss from the pain long gone. *What does he mean get undressed?* He's never come to my room before. He's always made us go outside to their piece of shit car—when they had one—or even to the shed in the backyard, as creepy as it is, but never in my room.

My room is my sanctuary away from all of this bullshit. This can't happen here. It can't.

"Please not in here. We can go where we usually go, or literally anywhere else, but not in here. Holley could wake up or something." I beg him with everything in me, the words sounding sour on my tongue, but I fight with myself to spew them out. I can't lose this last piece of myself. He swings his arm out and slaps me so hard across my face, my eyes instantly water. I feel as my lip splits open and blood floods the back of my throat.

"I didn't ask for your commentary on the situation. You're acting like I give a shit about you or anything you want. You're only good for one thing, so take off your damn clothes, Essa."

Not wanting to risk waking Holley and having her walk in on this, I stop fighting him. I stand on shaky legs and pull my jeans off, throwing them to the side. Gripping the hem of my sweatshirt, I pull it over my head and drop it next to me. I sit back down and close my eyes, shutting it all out. I barely even notice his hands on my hips, pulling me to him while pushing until my back hits the floor.

His wretched odor smacks me in the face as he crawls over me. I gag at his putrid smell and swallow the vomit shooting up my throat. The acidity of the bile burns my throat.

I scream at myself to shut off the pain, the agony, all of it.

Moving his body over mine, he spreads my legs wide enough to bring pain even before he starts, but I know it's nothing compared to what I'm about to feel. He thrusts inside of me and as much as I try to fight it, a scream tears from my throat anyway. I fling my hand to cover my mouth, hoping to muffle the noise. Tears stream down my face as I quietly sob in pain.

Someone please come fucking save me.

Pain.

The fucking pain.

I feel the familiar wave of disconnect come finally over me. I don't always have the option to detach myself from what happens, but tonight I fight like hell with my head to stay this way, and by some miracle, it does.

CHAPTER TWO
ESSA

The next morning, I wake to the sound of shit hitting the walls. I let out a huff, already exasperated with today. I push myself off of the floor with a groan. My body screams in pain with every move I make. Ignoring my body's way of telling me to relax and try to heal, I throw my favorite Bring Me the Horizon hoodie on to cover my arms. I don't need Holley seeing them and finding another excuse to stay here.

I found the hoodie at the same garage sale we found Holley's mattress at, but obviously I didn't have the money for it. Once we got her mattress to the house, I went back, shoved it in the backpack I was wearing and took off. It was worth the risk too. I have a massive weakness for band merch.

On my way to the kitchen, I stop at Holl's door to check if she's awake, but it's already open. I push it open all the way, but she's not even in her room. *Fucking great.* She's been dealing with their deranged behavior by herself. I've told her a hundred times, hell, even more than one hundred, to come and get me when she wakes up so she doesn't have to be alone, but apparently she can't fucking listen to me.

While searching for Holley, I trip over a patch of carpet sticking up. I tumble to the floor, but as is usual with my luck, my face breaks the fall. My nose gushes blood and it just starts spewing everywhere like a fucking fountain. *Great, this is just the type of shit I want to be dealing with today on top of everything else.*

I *just* woke up and I'm already annoyed. I push myself up while pinching my nose with one hand. Sprinting to the kitchen, I grab the pale yellow hand towel which is lying on the counter. I bring it to my nose and pinch the bridge with it to stop the flow of blood. It's not my first nosebleed and it definitely won't be my last. *Fuck you very much, Benjamin.*

I roll my eyes, but wince when my head begins to throb. I keep my nose pinched and while waiting for the blood to stop flowing, I roam my eyes around the open floor plan of the kitchen and living room. It's basically just one big room, except the living room has a smaller doorway to make the rooms seem separate. It's a stupid fucking design if you ask me, but beggars can't be choosers, I guess.

Holley's seated on the couch with a bowl in her hands, watching a movie on our small box TV. I sit down next to her and glance in her bowl to see what she found to eat. A bowl of fucking Corn Flakes. She claims they're her favorite, but I know they're not, because who's favorite fucking cereal is Corn Flakes? Froot Loops are actually her favorite, but she knows we can't afford them. To try to make me feel better, she lies and says these are her favorite. *Always the fucking people pleaser.*

I plop my ass down next to her and push myself up against her, resting my head on her shoulder while still holding the towel to my face. Holley tears her eyes from the television and darts them over to me when she notices the blood on my hoodie. Blood from my nose and not my arm thankfully.

"What the hell happened to you?"

"I fucking tripped on that patch of carpet sticking up in the hallway. *Again.*"

Holley snorts and laughs so hard she has to set her bowl on the floor so she doesn't spill it.

"How many times now have you tripped on it? Seven, eight? You think you'd remember it was there and watch where you walk, Ess. At least you haven't hurt yourself before now."

I laugh right alongside her, but not for the same reason. My laugh is more sinister, cold. *If she only knew how her words could really be taken.*

"Yeah, yeah, I know. Shut up and give me a bite, I'm starvin' over here." She laughs while handing me her bowl and we sit there, taking turns every bite while watching a lame ass movie which is playing on antenna TV.

Later that afternoon, I'm in my room once again jamming to music. "The High Road" by Three Days Grace is blaring through my earbuds when my door gets pushed open. I know Holley's in her room drawing, practicing for her classes starting soon. Which only leaves one person because I know for a fact it isn't my mom coming in here.

MARIE ANN

She doesn't even acknowledge my existence anymore, not like she ever did to begin with.

No amount of preparation could ever prepare me for how I feel when Ben walks into the room. I hold on to every ounce of strength I possess, but fear is a fickle thing. It doesn't care if you're strong or not. It grips onto every nerve in my body, spreading through me like wildfire, but he doesn't need to know he still affects me. I can fight it, so I do.

I subtly square my shoulders and turn myself to face him as he steps into the room. Shutting the door behind him, he comes to where I'm sitting and takes a seat right next to me, as if there aren't other places he could sit.

Last night changed things, apparently, because now he's coming to my room whenever he fucking feels like it.

"What are you listening to, sweetheart?"

I swallow down the ever familiar taste of vomit when that word leaves his mouth and glance over to him, deciding to play along with his fake niceties.

"Three Days Grace."

"Ahhhh. I see it's still a favorite band of yours." he raises his eyebrows in acknowledgement.

I shrug my shoulders. "Yeah, sure."

I don't know what the hell is going on and it's confusing the hell out of me. He's never made small talk with me, *ever*. And now he wants to? No. Something's going on and it's scaring me, but I don't have the slightest clue as to what it could be. *All I know is I don't think my life can get much worse.*

CREEP

The fear begins to consume me as my thoughts run rampant. It happens every time he is in my vicinity. I fight like hell not to be afraid, but knowing everything he is capable of trumps any rational thought, and the fear always swings forward, full fucking force, every single time.

He's leaning against the wall with his head resting against it. He closes his eyes for a moment and then looks over to me. The look on his face gives me pause.

"Look, Essa. I came in here for a reason." *Doesn't he always.* "I need to talk to you and you're not going to like what I have to say. I didn't want to give you up because I wanna fucking keep you all to myself, but the situation called for this and you'll do well to remember you don't have a choice in shit."

As if I didn't already have a million thoughts swirling in my head, now they swallow me whole and I shut down, unable to process a fucking thing. *What in the hell is he talking about?* My stomach cramps and I feel sick. The possibilities of what he is talking about are endless. He's my fucking abuser for fuck's sake, how much worse could this fucking get?

As I sit here mentally panicking, he stares at me, but there is something about his eyes that captures my attention. The first thing I notice is his eyes look relatively clear, meaning he might actually be sober for once in his fucking life. Or at the very least, sober enough to have some fucking sense of clarity. A scoff leaves my lips at that thought because how fucking barbaric is that notion. In all likelihood, he just hasn't smoked yet today.

His eyes bore into mine, unblinking. Unease settles within me at the way he's leering at me. I jump up and start pacing the small space of my room, absently rearranging things to keep my hands busy while also attempting to squash my loud thoughts.

"What do you want Benjamin?" His name tasting like acid on my tongue.

"Oh, Benjamin is it? I'm surprised you even know my name seeing how the word has never left your mouth before, but it's fine. I don't really give a shit because you're about to hate me even more than you already do, so what you call me doesn't matter to me—it never has." He winks. *He actually fucking winks at me.*

I halt my movements and stand near my door—the only spot which is the furthest from him—and wait for him to continue.

"I made a deal with an acquaintance of mine. You're going to be his now 'cause I owe him a lot of fucking money and since your mother and I obviously don't have the cash to pay him back, you're the next best thing." He looks up to me and our eyes lock.

My palms itch with sweat and I rub them against my pants before bringing my hands back together. I interlock my fingers and twist them together as I take in what he just told me. *But this has got to be some sick fucking joke. Surely he's joking?*

I spew my thoughts out loud, desperate for him to confirm them. "This is a sick fucking joke, seriously. Why the fuck would you think this is funny?" I spit the words out in a jumble because my brain is not working properly. The panic takes hold of everything, including my bodily functions. My legs give out and I slump to the floor, dejected, because deep down inside, I know he's being truthful.

How fucking sick is that?

"No, Essa. I'm not being 'funny'. I'm being fucking serious. Sierra and I owe this man a lot of money and the only way he won't kill us is if we find some way to pay him. You and everyone else know we don't have any money so we offered you up for trade. For you to be whatever he wants.

"This guy has a well-known reputation about how he treats women, and it's nothing you're not already used to." He flips me a wink as he continues. "He already talked to me about what he wants and how we'll go about this. He said you get to stay here at home the majority of the time 'cause he just wants you one night a week. Just one, Essa, so you'll have no problem fulfilling what he wants.

"Do you understand? I know you're not stupid. Just know if you don't do it, I'll just offer Holley to him instead. I'll go to wherever the fuck her school is and bring her little ass home to pay my debt—you best remember that."

He casually throws her name out because he knew the second her name got brought up, I would say yes. I would do anything, *apparently any—fucking—thing*, to protect my sister from their poison. I know I've been through some shit—shit no one should *ever* have to endure—but being pimped out by my own parents to pay off a debt? Yeah. I'm about to lose the last piece of myself that was actually mine and mine alone. *My fucking soul.*

Anger courses through my veins and any fear I had is now quickly being replaced by the toxicity surrounding me.

"Pimping out your daughter to pay off your debts? That's the lowest of lows you fucking fiend. Y'all will really do anything for those fucking drugs you love so much, won't you?" I scoff in disgust and cross my arms over my chest, hoping the act will help calm me down and maybe bring me comfort.

"But it's not like I have a fucking choice in anything, anyway, right?" I sneer at him. Nothing is helping to curb the anger I'm feeling. It's devouring me and there is only one thing I know will help, but in order to do it, I have to wait for him to hurry the fuck up and leave.

He continues to stare at me with a bored expression while I've been trying to process all of this bullshit he spewed.

"Exactly sweetheart." he sniggers. "You don't have a fucking choice. You never have and you never will. Besides, this arrangement doesn't get you away from me, so you don't even have that to look forward to.

"No one fucking wants you. Not me, not your mother, not even Holley. You're a waste of fucking space and a goddamn mistake that never should've survived. If your dumbass mother would have listened to me, you wouldn't even be sitting here right now. But it's fine, because I make up for her mistake every time I stick my dick inside of you. It's the only thing you're good for, anyway."

I fucking lose it. I scream and run to him, throwing my fists towards his face. I can't fucking believe how sick in the head he is, and I want nothing more than to fucking kill him. Enough is enough. In my fit of rage, my fist connects with his jaw and I hear a crack. Pain flares through my hand and up my entire arm, but I don't fucking stop—what's a little pain when the end result is so great.

I keep swinging aimlessly, hoping to hurt him in any way I can. I can't focus on anything other than that. I need to hurt him like he's hurt me over the years, but much to my frustration, it doesn't last nearly as

CREEP

long as I had hoped before he yanks my wrists behind my back, both locked in his tight grasp. He spins us around until my back crashes into the wall. He grips my chin hard enough to bruise.

"You think you're tough enough to put your hands on me? If I were you, I'd think twice before doing something like that again. You can be mad all you want, but you don't have a fucking choice so don't waste your energy. I'm sure you'll want to preserve it for when you're with him. Unless you want Holley to trade places with you, hm?" He brings his head down to the same level as mine and raises his brow in question, knowing he has me backed into a fucking corner.

"Huh, sweetheart? You want me to go talk to Holley instead since you seem to be so against the idea? I'll make her stay and quit college to pay my fucking debt, Essa. Don't push me. Or if you decide to be fucking stupid after she leaves, I'll drag her ass back home." I can barely breathe with how tight he is gripping my chin, my neck angled up as far as it can go. I manage to shake my head no just enough for him to notice, but I can't let him have the last word—not when he keeps bringing Holley into it when it has nothing to do with her.

"Fuck you, you disgusting piece of shit. Leave Holley the hell alone. You already know I'll do whatever I can to protect her so just leave her out of it." He shoves my face away from his hand, as if I'm the one who is fucking disgusting.

He trails his index finger down my neck to my cleavage, which just so happens to be exposed in the black tank top I put on for bed not even twenty minutes ago. His finger moves lower in between my boobs, moving up and down, tracing my skin back and forth. I keep screaming at myself to move, but just as quickly as it came, the anger is gone and replaced with my constant fucking companion, fear.

I have never felt more disgusted with myself and in that moment, I snap out of it and smack his hand away. My emotions always come barreling back and forth like the continuous flicker of a light switch.

"Don't fucking touch me." My stomach is churning with the need to vomit and beads of sweat trail down my spine. I need him to leave right now. I need to process this, if it's even something that can be done.

No, fuck that. I need to bleed. I need the pain.

"Get the fuck out of my room you piece of shit druggie. You got what you wanted, now leave me the fuck alone." My chest heaves with my anger. *I'm giving myself fucking whiplash with the constant back and forth of feelings.*

I flick my eyes to his retreating back in surprise when he turns around and walks to my door. He opens it but glances back at me before leaving.

"I'll leave you alone for now, but I won't forget what you just said to me and you'll fucking pay for it. Not a word of this to anyone. If a single person finds out, your sister will trade places with you, you hear me?"

"Yeah, I fucking hear you. Now get out."

He smirks at me, trailing his eyes down my body again and then leaves, closing my door behind him. I have goosebumps all over my body and not the good ones. The kind that makes you feel like you want to crawl out of your own skin. I'm so fucking disgusted with myself.

I wish I had the power to fight back, more than just with my words, but that pesky fear takes over every time I even think about it. I want to fight back against my parents, hell, even against myself for being so fucking weak.

    I desperately need to forget the last twenty minutes, at least for a while anyway. I lean over to my nightstand and pull out my knife. I flick it open and watch the blade sparkle as it hits the light just right. I twirl it around in my hand, my thoughts dragging me further into my own head.

    Every voice inside of my head is screaming at me. Desperately needing to drown them, I bring the blade down to my arm, pushing hard and sweeping it across my skin in a flurry. White hot flames shoot up my arm as I see my flesh being torn open. It's fucking brutal but I can't help but to smile as I watch the sight.

    Pain is so fucking beautiful.

    Pain.

    In a matter of seconds, I go from freaking the fuck out about my entire existence, to not giving a shit about anything and just basking in the bliss pain brings. I may not be an addict like my parents, but I sure as fuck have my drug of choice.

    I lose count of how many cuts I give myself and drop the blade when I feel myself losing my grip on it—either from the blood being too slippery or because of the numbness which travels through my body.

    I fall to the side and collapse on my pile of blankets. I lay, staring at the wall, thinking about absolutely fucking nothing. I know it won't last long, but in a few days, hell maybe even a few hours for all I know, my whole life is going to be turned upside down, *again.*

CHAPTER THREE
ESSA

When I glance down at my iPod lying next to me on my bed, I see it's already two-thirty p.m. I've been lying in bed all day listening to "I Feel Like I'm Drowning" by Two Feet on repeat and I can't bring myself to move. Everything is surreal. It's almost like I'm floating above my body, peering down and observing everything like it's all happening to someone else.

I don't know how to fathom what the fuck is going to happen. Well, besides the obvious, I guess. The obvious is some fucking man my parents owe money to is going to do whatever he wants to me and I don't have a choice. But what is almost worse than that, is the fact I have already accepted it. What could this man do that is worse than what I have been going through for years?

And when it comes down to me or Holley, there isn't even a choice to be made because how could I be so selfish, I would let her go through something like this? Exactly, I couldn't.

So here I lie, already accepting whatever is going to come my way

CREEP

and just waiting for the inevitable to happen. I guess I can be happy about the fact Holley doesn't have to be stuck here alone when I'm not here because she's leaving for college tomorrow.

Speaking of Holley, I wonder where she is. I know our parents aren't home because I heard them leave early this morning and they still haven't returned. *Thank God.* The longer they stay away, the better for us.

Maybe she and I can have a girls' day and spend some much needed time together before she goes off to college. It would be nice to have at least one last day of something normal before my life gets even worse than it already is, which is really saying something.

I'm still pissed at the fact she put it off for a year to stay home with me. She made the excuse she didn't want to leave me here alone with our parents, which I understand to a certain extent, but I just wish she would realize I am more than capable of taking care of myself. Hell, I have been taking care of myself *and her* all these years, so what makes now so different? If only she knew the shit that was really going on, she might change her stance.

Ha, if she did, she would never leave then, so scratch that thought.

I get up and throw my hoodie on and I make my way to Holl's bedroom. I push open the door and see her sitting on her bed drawing. Packed bags and boxes are scattered about her room in complete disarray. Where I'm the organized clean freak, Holley's the messy, "I don't care" one. Even though the messy state of her room drives me nuts, it also instantly brings a smile to my face as I make my way over to her.

"Hey Holls. Whatcha drawing?" I plop down on her bed, making all of her supplies shake. She looks over at me with a smile. A genuine smile and it does nothing but solidify the fact I made the right decision—not that it ever occurred to me I didn't. I can't imagine being so selfish I would never do something to take her smile away. She truly is the light in my life and the only reason I'm still breathing.

Her eyes narrow as she takes in my face now that I'm closer to her. I'm sure she can see the bruises already forming on my face from Ben's rough handling of me the other night, but I subtly shake my head at her, not wanting to get into it. Her brows pull together with worry, but she gives me a weak smile before looking back down at the pad of paper in her lap.

"I'm drawing you, you wanna see?" She pushes the sketchbook I got her for her birthday into my lap. I glance down at the heavy paper she just threw in my lap and can't help the gasp leaving my mouth when I see it, my eyes going round with shock.

"Holy shit, Holley, this is beyond amazing! I can't believe you drew this! I'm so honored you would want to draw me." I look over at her with a smile so big, my cheeks ache, not used to making the expression. My eyes brim with tears. I'm trying so hard to fight from falling down my face.

"I am so proud of you, Holl. You're going to do so well at Rhode Island, I just know it."

"I— I don't know Ess. Rhode Island School of Design is relatively elite and I'm probably not going to do well enough to keep my scholarship. This school is the only way I'm getting out of here.

"I feel like I'm suffocating, Ess. Mom and dad are just too much for me to deal with anymore. But I don't want to leave you here, alone.

You don't deserve that."

She has tears in her eyes when she glances up at me through her lashes. They begin spilling down her high cheekbones. The tears make her already vivid blue eyes seem even brighter—eyes she got from our mother. But I let the thought go as I try not to think about our piece of shit mother right now and completely ruin my mood.

I grab her hands as I regard her. "Holley. You never have to worry about me, I swear to you. I know our lives haven't been the easiest, hell, that's the understatement of the century, but you deserve to get the fuck out of here. To live, to chase your dreams. You are so talented, and they are going to see it. You just need to put yourself first, okay?" I beam at her as I tell her how I truly feel. I need her to know how desperate I am for her to get out of here and away from all of this shit. She deserves it, more than anything.

"I love you so much, Essa. You are the best sister anyone could have ever asked for. I promise to call and text you every single day, okay?" I burst out laughing at her eagerness.

"You know you don't have to *every* day, right? You're going to college, Holl. Don't be that one weird person to call home every day. I'll be fine."

I don't tell her this, but the real reason I don't want her calling and texting every day is because Ben and Sierra don't know we have phones. They're nothing special, just those low-income government issued flip phones, but still. I don't want them to find out we have them and then lose my ability to be able to talk to her at all.

She laughs right along with me, slapping me on the arm "Oh shut up, I want to. Graduation is this weekend, you know?" She apparently feels the need to remind me. I try to resist rolling my eyes, but fail miserably. She shoots a glare at me.

"I haven't forgotten, I just don't care. It's just another day to me. You know that." I quirk my brow. She knows how I feel about all of that mundane shit. She just rolls her eyes at my indifference.

"Yes, yes, I know you don't care about those types of things, but I do because it's a great accomplishment for you. You should be proud."

"Yeah, all right. Changing the subject now." I push her and laugh. "Want to have a girls' day? I noticed Sierra and Ben bought some food for once, so do you wanna veg on the couch with some popcorn and watch a movie? I rented the whole *Fast and Furious* series from the library." I grin at her because the *Fast and Furious* movies are her all-time favorites and I know she'll make me stay up all night binging them with her.

"Ah damn, you know those are my favorites, otherwise I would have *totally* said no." I roll my eyes at her, then jump off bed before she can smack me for it.

"Oh shut up, you know you're full of shit. You love me and you love these movies, so it's a no-brainer. I'm going to throw the popcorn in the microwave and meet you on the couch. Don't take forever or I'll start without you!" I yell at her as I skip down the hallway.

Shaking my head and laughing to myself quietly, I realize how easy it is to forget all of the bullshit in our lives when we're together. She is the light in any room you walk through. Her genuine happiness rubs off on anyone and anything, except our piece of shit parents, of course. They don't give a fuck about anyone or anything but their drugs. Not even Holley's light can penetrate their dead hearts. They simply remain completely indifferent towards her ninety-nine percent of the time, which is better than the way they could treat her, so I take it as a win in my book.

Scoffing in annoyance at myself for even allowing my thoughts to venture there right now, I pull open the microwave door and throw the popcorn in. Kettle corn of course, because the butter one is disgusting and you get this gross film on the roof of your mouth when you eat it. *No thank you.*

I stand, twiddling my fucking thumbs until the microwave beeps two minutes later, then carefully grab the corner of the bag and walk over to the couch. I turn the movie on, and flop my ass on the couch to wait for Holley.

I remember the last time we were able to do this and how I burnt my hand on the popcorn bag. When I yanked it out of the microwave, impatient as ever, the steam from the open top burned my hand so bad I had blisters for over a week. I laugh at myself as I sit here eating, this time being diligent of the steam.

"What's got you laughing at yourself, crazy ass." I glance over at Holley as she walks in. She sits literally *right* next to me on the couch, our thighs squished together.

"Do you remember the last time we were able to do this, just us, and I ended up burning the fuck out of my hand because of the damn popcorn bag?"

Holley shouts her laughter, bending over and holding her stomach from laughing so hard.

"What the fuck is so funny? I try to sound annoyed but I can't help the huge smile spreading across my face. Her laughter is contagious.

MARIE ANN

"You look like a fucking hyena laughing like that, by the way."

"A hyenaaaa!" she screeches in between her fits of laughter. Still holding her stomach, she seems to get it together for a second, though tears from her laughter are running down her cheeks. "Oh my god, I'm sorry but it's so funny! You chucked the popcorn—which you burned by the way! And then started screaming at the microwave like it was a person who pissed in your Cheerios all because you weren't paying attention. Seriously one of the funniest things I have ever seen!" she starts her laughing fit up again.

I huff out a breath and roll my eyes. Ignoring her, I turn to the T.V. again and push play. I pretend to be annoyed, but I'm genuinely happy for the time being. I'm going to miss the banter between us.

"Are you going to shut up so we can watch these movies or what?"

"Yeah, give me some popcorn, would ya?" I hand her the bag and turn the volume up a few notches. I kick my feet up, getting comfortable, because I already know we're going to be here all night.

Tomorrow she leaves for college and then I'll truly be all alone. But I wouldn't want to spend our last night together any other way.

CHAPTER FOUR
VINCENT

The second my eyes land on her, my cold, dead heart thuds inside of my chest, beating for the first time in years. But fuck if I can help it. She's the most beautifully broken girl I have ever laid my eyes on. From what I can see of her exposed skin—which isn't much with all of the clothes she has on—she has shadows of bruises peeking out from her clothing and a few smattered on her chin and defined cheekbones. Her clothing barely does the job of keeping them covered, which I imagine is why she's wearing so much.

She's in a Sublime hoodie which has holes in it, telling me it's been worn hundreds of times, and black ripped skinny jeans. She has these thick thighs that make me instantly think what it would be like to have them wrapped around my face, squeezing hard while I make her come all over my tongue. Her hands bound behind her back, unable to move.

Forcing my eyes from her thick thighs, I make my way up her body again. She has long, shiny black hair which hangs all the way

MARIE ANN

to her ass. Fuck me, that ass. I envision it bouncing up and down on my dick, her screams so loud my ears ring while her blood makes our bodies slip together effortlessly.

I feel my dick jump in my jeans—*woah, calm the fuck down.* This is not the time, nor the place. *Well, not yet anyway.*

Fuck, I need to get my shit together. I shove my thoughts away—ignoring them has become my specialty. One I am going to have to utilize constantly with this girl around, apparently, seeing as I've been distracted multiple times already in a matter of minutes. This is not the time nor the place because as much as I want to wrap my hands around her throat and shove my dick down her throat, I have to have my fun with her first.

Her eyes swing over to mine and my heart thuds again.

Thump. Thump.

She has the palest green eyes I have ever seen, but it's not the color of them that fucks with my heart. It's that even with pure hatred in them—hatred towards me, I'm sure—they are full of pain. Pure, unbridled pain. Pain I recognize all too fucking easily. I feel as if she can see into my soul—a soul I don't even fucking have. Which, quite frankly, makes me uncomfortable as fuck, but my dick doesn't get the memo because I can feel it growing harder inside of my jeans just from her scrutinizing me.

Pain turns me the fuck on like nothing else, and this girl is just *oozing* pain and daddy issues. *This is going to be even more fun than I thought.* I'm going to enjoy breaking her body. And her mind. Her body is going to become my playground.

When her father offered her as payment for all the money they owe

CREEP

me, I was quite frankly, surprised as fuck, because who the hell in their right mind would offer their child as payment to a fucking drug dealer? Oh right. Drug addicted pieces of shit. Parents of the year. I mean, it's not like I give a shit. They told me she was eighteen and attractive, and well, I've been bored out of my fucking mind, so I said, "Why not?"

Standing here now, in this kitchen, staring at her, I'm glad I said yes. I'm already thinking of hundreds of different things I want to do to that little body of hers.

I came to Ben's place today to handle the semantics of everything, but now I'm standing here staring at her, I know this deal is going to change. Originally it was supposed to be once a week, but now I think it needs to be way more often.

I already know I'm going to do a bunch of fucked up shit to this woman. The icy glare she's giving me is only making me harder. Jokes on her, because I'll show just how much I crave the hatred she's giving me.

I continue to hold her eyes and watch as she takes a deep breath, like she's steeling herself for our conversation.

Yeah, baby doll. You feel it too, don't you? That right there is our monsters mingling—recognizing one another.

Realizing we're just standing in the kitchen staring at each other, I clear my throat and make my way over to one of the mismatched chairs and take a seat. The rickety chair creaks and scrapes against the ripped up vinyl flooring as I move it to face her. Focusing on her again, I stretch my arm out and gesture for her to take a seat too. She glares at me but moves to the chair that is furthest from me and sits, facing me.

She's glaring at me as she spits out, "So how the fuck is this supposed to work?"

Fuck, even her voice is sexy. Low and rough, yet still feminine as fuck. I don't even know how it makes any sense but it's just the truth. I can only imagine what it would sound like while I drag a knife across her thigh in the middle of her climax, screaming my fucking name, again and again, begging me to stop and to keep going.

Annoyed with myself again, I keep a blank look on my face as I stare at her. It's a look I've managed to perfect over the years. Being a dealer means I handle a lot of people who seem to think they can try to intimidate me. *It never fucking works and they learn real quick to never try that shit again.*

I let a smirk pull at the corner of my lips. She's still glaring at me, but I see her steely gaze falter for a moment as her eyes drop to my mouth.

I can't help but admire the pain which surrounds her like an aura. She's obviously seen some shit and something inside of me recognizes her pain and suffering because as much as she tries to hide it, she still fails miserably.

"Are you going to answer me or just continue to sit there staring at me like a fucking idiot?"

"You're a feisty one aren't you, little girl?" I goad her, unable to resist her attitude. It's doing things to me I'm not sure I like, but apparently my dick certainly does.

"Don't fucking call me a little girl unless you want to be punched in the jaw for talking shit." She sneers at me with hatred burning in her eyes.

"You've got balls, baby doll, but you might want to watch that mouth with me. I see I have hit a nerve, which is good to know." I smirk. "I'm sure your father has filled you in on the situation?" I'm assuming she knows, but these are drug addicts we're talking about, so who the fuck knows.

"Yeah, I know you're going to use me until you've gotten your fill and you feel like you've been paid in full." The disgust is evident in her tone, but her eyes tell a different story.

"Look, little girl. I don't know what your father said to you about this arrangement, but let's make one thing clear right now. I fucking own you and you don't get a word in edgewise, so the attitude is really fucking annoying. Although, my dick isn't complaining. So, unless you want me to make you shut the fuck up by shoving my dick so far down your throat you can't breathe, I'd zip up your attitude real fucking quick."

I grab my already hard dick through my jeans to emphasize my point. She looks down at the bulge and her eyes practically bug out of her head. Her cheeks flame the most beautiful shade of red and she throws her gaze back up to mine, furious.

"If you think you're getting anywhere near me with *that* thing, I'll fucking bite it off."

"That would mean your mouth would be on my dick, baby doll. Don't threaten me with a good time." I chuckle as her cheeks redden even more. My retort has her snapping her jaw shut and swinging her head away from me.

Fucking with her is going to be prime entertainment.

"Well, I need to go speak to your father. While I'm doing that, why don't you go pack a bag or grab some things you want to bring with you. I'll come get you when I'm ready to leave."

She shoots up, and the chair she was sitting on screeches as it's shoved across the floor behind her. It crashes to the ground with a bang.

"What the fuck do you mean pack a bag? Ben said it was just for one night a week. What would I need a bag for?" She's speaking so fast, the fear in her voice evident as she stumbles over her words.

I keep my face blank, not answering her. This little bitch is going to be in for a rude awakening when she realizes what this deal actually entails for her. I can't wait to show her just how much she shouldn't run her fucking mouth.

"I know the deal that was made, but I'm thinking I might want you a little more than once a week little girl. You intrigue me and your attitude makes my dick hard for some reason, so I'm going to need to deal with it. More than once a week. And besides, do you really think your father will care?" I quirk my eyebrow at her because she knows he won't care. He doesn't give a shit about anyone or anything but his drugs. Drugs I supply to him. I know I don't even have to ask him— not that I was going to anyway. I'm going to tell him how shit's going to go and that's what is going to happen.

She glares at me because she knows I'm right. She turns on her heels and storms to what I'm presuming is her room, but it actually looks more like a large closet with a makeshift door. *Jesus, what a shit show.*

Wanting to get the fuck out of this shithole of a house, I head down the hallway to Benjamin and Sierra's room, or dumb and dumber, as I usually refer to them as. These two give me a fucking headache, but I only have to deal with them long enough to tell them what's going on and then I can leave with my baby doll. *My? Where the fuck did that come from?*

Shaking my head in annoyance with myself, *and* pushing the disturbing thought from my head, I shove their door open without knocking and duck my head past the door frame as I take a few steps into the room. It's small with just enough room for a large bed and a dresser, both of which have seen better days. It also smells disgusting. The scent of mold and body odor lingering in the air.

Scoffing and wrinkling my nose in disgust, I look over and see them both sitting on their bed, talking to one another. They glance up when they see me and I notice their *very* blown pupils, along with fear in their eyes.

Ahh, the fear. I crave it. I fucking live for it.

I tilt my head to the side and keep my face a blank mask. "So, the plan has changed. I decided I'll have Essa stay with me more than once a week, though I'm not sure how long yet. I'll make sure she attends her graduation Saturday, but other than that, you'll see her whenever I decide to bring her home.

"While she is with me, you are not to try to contact me or her. If you do see her you are also not allowed to talk to her about me in any way, is that understood?"

I observe as they look back at each other for a second, like they're trying to communicate silently. *I really don't have the time for this shit.*

"You're both acting like you have a choice in this situation. Let's make one thing clear so this doesn't get confusing. What I say fucking goes. You are the ones who owe me thousands of dollars and since you can't pay me what you owe me in cash, I'm taking the next best thing.

"So, with that said, I will have Essa as much as I fucking want her. Don't get shit twisted. Do I need to write it down, or can you not fucking read either?"

They start stammering, trying to get their words out. Fear is such a funny thing, the way it fucks with normal bodily functions.

Benjamin is the first to get his words out coherently. "Y—yes, sir. We understand. We won't bother you." They fidget on the bed, their bodies swaying from side to side and they look like they haven't showered in days.

Fuckin' pussy.

"Good. Now this exasperating conversation is over. I'm taking Essa and we're leaving. You'll see her Saturday." With that, I turn around without waiting for a response and make my way to where I now know Essa's room to be. She better have her shit ready to go because I don't feel like being in this shithole much longer. Dumb people, especially dumb druggies, make my fucking trigger finger twitchy.

I don't know how she lives here. Well, I guess I do—it's not like she has a choice with parents like hers.

I get to her door and rasp my knuckles against it once. The force of my knock is enough for the makeshift door to rattle and she yanks it open, shoving her way past me. *Well damn, she looks pissed.*

I laugh at her audacity. I'm going to fix that attitude of hers real quick. But do I really want to fix it? As irritating as it is, my dick gets so hard every time I see even an ounce of it.

I turn and follow her out to my car, choosing to let it slide for now.

CREEP

"This—This is your fucking car?" she swings her head around to look at me with wide eyes, her mouth agape.

"Yeah, baby doll, this is my car. Why? You like her?" I quirk my eyebrow at her and then turn to look at my car with pride. I worked my ass off to get this car. She's a fucking beauty. A 1969 Camaro SS with glossy black paint and black leather interior.

"Do I like her? I fucking love her. This is so similar to my dream car. I never imagined I would ever see a car like this in person." I can see her smiling so wide while she walks up and runs her hand along the car door. I can't help but smile myself. However, I snap myself out of it before she notices.

I round my car and jump in the driver's seat. I roll the passenger window down where she's still standing, admiring. "Get the fuck in the car so we can out of here. This place is disgusting." The smile she was wearing immediately dissipates when she hears me speak.

"You don't have to be such a fucking asshole," she snaps as she opens the door, carefully I observe, and sits down. Even though she hates my guts, she still treats my car with respect. I like that.

"We both know I'm not happy about this, but I obviously don't have a choice. So if you could refrain from being a complete dick to me, that would be great."

"Oh, baby doll. Tsk Tsk. You're in for quite the treat. You have no fucking clue how much of a dick I am. You might want to learn to reign in that attitude before I make you." I glance over to her and then my dick to remind her of what I said earlier. It seems to shut her up, thankfully. I don't know how much longer I can stand the feel of my dick strained against my jeans, the zipper digging in painfully. Though

I love pain, that's a type I could do without.

I turn the key in the ignition, starting the car and driving down the road, toward the highway. As I glance over at her, I notice she has her hands in her lap, twisting her fingers. Probably a nervous habit.

"So, where exactly do you live?" I flash my eyes to her as I shift the car to fifth gear now we're on the highway.

"Wouldn't you like to know, little girl." I can't help the smirk fighting its way onto my face when she swings her head over to scowl at me.

"Like I said, you don't have to be a dick. All I did was ask a fucking question. Since I'm being forced to stay with you, don't you think I should get to know where exactly it is I'm going to be staying?"

"No." I keep my voice tight and face expressionless. I don't want her knowing where my house is just yet. I'm sure she will find out eventually, but for now, it just adds to the mind fuck of it all. And the more I can fuck with her, the better.

We continue the ride in complete silence. "Californication" by The Red Hot Chili Peppers playing quietly in the background.

CHAPTER FIVE
ESSA

About half an hour after we leave my parents place, we pull up outside of his house—if you can even call it a house—because it's massive and I mean fucking massive. *How the fuck does a drug dealer afford a place like this?* I don't think I have ever been in a house of this stature and it's kind of intimidating if I'm being honest.

The sun has almost set, so I can't quite make out the features of the house other than the fact it's beautiful. The outside is made of glass walls and it's completely surrounded by trees. Woods surround us for miles upon miles. In fact, when we pulled into his drive, we drove for ten minutes before we actually reached the fucking house. So, I'm stranded in the middle of nowhere with a man I do not know and no way to escape. *How fun for me.*

I reach behind me in the car to grab my bag out of the backseat. Once I have it in hand, I step out of the car and shut the door carefully behind me. Not knowing what to do, I stand next to the car and stare at the open abyss of trees, waiting for him to make a move.

MARIE ANN

I won't ever admit it to him, but I'm scared out of my fucking mind. I don't know what to expect from this whole situation. Obviously, I'm not dense and I understand the fact he's going to want to fuck me. Which is most definitely not going to happen, but I have a very strong feeling he's the type of man who doesn't care about my consent. *He wouldn't be the fucking first and I don't even know his damn name.*

Sighing, I look over to where he is leaning against the side of his gorgeous car, staring at me. I don't know how I didn't hear him get out. I must've been too lost in my head.

His face is completely stoic so I can't read his mood or what he's thinking. I'm already annoyed as hell by this whole situation and by him, so I decide to ask, "What's the plan? Are we going to stand here in your driveway all night or are we going to go inside at some point? It's getting kinda chilly out." Living in Oregon usually isn't too bad with it being the end of May, but the weather tonight has a chill to it and my dumbass didn't grab an extra hoodie.

His jaw ticks in irritation before he turns toward his front door, downright blowing off my question. I roll my eyes in exasperation at his retreating figure—with the knowledge he can't see me—and follow him to the front door. As I get closer, I notice the door is a matte black, matching the rest of the house and there are also wooden planks running along the side as well. It's an interesting concept, but I actually like it a lot.

The man pushes the door open after pulling his key out of the lock and moves to the side, gesturing for me to go in front of him. *Oh, what a fucking gentleman.*

CREEP

Steeling my spine, I push my way past him, my arm brushing his chest in my haste. My breath catches in my throat, the instant heat traveling up my arm from his touch is unnerving as hell. Goosebumps cover my arms despite the heat I'm feeling all the way to my bones.

Behind me, he flicks the lights on and the room suddenly comes to life. I walk into the massive space and look around, my eyes flicking between multiple focal points because everything catches my eye at once. The house looked huge from the outside, but now I'm inside with fucking light, I realize it's much bigger.

As I already saw outside, the walls are mainly made of glass, giving an exquisite view of the trees right outside. The sun has completely set in the time it took us to get inside, so as I peer out of the window, all I see is the dark surrounding the trees. It's eerie as hell and causes chills to run through my body. For some reason, there's something about the woods out here that gives me the creeps.

Turning back, I keep looking around, avoiding the man's eyes but I feel them on me like I'm his prey and he's the predator, preparing to pounce.

I do my best to ignore his gaze as I check out the rest of his house. From what I can see, it's all one big room for the most part with the exception of a few doors off to the back down a small hallway. The modern looking kitchen has its own space and the living room takes up the majority of the remaining area.

The walls that aren't glass, are painted a steel gray with nothing but a few abstract paintings hanging sporadically around to divert from the fact the house has absolutely no personal effects. *Well, isn't that interesting. If this is his home, why don't I see anything personal?*

MARIE ANN

Not knowing what else to do because it took all of five minutes to look around, I walk over to the massive light gray sectional which takes up half of the floor space in the center of the room and gingerly take a seat.

The entire time I was walking around, I could feel his eyes trailing me. It was easier to ignore it when I had a way to distract myself, but now that I am just sitting here, his eyes burn a whole straight through me. I shift from side to side a few times, utterly uncomfortable with the undivided attention he's giving me. Mainly because it's something I haven't experienced before.

Earlier, at my parents' house, it was a thousand times easier to give him an attitude because I had the security of my own home backing my resolve. But now? Now I don't have anything but nerves eating away at me. I look up at him through my lashes and hold his gaze. I'm fucking terrified, but I will never show him a sliver of fear. I have been through a hell of a lot worse than this man or anything he can put me through. And if it does get to be too much? I can always cut.

Just thinking about it brings the level of comfort I need to start this unwanted, but apparently fucking necessary conversation with him.

"What's your name?"

"That's really your first question to me baby? Aren't there things you want to know more? And if I were you, I'd ask shit you truly want the answers to you because in case you haven't noticed, I'm not really a man who answers people's questions if I don't feel like it."

I stew for a minute, thinking about the things I want to know, but the only one I can think of, is I want to know his name. Everything else is purely semantics when you're being forced against your will.

CREEP

Sure of my answer, I respond to him, "Yes, that really is my first question to you. Actually, it's my only question. I don't give a fuck about the answers to anything else because they won't change a goddamn thing." *No matter how much I wish they could.*

"Name is Vincent, baby doll, and if I were you, I'd get real acquainted with it. I plan on having you scream it, *a lot*. Depending on your attitude, it can be in pain, *or* in pleasure. But my personal favorite is both."

My skin heats for reasons I don't know. I didn't think I was attracted to him in any way, but of—fucking—course my body doesn't feel the same way. I can feel the heat work its way up my neck and onto my cheeks, showcasing my feelings right to the asshole.

When he notices, he bellows a laugh and I swear on everything, I want to punch that stupid ass smirk off of his face. Clenching my fists, I shoot off the couch and march over to him.

Just like every other time I get pissed off, I let it overtake my body as I shove myself right into his space. My hands on his chest throws me off for a moment as heat travels up my arms. *Fuck. He feels so warm.*

I push him as hard as I can, but of course he doesn't move an inch. Ignoring his tall, lean, and statue-like persona, I tilt my head as far up as it will go so I can look him in the eyes. *Motherfucker is tall. Like well over six foot or something.* I don't know anything other than the fact it hurts my neck to look at him. Annoying.

"I want to get one thing clear, motherfucker, I am not your goddamn *slave*, toy, or whatever the fuck. You will never put your hands on me in a manner I am not okay with. And to make another thing clear, that is something I will *never* be okay with.

"Second, you are not going to tell me what to fucking do. I am here because I don't have another choice, but it doesn't mean I am going to roll over like a fucking dog at your commands. If you think that's what's going to happen, you're in for a rude awakening." I spit my words out with as much venom I can manage, but being this close to him is causing my confidence to wane and my anger to dissipate.

Touching him is really fucking with my head and I haven't the faintest clue why. All I can feel is his touch burning against my skin and I'm not even touching him.

Suddenly his hand shoots down to grab my throat in a harsh, unyielding grip. He spins around and shoves me back, my skull smacking against the wall with a punishing blow. My head instantly starts throbbing, but I can't think about that when his hand squeezes, blocking my airways.

He continues to squeeze until I swear he's crushing my fucking windpipe with the palm of his hand. Panicking, I grip his wrist with both hands and attempt to yank him off to no avail. He merely laughs at my weak attempt and I don't fucking know how he does it, but he manages to squeeze even tighter.

My head swims with the loss of oxygen and black dots dance around the edge of my vision. Right as I think I'm going to pass out, he loosens his hand enough to let me suck in a ragged breath before clamping down again.

"I want to get another thing clear, baby doll," he says in a mocking tone. "It's fucking cute you think you can tell me what to do. Let me just say this so we can have all of our facts laid out on the table.

CREEP

Goosebumps crawl across my skin as he speaks, terrified of what it could mean.

"But anyway, fact number one. You *are* my fucking slave. You will do whatever I say, whenever I say it. Free Will? That doesn't exist for you anymore and the sooner you realize it, the better things will go for you. But let me tell you a little secret," he bends his head down, lips brushing my ear as he whispers, "I fucking love that attitude of yours just as much as I hate it. It makes my dick the hardest it has ever been."

He trails his tongue along the shell of my ear as he talks and his words are making my pussy impossibly wet and I fucking hate myself for it. *Well, as much as I hate myself at this moment, I don't think I can make it much worse.*

He loosens his hold over my throat just enough I manage to shove away from him. I back away, putting as much distance between us as I can.

"Fuck. No," I say with defiance as I spit the words at him. He can get fucked if he thinks I'm going to do anything he wants me to do without a fight.

"What did you just say to me?" he asks me as he begins to stalk towards me again. He has this gleam in his eyes at my defiant words, like it's what he wanted me to say. I instantly regret it, but I can't give him the power of that knowledge, so I fake my confidence as I cross my arms over my chest and square my shoulders.

"I said no. Do I need to repeat myself or are you too stupid to understand the word?"

A barrel of a laugh leaves his chest, though it doesn't meet his eyes. If anything, his dark brown eyes grow even darker, looking almost black. The eyes of a predator, of a monster. Eyes similar to ones I have seen far too many times in my life. Fear licks up my spine and I take small steps backwards, slowly working myself farther away from him and out of the room.

Hopefully, I can make it to a room that has a lock while he calms down because the look in his eyes is one I have truly never seen before. And I have seen evil. But this man tops the fucking cake and my ass wants nothing to do with it. *Nope. No thank you.*

I keep my eyes on him but his steps are quicker than they were moments ago. Fuck. I whip around as fast as I can and dash out of the room. I have no fucking clue where I'm going because we just got here, but I run up the floating stairs and make my way around the corner. I see a door that's cracked and without hesitation, I launch myself into it and slam it behind me. I twist the lock and throw my back against the door as I try to regulate my breathing now I am somewhat safe from him—for the moment being anyway.

I look around quickly and realize I must be in a guest bedroom. The room has a full sized bed with white sheets and the curtains are white, as well as the walls. Very plain and boring, but whatever. I don't even know why I'm thinking about the furnishings in the room right now. I have more pressing matters to think about.

I close my eyes and strain my ears, trying to listen for his footsteps coming up the stairs, but I don't hear a fucking thing. Not one sound coming from this ginormous house. Only the sounds of my haggard breathing. *Well, that's just fucking great.*

I really don't want to know what happens if he catches me. Who the fuck am I kidding, when he catches me. But maybe a small, very

CREEP

small, dark part of me does want to find out. *No. No, I don't.* I cannot think like that right now. Not when Vincent looks like he wants to murder me and do something like lick the knife afterwards while smiling down at my corpse.

My whole fucking life is one big joke, I swear. At the feeling of my backpack squished between me and the door, I praise myself for not taking it off when we got inside. As I was throwing my shit together to leave, I made sure to put my knife in with everything else. I never go anywhere without it because I never know when I'm going to need it.

A sense of relief floods over me at the notion of having it. I rush to the bathroom, slamming and locking that door behind me as well. The more doors between me and that monster, the better.

Taking a seat on the toilet, I shrug my bag off my shoulders and place it between my feet. Opening up the hidden zipper pocket on the left side of the bag, I pull out my knife. I yank my sleeve up and flick the knife open. My hands shake, the need for a release too great, but I manage to push down as hard as I can, dragging the blade across my skin like I always do—fast and repeatedly. Over and fucking over again, until my arm looks like a mutilated mess and everything goes numb with the pain. I don't even care about my old wounds being ripped open again, on top of new ones. I love the sudden feel of nothingness ripping my flesh open brings me. Because now I don't give a shit if he finds me or not.

Pain.

Pain.

Nothing but pain.

The blade slips from between my fingers and clatters to the floor somewhere next to me. My body sways so I shift myself to the side and flop to the floor, unable to keep my body upright on the toilet. I rest my head against the wall behind me and my eyes flutter closed. I can feel my blood running off my arm in fast trails, splattering onto the pristine white bathroom floor. I manage a smirk at the fact he's going to have to clean this up, bitching at me all the while probably.

Hopefully it'll stain his floors, the bastard.

While my thoughts are slowly starting to dwindle as I lose consciousness, I'm jolted awake when I hear the bedroom door smash against the wall.

Well shit. That didn't sound good.

Unable to process much more than a single thought, I lie here waiting for him to get to me. There's no point in fighting it when I'm like this, so I enjoy the bliss for a little while longer. But that little while longer doesn't last for more than five more seconds, much to my disappointment, because the bathroom door is smashed to pieces in an instant.

Well, that was dramatic. He could've simply knocked on the door and saved himself the money of replacing the damn thing, but what do I know?

I manage to peel my eyes open and peer up at his domineering figure. I never gave myself a chance to *really* look at him before, but I do now. He resembles a wild beast; his chest huffing from his exertion. His very naked chest because apparently he lost his shirt in his struggle with the door.

My gaze rakes over his body, admiring what I see, starting at his deep, chocolate brown eyes. He has dark brown hair which is just long

CREEP

enough to run my fingers through and yank, a chiseled jaw with a bit of scruff which would feel rough against me, burning its way across my skin as he moves his mouth from place to place, devouring me.

The direction my thoughts have taken me throw me for a loop. The blood loss becomes something great, and prohibits me from having reasonable thoughts. At least I'm choosing to blame it on the loss of blood because any other answer is not feasible right now, even though I know I'm not losing enough blood to blame it on that.

He remains still as he regards me on my journey of blatantly checking him out. I move my eyes down his lean, but sculpted body. A body gloriously covered in fucking tattoos. I run my eyes over all of the ones I can see, but there is one in particular which catches my eye.

It's a poppy plant wrapping around his right forearm, up towards his elbow. There aren't many details to it, just a few flowers in black and white. It piques my interest 'cause it seems like all of his other tattoos—the ones I can see anyway—are in some way centered around that one in particular.

When I manage to tear my eyes away from it, I glance up at him to ask about it, my curiosity getting the better of me, but the words freeze on the tip of my tongue when I notice the look in his eyes. He's looking at me with so much rage, the words fall silent upon my lips.

"What. The. Fuck. Do you think you're doing running away from me?" he spits the words out between his perfectly white clenched teeth. His fists clamp tighter as the words leave his mouth. I refuse to answer him, choosing to remain silent. I don't owe him any explanations about anything I decide to do.

"You're a dense little girl, you know that right? Let me guess, your life is too fuckin shitty for you to handle, so you take that pathetic little blade to your skin to make yourself feel better, hmm." He moves forward until he is standing over me, staring at me like I'm a tiny little bug he is going to squash under his shoe.

"I'm right, aren't I?" He smirks.

I push myself further into the wall to escape his dominating aura, but the attempt is a pathetic one at that. Never taking his eyes off of mine, he crouches down next to me, until his lips are a mere whisper away from mine. The feel of his hot breath mixing with my own is enough to cause my heart to flutter in fear.

My head starts to swim, from the blood running down my arm or his intoxicating presence, I'm not sure. Either way, I can't help how fucking screwed I feel. Keeping my cold green eyes locked on his soulless browns, I take as deep of a breath as I can, causing my own lips to skim his in the process. I gasp at the split second of contact and he grins.

Breaking eye contact with me, Vincent moves his lips to my ear, running his tongue along the shell while whispering, "Let me tell you a secret baby doll. Taking a blade to your body doesn't solve a single fucking thing other than marking your skin in your pathetic attempts to feel better. You think it takes everything else away, but it doesn't. It merely masks it. You have a pathetic excuse of a life. Just fucking own it, because there is nothing you can do that will make you feel better."

The second the last word leaves his mouth, his words crawling over my skin, my brain finally registers what he said. I only met this motherfucker a few hours ago and he's already telling me shit about myself and my own damn life...I don't think so.

CREEP

I quickly rear to the side and smack my head against the side of his, causing him to stumble backwards. With rage boiling through my bloodstream, I scream at him. "As if you have any fucking right to tell me anything about my own body! My decisions for doing what I do are of no fucking concern to—" My words are cut off because before I can even finish, everything goes black.

CHAPTER SIX
VINCENT

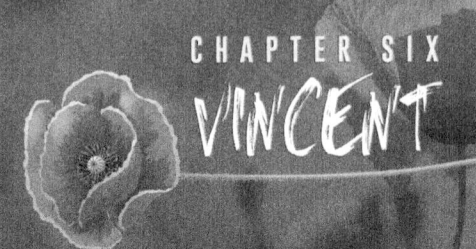

I'm honestly shocked, which doesn't happen often anymore. I've seen and dealt with a lot in my line of work. I'm not a big player in the drug business, I just happen to know people who know people—keeping my life on a pretty low scale—but enough to keep me more than comfortable. I used to do a lot of dirty work. Such as tracking people down to get their money, running the streets, et cetera.

Now I've earned my place at the top, but choose to stay hidden in the shadows. I mostly do my boss's dirty work, but to earn quick, easy cash on the side, I sell to people where and when I want, which entails mainly parties. Those always get me the big bucks around here. When I do decide to hit them up, I always make my rounds at the ones the rich kids are throwing. Stupid ass rich kids love throwing away their money on blow.

Then there are people like Essa's parents. The ones who keep coming back time and time again—the true fucking addicts. Those are the worst to sell to, but the most profitable because of their desperation.

CREEP

Or at least they are supposed to be, but of course I got pieces of shit ones who continuously blow off their payments until it gets to the point of pay or be killed.

Which happens to be my favorite part if I am being honest, but I haven't had the opportunity in a long while and my body is itching for it. So when it came to the point of getting rid of dumb and dumber, I was more than willing—until they threw a curveball at me. By the name of Essa Jaymes Monroe.

The words "not a fucking chance" were resting on the tip of my tongue, but I don't know what happened. I remembered how utterly bored I have been in every aspect of my life and how fun a slave would be right now. But not just my typical willing slave which I could go pick up right this second. I wanted someone who was truly unwilling. I wanted a challenge. I wanted someone to entertain me and *that* sounded like a good fucking time. So before I thought much more about it, the words "why not" spilled from my lips, solidifying the situation.

Now though, I'm regretting the unwilling part just a smidge. That little bitch headbutting me as she was bleeding on my bathroom floor sure as hell surprised me.

I bring my hand to the side of my head and rub at the lump now forming. Fucker is throbbing and it's pissing me off even more. I stare at her in irritation as I watch her sleep. I'm sitting in the chair in the corner of what is now her bedroom, waiting for her to wake up so I can show her what happens when she throws her ass around.

After she headbutted me, I shoved her away from me and her head smacked against the side of the toilet, knocking her out. I didn't mean for that to happen, but it's not like she didn't fucking deserve it. I took a cloth, cleaned her up and carried her to the bed, deciding to let her sleep for a bit. She's going to need some of her strength for what I am about to put her through.

    I chuckle sarcastically as I think about her little fiasco in the bathroom. I wasn't even irritated about having to clean it up. It's too amusing to me. Little bitch cuts herself to feel better like she has the slightest fucking clue as to what real pain ensues. I remember doing the same thing at her age, but it never fucking works.

    I can show her what does.

    I rise from the chair and leave the room. I slowly close the door behind me, careful not to wake her. I don't want her awake until I get back.

    Turning to the right, I make my way down the long hallway to my room. I close the door behind me and walk over to my dresser. Opening the top drawer, a million different ideas come to me all at once. I rummage around, looking for specific things to take to her room.

    I decide to grab the rope, my whip and a fucking ball gag to shut her mouth because as hot as her attitude gets me, it is really starting to get on my nerves. I'm not used to any kind of disrespect, especially coming from my playthings. I realize the irony at being pissed off at her blatant disrespect because it's exactly what I wanted. I didn't anticipate how fucking *exasperating* it would be.

    My heart rate kicks up and my dick pushes against my zipper in anticipation of what's to come.

    Let the fun begin.

CREEP

Essa

Throbbing. That's all I feel as I peel my eyes open, struggling because of the pain in my head screaming at me to keep them shut. Once I manage to open them after blinking a few times to help clear my vision, I realize I'm lying down which is different from the last memory I have.

I shoot myself into a sitting position when I realize I'm lying on a bed and not the hard bathroom floor like expected, but vertigo hits me hard. My head swims and throbs a thousand times worse than before, causing tears to leak from my eyes.

That motherfucker. My head has never felt this terrible before. I rub my fingers in circles over my temples, trying to ease the ache, but it's not helping like I'd hoped it would.

I look out the window, well, would it be called a window or a wall since the entire wall in here is made of glass as well? Either way, it's dark outside, probably late into the night, though I'm not sure the exact time because I was *fucking knocked out.*

I stare into the wooded area and even though it creeps me out, I can appreciate how peaceful it is being in the middle of nowhere. There are no lights from the city to pollute the sky so you can see every star in the abyss of inky black. There is not a cloud in sight, just millions of tiny balls of gas. In fact, this night looks similar to the night I realized the truth—I'm all alone.

I used to love stars when I was a kid. Almost every night, starting when I was six, I would go outside after my parents would leave to the neighbors down the road, and sit, staring at the sky. I remember hearing one time how you could wish on stars and they would come true. At six years old, I thought it was the coolest thing in the world, exactly what Holley and I needed. So, every night I sat outside, staring at the sky, making one wish over and over again.

Twinkle, twinkle, little star. Save us. Someone please come save us.

Hundreds of nights I sat there, making that wish, thinking for some pathetic reason if I devoted myself to it, my wishes would actually come true. But two years later, every single dream I ever had, every single shred of hope, of being free, was ripped to shreds in one night.

Losing yourself that young, you finally realize how fucking dumb wishing is. You can't depend on anyone but yourself. Nothing or no one was coming to save Holley and me. We were on our own. The day my innocence was ripped from me, I made the decision to protect us. If the stars couldn't save us, then it was up to me.

All of a sudden goosebumps crawl their way across my skin. I slowly turn my head to the corner of my room, a strong desire pulling me to look in that direction. Vincent's sitting in the chair in the corner of the room with one leg crossed over the other, resting on his knee.

He has a cigarette dangling from one hand, while the other is holding onto something I can't quite make out in the darkness of the room. Not knowing what to do, per usual, I sit and stare back at him, thankful my thoughts are taken away from my childhood for the moment.

It feels like we sit with our gazes locked on one another for an eternity, but it's only long enough for him to smoke two cigarettes back

CREEP

to back. He smokes each one without ever moving his eyes away from mine. I don't know how he didn't burn himself with the lighter, but somehow he managed to light each one effortlessly as if he's done it many times before.

The tension building in the air is nearly palpable. I shift, making myself comfortable again when I notice the bandage on my arm. *He bandaged my arm?*

"Why do I have a bandage on my arm?"

He grunts out his response as if it's obvious. "I didn't want your blood all over my bed when it's not because of me. You already bled all over my bathroom floor." He takes one last drag of his cigarette before smashing it into the ashtray on the end table next to him.

"I don't understand how this hasn't gotten into your thick skull already, but keep your fucking hands off of me. You fucking knock me out and then think it's okay to bandage me up like you give a shit? Please, don't even fucking bother. I don't want you anywhere near me, so get the fuck out of the room so I can go back to bed." He smiles as I talk, making me more wary of him.

How the hell does he go from a completely blank face to smiling that sinister ass grin at the flip of a switch? It's getting fucking creepy.

With the same eerie grin plastered across his face, he begins swinging something around on his finger—the same object I noticed him holding earlier—but I still can't make out what it is.

"What the hell is that?"

"You wanna know what this is, baby doll? I'll show you." He gets up and makes his way to me, his smiling growing wider. But now that he's moving closer, my defenses rise to the max and I crawl backwards across the bed to move away from him. Before I can move more than a few inches, he shoots his arm out and wraps his long fingers around my arm in a hard grip, his fingertips digging into my fresh wounds, causing me to hiss in pain.

"Sit fucking still little girl. You're not going anywhere. You've pissed me off enough already today, so if I were you, I'd play nice. It's the only way things won't get worse for you." He yanks my arm until my body is flush against his, both of my legs wrapping around his knee which is resting on the bed. Our chests touch with every heavy breath I suck into my lungs. "I'm sure you know by now how much I hate to love you acting up. I have a room full of things I want to use on you baby doll, but don't worry, we'll get to that. So, please keep running your pretty little mouth. I'll show you real fucking pain."

He seizes my chin, squeezing hard enough to bruise, and also making my lips pucker from the pressure of his fingertips digging into my cheeks. Soon enough, I'll be able to play connect the bruises on my face.

I can't help the rapid rise and fall of my chest, which worsens the tighter he squeezes my face. But not from fear, no. My pussy throbs and my panties dampen with what I can only assume to be arousal. I think I'm getting turned on by this fucking maniac.

What the actual fuck?

"Ready to play, baby doll?"

Oh, hell no. There is no way I'm doing whatever the fuck it is he has in mind. And I'm sure it's nothing good, but he doesn't wait long enough for me to react before he's pulling both of my arms to the junction of our bodies and wrapping rope around both of my wrists.

CREEP

The bandage covering my cuts is ripped off of my right arm in the process and I struggle against his grip, completely panicking.

Once he gets this rope secured, I'll be trapped—completely at his mercy.

Would it really be a bad thing?

Yes. I force the thought to override the other and repeat it over and over in my head like a chant.

Of course, while lost in my thoughts, I lose track of what's going on around me and it takes me a moment to realize my hands are already tied and bound together. I didn't even get a chance to fucking fight him off because of these damn thoughts that won't shut up and my stupid fucking body reacting in a way it shouldn't. In a way which terrifies me.

My hands shake as they rest against my lower stomach. Vincent's face is back to the blank mask he wears so well, but his eyes, however, tell a different story. They burn with anger and need he has no problem showing me as he drags me over to the foot of the bed. The ropes around my wrists chafe my already raw skin. A drop of blood forming on my right arm—the arm I mutilated mere hours ago—catches my attention. I zone in on the blood and watch as the drop doubles in size before falling to the mattress below.

Apparently he doesn't give a shit about blood on his bed now. Cue eye roll.

I thrash around on the mattress, flailing my legs hoping one clocks him in the face but he still manages to keep his grip and tie the ends of the rope to the foot of the bed, leaving me bent at an angle so moving my arms is virtually impossible.

He moves to the chair he was sitting in before and grabs a few objects which are gathered on the floor next to it. He slowly turns around with them in hand and drops them right next to me, a few of them smacking against my leg. Even in the dark of the room, the close proximity and the available moonlight gives just enough light to see what he dropped.

My heart hammers and my skin gets clammy with my anxiety. My breaths become more rapid and shallow as it becomes harder to breathe with every second passing with no reprieve.

I can't do this. I can't fucking do this.

His hands on my legs.

He breath fanning my face as he moves on top of me.

The pain.

The agonizing, brutal pain.

No. I can't.

I suck as much air into my mouth as I can, but none of it enters my lungs. My chest heaves as my lungs burn with the need for oxygen. Heat floods my cheeks as a cold sweat breaks out across my forehead.

I can't pass out. *I have to fight this. I have to fight him.*

I don't know what he would do to me if I lost consciousness and that's a risk I can't take, not again. Never again.

I somehow convince myself to take deeper breaths to calm my racing mind and my racing heart, but it becomes impossible when I see him pick up the whip in my peripheral. A fucking whip. All previous thoughts forgotten, the panic comes surging back into the forefront of my mind and black dots dance around the edge of my vision. A loud ringing sounds in my ears and my skin heats. I feel like I'm on fire.

CREEP

Fire.

Pain.

I need to cut. It's the only way I have ever been able to erase the thoughts of my father from my mind, or anything I can't deal with. Ironic, I know. Masking one pain with another, but it's the only thing that works and I'm not about to start changing it now. In my desperation for the one thing I know will save me, I resort to the lowest of lows—begging.

"Please, get me my knife. I need it!" I sob. He keeps his gaze locked on mine, but his expression remains stoic. His eyes now blank as well.

"Please, Vincent, I'm begging you! I need you to untie me. I can't fucking do this!" Tears stream down my face, leaving a trail in their wake. Vincent moves until he's standing right beside me, never taking his eyes off of me. I don't even think he's blinked one time. It sets chills bone deep, but a dark cloud settles over me and exhaustion sets in.

CHAPTER SEVEN
ESSA

I rouse for the second time that night, or was it early into the next day? That's one of my fucking problems. I don't know what day it is or even what time it is because I've been unconscious most of the fucking time.

I yank on my arms, but they're still tied to the fucking bed frame and my body is lying sideways. My arms are stretched to my right and they ache from having been stuck in the same position for so long. I'm uncomfortable as fuck.

While shuffling my body into a sitting position the best I can, I inspect the room for Vincent, but I don't see him, which means he probably stepped out for a few before coming back for me. I need to hurry up and find some way to get out of this hell hole. I don't know what I expected, but this is a whole other level of fucked up.

But Holley. Fuck. I can't be sure if my dad was bluffing about her or not. He has never laid a finger on her our entire lives—only lucky 'ol me—so it makes me question him. He's never laid a finger on her because she's actually his biological daughter and I'm not, but it's not like it matters at this point.

    Her life and her freedom are a risk I'm not willing to take. My one purpose in life is to protect her at all costs. With that in mind, I know I can't leave, but I at least have to get out of these fucking ropes. I pull against them, testing the strength of the knots. Naturally, they don't budge, but I try a few more times anyway because why the hell not. It's a start at least.

    I shuffle myself around on the bed, being as quiet as I can so I don't alert Vincent I'm awake, wherever he may be. I manage to maneuver myself to the bedside table and use my toes to grip onto the handle. I pull it open but snort when I realize it's empty. *Of fucking course it's empty. Why would I assume he would leave a fucking knife or something sharp lying around where I could reach it?* Sometimes my own stupidity makes me want to scream. I slam the drawer shut, pissed off. If that's not my luck, I don't know what is. There's nothing else I can reach while tied to this damn bed.

    I scooch to the other side of the bed, the side nearest to the door, while moving slowly and deliberately. I think I can flick the lock on the door if I can stretch far enough. It won't do much, but when he comes back, maybe it'll buy me enough time to figure something else out.

    Stretching my body with my arms raised high above my head, I lay my body across the end of the bed, stretching my foot to reach the door handle a few feet away. My limbs scream in protest, but I fight against the urge to give them relief.

    Once I get my toes on the lock, I curl them and twist my foot to turn the lock but my foot slips. I humph out an exasperated breath and try it again. On the third try—*third time's a charm*—I miraculously manage to wiggle my toes enough to turn the lock. Satisfied, I finally bring my screaming body back to the edge of the bed. I bite my tongue to stifle the cry which almost slips past my lips when my body is finally settled back onto the bed.

    I lie back on the bed, attempting to get comfortable in my compromised position as my thoughts overrun my brain. I have no fucking clue what to do. I don't think I can stay with this man, but at the same time, I know I don't have a choice. I never fucking did. Even though Holley's gone to college, I don't know if it will stop Ben from bringing her back here to pay his debt. He's a druggie for fucks sake. He's never given a shit about anyone or anything but his next fix.

    But for some reason, he has had a soft spot for Holl a time or two, or as much of a soft spot someone like him could have. It's never been anything big by any means, and almost nonexistent to the point I would've never noticed if I didn't see it for myself once before. Don't get me wrong, we were both neglected plenty, but he kept the physical shit to me and me alone.

    We were at the park playing one day because Ben had brought us. We were probably only at the park because he was buying drugs, but I guess ignorance is bliss, especially being a child. Holley was probably eight, and I was seven. It was a beautiful day. The sun was shining down, warming everyone and everything in its path. A few clouds could be spotted throughout the sky making it look as if they were painted on.

    We decided to slide down the giant metal slide together because it was always more fun that way. On our way down, Holley burnt her legs causing blisters to instantly pop up against her skin. The heat from the sun turned the metal so hot it burned to the touch, but we didn't realize it before it was too late.

She started crying in pain the second we jumped off and when she realized what happened, she ran to our father. She ran right up to him and jumped into his arms without hesitation. I stayed by the slide, watching it all, but not saying a word. For one, I thought it was strange as hell she sought him out in a moment of pain when all our mother and father had ever brought us was a life full of suffering, but Holley was always a forgive and forget type of person from the time she was a little girl.

He froze at her touch, hunched over with his arms dangling by his side while his daughter clung to him like a monkey. He stood with a stupefied look on his face for a solid minute before he got himself together and wrapped his arms around her.

I gasped, completely surprised. He had *never* hugged either one of us before. He usually preferred to act like we didn't exist. My heart clenched in pain, wanting affection from him, but knowing it would never happen.

Thinking about Holley makes my heart ache. I miss her so fucking much and she's only been gone for a few days. Has it been days already? Or is it still the same day? I don't even know, with everything that has been happening. I haven't talked to her since the morning she left, which was also the day Vincent showed up. Hopefully, she hasn't tried to call me because I don't even know where the fuck my phone is and she would worry if I didn't answer. She doesn't need the stress right now. Not when she's trying to get settled. So, for right now, I can only hope she's doing okay.

I strain my eyes trying to see if I can find my bag but it's fucking useless in this darkness. Clouds must be thick in the sky for there not to be much moonlight shining in.

The urge to cut again seeps into my veins, and I rub my arms together against the rope in hopes of satiating the feeling. At least temporarily, but it does nothing for me. Growing more frustrated by the second, I yank my arms up against the ropes a few times, making sure to pull hard. The chaffing from the rough rope creates enough friction for my cuts to seep open easily. Blood beads in a few different spots and begins to drip down my arm. *Fucking finally.*

Tugging harder, I cause even more cuts to split open and start bleeding again.

But it's not enough. I need more.

Getting creative, I twist my wrists from side to side as I continue to tug and I *hit the motherfucking jackpot.* Blood gushes out of the worst of my cuts, which just so happens to be my most recent one from the bathroom earlier. A feeling of ecstasy washes over me, the force of it so strong, I close my eyes.

Pain.

The pain.

The fucking numbness.

I don't know what's wrong with me. All I do know is cutting myself is the only fucking way I can keep surviving. I need this pain and I need the control it gives me. I know it's ironic I need to hurt myself to deal with the pain in my life, but it's just the way it is. One pain masks the other and makes it a little more fucking bearable. But more than that, it's about the *control*.

When you lack control in every aspect of your life, you search for something that is purely yours and yours alone. Mine just so happens to be my own pain and it's something I've come to accept over time. I used to feel ashamed of myself, for this need I have, but not anymore. This is my normal. Everyone has their own way of dealing with the baggage life gives them, and my method is more unconventional than most.

Hiding it from Holley has been a major challenge over the years. She has questioned me a lot about my attire, asking why I always wear hoodies even in the middle of summer when the temperature can reach over eighty degrees. I'd blow her off by shrugging my shoulders and saying I liked wearing them. Over time she grew to accept my answers as the truth and left it alone.

Lying here now, I realize how fucking dumb I was, expecting her to never catch on. But then again, she never did, did she? Maybe she never cared enough. Maybe she never cared at all. After all, she did leave me to go to a college all the way across the fucking country, ensuring we wouldn't see each other in person for a long time.

I obviously don't have the money or the option to go there and I know she doesn't have the money either. The only reason she was able to make it there to begin with was because the flight there was included with her full ride scholarship.

How could she leave me? I can't help the blistering rage simmering in the pit of my stomach. I wasted my entire fucking existence to protect her, solely surviving to take care of her. It all feels like a huge fucking waste now. What did protecting her give me other than a life full of pain and torture? I can't even remember a time when I wasn't covered in bruises and scars. I've been covered in both for so long, I don't know what I look like without them.

After that night outside, the night everything changed for me, that's when Ben first started slapping me around. Over the years, his open handed slaps turned to closed fists. After he got tired of splitting his knuckles against my body, he took to kicking me, to fucking *beating* me, within an inch of my life.

I vividly remember how he would swing his leg as far back as he could before swinging the fucking thing forward to connect to my ribs. My stomach. My back. It really just depended on his mood and how high he was.

He was always in a bad mood and high out of his mind.

The majority of the time, whenever he put his hands on me, I would be in bed for days after, trying to heal enough to go to school without drawing notice to the fact I was black and blue. Every shift of my body felt like a sledgehammer being swung over me repeatedly and made it pretty fucking hard to move, let alone go to school. I can't even remember how many broken bones I've endured. I only ever went to the emergency room when it was an injury too severe to be bandaged up myself.

Every emergency room trip we took was the same. My mother would accompany me, never leaving my side to make sure I didn't say a word about what had really happened—not that I ever would. They threatened Holley the same fate as me every time, so the unwelcomed company was always unnecessary. They knew that, but I know they liked thinking they could intimidate me.

CREEP

I shriek when a banging sounds against the door, yanking me out of my torturous thoughts.

"Essa. Open the goddamn door. I'm about sick of your fucking shit." He beats his fist on the door again as if I can't hear him.

"How can I do that when I'm tied to the bed, dumbass?" I genuinely can't help but goad him. I always did the same with Benjamin too. I knew running my mouth would make things a thousand times worse, but it's like my brain to mouth filter malfunctioned, and I'd spew shit I knew I shouldn't, even knowing I would later regret it.

"You do realize if you make me break another one of my doors to get to you, you won't be able to move for a fucking week, right?" The threat evident in his words, his tone dropping decibels in his anger and becoming rougher, sexier.

"Well, it sure as hell wouldn't be the first time, so bring it on, baby. I'm sure you can't hurt me more than I already am." *Again with the filter malfunction.*

At this point, I'm not even surprised when I see the door bust open, smacking against the wall with a thundering crack. Vincent's body takes up the entire doorway, looking like the fucking Hulk after he smashed something. A smirk pulls at the corner of my lips thinking about comparing him to The Hulk, their similarities not too far off in this moment.

He stalks over to me, not sparing me another glance. Reaching down, he grabs my arms and yanks them up, causing a few more lines of blood to run down and drip onto the bed.

"I thought you didn't want me to bleed on your bed, Vincent. That right there," I gesture to my arms with my head, "is kinda causing blood to drip all over the place." He grunts in response. *Fucking grunts like he's some caveman incapable of using words.*

"So, what's the plan for the rest of the night? Or is it tomorrow night already? I'm not sure because, for some reason, I keep either getting knocked out, or passing out for hours." I find his eyes and quirk my brow.

"You're funny, little girl. Who would have guessed behind all that attitude you can be a smartass as well. Too bad for you, I prefer the attitude, because your smartass mouth isn't getting my dick as hard as that does. You shutting the fuck up is preferable to me right now. Unless you want me to be the one to do it for you? I've already told you my favorite method, but if you would like a reminder, I don't mind giving you one."

I lose my snarky remark the second he references shoving his cock down my throat. My stomach flips in disgust. *Or is it in arousal? What the actual fuck is wrong with me?* This man is talking about fucking my mouth against my will and my dumbass is sitting here getting wet from it. *Yeah, I'm most definitely all kinds of fucked up.*

He shifts my arms to the side, bringing them to rest on top of the bed instead of the side. He drops them and reaches over to grab my hips from my lying down position. I jerk myself up, squirming out of his grip, but he squeezes tighter, moving me until my bottom half swings off the bed in a doggy style position. *Well, this definitely isn't good.*

I can't even fathom the different things that could happen in a position like this. Yeah, scratch that. I definitely could, and I don't like a single idea that pops into my head. *Or do I?*

Suddenly, my jeans are ripped down my thighs and thrown across the room. I whip my head around to look at Vincent but he's not even looking at my face. The fucker is blatantly staring at my ass.

"My eyes are up here, motherfucker. What the fuck do you think you're doing right now? Untie me and give me my jeans, right the fuck now." Anger boils through my veins, but more than the anger is the fucking fear I feel.

"What makes you think I give a shit about your eyes, hm?" he quirks his brow. "What I'm doing is playing with you, my little slave. Teaching you a lesson. Enjoying myself." He leans forward, resting his hand on the top of my head. He runs his fingers through my long, tangled strands. Wrapping my hair around his fist in a tight hold, he shoves my face into the bed.

"I've told you to shut the fuck up way too many times today baby doll. Please, make me say it again."

The pressure he's putting on my skull is so immense, I can barely breathe, let alone answer him. I try to nod my head, but it must be good enough for him because he relieves the pressure on my skull, though he doesn't let off my hair. My body is screaming at me to move, but I decide it's best if I stay still for the time being. I'm beginning to realize this man does not fuck around and I don't know how to react. With Ben, I always knew what to expect, but this is uncharted territory for me and I'm reacting poorly out of my fight or flight instincts.

Satisfied I'm where he wants me, he leans back, pulling my hair with him and my back arches at an incredibly painful angle.

"Hmm." He runs his nose along my neck, inhaling, causing

goosebumps to crawl across my skin. "You smell fucking divine, baby doll, and you look irresistible like this, but I think you'll look even better when your ass is blistered red and tears are running down your face. What do you think?" *Fuck, okay. I'm panicking.* Yep, I'm panicking. I wrench my body up and away from him, but as if he already knew what I was going to do, he grips my hips, halting my movements.

"Times up, baby doll." He removes his hands from my hips as he reaches for the whip lying on the bed. Without warning, he steps back and swings it down against my backside in a brutal blow. Fire rips across my ass, a scream tearing from my throat simultaneously. Before I can manage more than a scream, he brings it down again, in the same spot as before, but impossibly harder. Tears burst from my eyes, running down my already tear stained face.

Fuck, this is beyond brutal. I don't think I can take this kind of pain.

Vincent steps forward until his groin is right against my ass, rubbing against the fresh wounds. I hiss at the contact, trying not to show him how much pain I'm in.

He brings his lips to my ear. "I'm sick and fucking tired of your constant disrespect. I told you I'd show you what real fucking pain is, baby doll. You think the pathetic little blade you use will help you forget your shitty life? News flash, you're wrong."

"You know what I'm doing, baby? I'm showing the kind of pain you need. This is the kind of pain that makes you forget absolutely anything and everything except what you're feeling in this very moment. I know you already know what I'm talking about because you can feel it, can't you?"

He traces his tongue along my cheekbone, pulling back enough to bring his eyes to mine "Since the first lash, you haven't thought of a single thing except the pain you feel, correct?"

Fuck, I hate he's right, because he is. This pain is consuming everything. I don't care about a damn thing because I can't think about anything other than what's happening right now.

"You better get real used to it, baby doll. Until you can learn to shut that fucking mouth of yours, this is what you will get every time. Three lashes."

"Three? You've only given me two." I manage to croak out, but I instantly realize how stupid of me it was to mention it, because in the next second, I feel the third across my ass and lower back. I arch my back in a pathetic attempt to escape the blow. Vincent grabs my hair again, pulling until my back is against his front and my hands are pulled down in front of me from the rope. He wraps his large hand around my throat and squeezes me against him until every inch of my back is touching every inch of his torso.

"If you think that was bad, you're going to be in for quite the surprise. That is *nothing* compared to what's to come, baby doll. It was just a little taste of what I want to do to you. Remember that." He smashes his lips down against mine. I gasp at the unexpected contact, giving him the opportunity to slip his tongue into my mouth. I run my tongue along his, twisting them together and reveling in the contact. Fire surges through my bloodstream, and I mold myself deeper into his body.

His grip against my throat tightens as he deepens our kiss. He becomes more aggressive and pulls me harder against him, causing our teeth to clash together. But the contact spurs him on even more. He pulls my bottom lip in between his teeth and bites down. My blood floods our mouths and unexpected pleasure rips through me. I can feel him harden against my backside and my ass screams in pain as I grind against his growing cock. My body completely took over the second his lips touched mine.

I don't know what the fuck this is, but whatever it is, is not good.

Snapping myself out of it, I yank my head away from his, gasping. My chest is heaving as if I just ran ten miles. It takes me a moment to open my eyes, but when I do, I notice he's already looking at me. Confusion rings loud in his eyes, his brow furrowing as our eyes stay connected. Both of our internal monologues are probably screaming, *What the fuck was that?*

Vincent shoves me away and I fall to the bed, my arms pulling against the rope. He's already almost to the door when I look back at him, "What the fuck? You're just going to leave me tied up?" He completely ignores me as he slams the door behind him.

I look down at my arms, the blood covering them has long since dried, leaving streaks down my arms. That was beyond fucking weird. And so fucked up. I can still feel my pussy throbbing, demanding a release. I've never had an orgasm, or even been turned on before, but apparently my body knows what it wants.

But why did it turn me on? He was violent, demanding, brutal. The exact things I *shouldn't* want, yet, here I am wanting to beg for more.

I roll to my side and hiss when my ass makes contact with the bed, but this pain is nothing compared to the shit Ben has put me through. I

can fight through this.
    Maybe.

CHAPTER EIGHT
VINCENT

I pace the kitchen, wearing a path into the floor. I run my hands through my hair, yanking the strands and ripping some out. *What the fuck just happened?* I fucking kissed her. I have never kissed another person before in my life, but I just kissed her. And I liked it.

No, scratch that, I fucking loved it. But I hate the little bitch and I want to hurt her. I need to hurt her. To wrap my hands around her throat and squeeze until she's blue and cold and no longer running that little mouth of hers.

But those plump lips, cracked and bleeding against mine felt like fucking nirvana. The taste of her blood still rests on my tongue. Seeing her bleeding in the bathroom after she ripped her arms open was one thing, but the second I tasted her blood, I knew shit just got more complicated.

One taste and I was fucking done for. There is something about her that's intoxicating me. It's almost like her blood is my own personal drug, specifically designed to fucking consume me.

CREEP

Thinking about her, I run my tongue along my lips, savoring the taste of her because I can't let myself lose control like that again. She needs to know who the fuck is in charge, and I can't let her get confused by thinking her pussy has any effect on me. She's just a toy who needs to learn her fucking place.

If I would've used that ball gag to begin with, then this is something I wouldn't have to worry about right now.

I halt my pacing and take a seat on the stool at the kitchen island. I run my finger over my lips, unable to stop thinking about her and it's driving me fucking insane. I wish I knew what the hell it was about this girl which has me breaking my own rules. I only met her for the first time yesterday, less than twenty four hours ago, *and* she's been unconscious most of the time—not like it stopped me from watching her.

I'm fascinated by her in ways I truly wish I wasn't. I mean, sure, women have held my interest before, but only long enough for me to stick my dick in them to come, and then call it a day while kicking them out of the door. Occasionally, I'll have a slave around for a month or so to play with, but it's been occurring less and less recently because even they aren't holding my attention anymore. I've been utterly fucking bored, or at least I was until Essa showed up in my life. Now, I'm just annoyed and slightly obsessed with a bratty eighteen year old who is about to graduate from high school.

This girl should have never piqued my interest. I'm a fucking twenty-four year old man, but the second I laid my eyes on her, something happened. My pain felt her pain and the monsters in us began to merge. The pain that is blatantly clear in her eyes is consuming me. That's not even mentioning the bruises covering her entire body, bruises I know aren't from me. Something's been happening to her and I'm going to find out what...

But enough of that shit. Shaking thoughts of her away, I get my head back in the game. It doesn't matter what this girl does to me, she's a fucking payment. Strictly a payment who needs to learn her fucking place.

Her piece of shit parents have been buying from me for years, therefore their debt has drastically built from *many* skipped payments. The money I wasn't receiving from them wasn't enough to put a dent in my future plans so I never paid it much mind—it was just fun to fuck with them. Tweakers are always so paranoid. They did pay me a little here and there, but they owe me way more than they could ever repay.

Hence, Essa.

A few weeks ago, Ben came to the pub and was waiting for me to get him his eight ball, which was his usual order. He started blabbing about his daughter, clearly already high out of his mind. Only half listening, I heard him say some shit like she was a waste of space, always in the fucking way, blah, blah.

I then tuned him out like I always do but then he jumped off of the stool he was barely managing to sit still on and randomly shouted about Essa not being his biological daughter and he hated her, so he made sure she knew it.

Thinking about him putting his disgusting hands on her in any way sends rage boiling through my blood. Ironic, considering I have her tied to my bed and crying right now, but I never said I wasn't a hypocrite. I want to be the only one to make her bleed, to make her cry, and to bring her pain. I *need* to be the only one.

Speaking of, her pathetic little attempt at hurting herself is quite amusing. I wonder what she's been going through that makes her want to do it. She obviously wants or even needs to feel pain to feel better, to center the bullshit she is going through. Something I understand all too well.

Exhaustion hits me like a punch to the face. I look over to the clock on the wall and see it's already after three a.m. I scoot the stool back and it scrapes against the floor. It creates a terrible screech, which actually makes me wince.

I walk into my bedroom and decide to shower then grab a quick nap before dealing with Essa and her bullshit. The little bitch is fucking exhausting. I walk into the bathroom, quickly strip my clothes, and step into the shower. I reach down and turn the nob all the way to hot, letting the ice cold water run over me until it warms up.

Later that day, I'm standing in front of my bathroom mirror straightening my tie when I hear a loud banging against the wall. Rolling my eyes, I take one last glance, making sure it's straight and then make my way to Essa's room. The little brat is probably annoyed. I left her tied up and alone all day. No food or even water because I didn't have the energy to deal with her. I still fucking don't, but it's three o'clock and her graduation starts at five so we have to get moving. I don't understand why there is a graduation at five in the evening, but whatever. The sooner we get it over with, the better.

I push her door open and step inside and see Essa curled up along the edge of the bed. Probably to stay off of her ass because it's still glowing a beautiful red and the welt are still raised against her skin. When she notices my entrance, she scoots herself into a sitting position, wincing when her ass touches the bed. She tilts her head up to meet my gaze, her eyes simmering with indignation.

"Watch those eyes, baby doll. You know how your defiance turns me on." I wink and she ignores me, continuing to glare, unperturbed by my comment. *Someone must have gained some confidence throughout an entire day of being left alone.*

"You feel like telling me why the hell you have left me in here all damn day? I have to piss really fucking bad so could you *please* untie me so I can use the bathroom." Sarcasm is dripping from her voice, but I ignore it, for now, only because we don't have the time for me to beat her ass right now.

I reach into my pocket to grab the knife I always carry on me. Slipping it in between her mutilated wrists and the rope covering them, I work it back and forth a few times until it frays and the knife slips through, releasing her. She rubs her wrists, attempting to bring life back into them. I pocket my knife again and step back.

"Your graduation is in two hours, you need to get ready. Your bag is in the bathroom." I turn around and leave the room before I can hear her response.

CREEP

I'm standing in the kitchen, leaning against the counter waiting for her, when she finally walks into the kitchen. She stops a few feet in front of me and stands, staring out the window while twisting her fingers, her nervous habit coming out again.

Damn, she looks good.

I run my eyes over her body, taking in her appearance. She's dressed in a simple black, long sleeved dress which cuts off midthigh, showcasing her thick thighs covered in fishnet stockings. She has on Chuck Taylor Converse and her long hair falls down her back in slight waves.

As I bring my eyes up to her face, I notice her lashes are coated in black. Such a mundane thing which makes explicit images pop into my head. The black of her makeup smudging from her cries and mixing with her tears, leaving black stains down her face as she chokes on my cock when it hits the back of her throat.

I clear my throat when she catches my eyes lingering on her. "I want to set some ground rules to make things clear to you before we go anywhere. I'm certain you know this, but the most obvious rule is to keep your fucking mouth shut. Second, I'm going to give you your phone back so you can talk to your sister. She hasn't called yet, but I'm sure she will soon. You already have a habit of pissing me off, so let's not make right now one of those times you decide to open your pretty fucking mouth, yeah? I'm feeling less lenient with you and your shit today."

She carries on fidgeting with her fingers, annoying the fuck out of me. This entire fucking time she's been constantly running her mouth and now she wants to shut the fuck up? Why couldn't she just fucking listen and start shit out this way?

Fucking women make no sense.

"Okay," she retorts while staring at the floor. I brush past her on my way to the door, already completely over this whole fucking endeavor. I make it to the door before I notice she's still standing in the middle of the kitchen, staring at my fucking floor like it's some interesting piece of art. There is something gravely wrong with this girl.

"Are you coming, or would you like to skip your own graduation? I don't really give a shit either way, but just know if you don't make the decision to move your ass in the next two seconds, I'm taking you back to your room and tying your ass up for the entirety of tomorrow for wasting my fucking time."

"Chill, I'm coming. I'm just fucking nervous," she snaps as she finally moves her fucking feet and walks toward me. When she gets in the same vicinity as me, I wrap my hand around her throat and push her against the very same wall I had her against last night.

I bring my face right in front of hers and gaze into her eyes. "You have every reason to be nervous, baby doll." I run my tongue along the side of her face, from her chin to her temple. I hear her sharp intake of breath and it makes me smirk.

"Because if you fuck up one iota tonight, I'll show you the side of me you haven't met yet. And he is someone you better pray you never meet. He would rip you to shreds little girl, and I'm not saying it figuratively either. Especially because he hasn't been out to play for a while." I wink at her and push off the wall, leaving her while I walk out to the car. I jump in and while waiting for her to follow, I start the car and appreciate the feel of it rumbling beneath me.

She gets in and I catch as she winces when her ass meets the leather. My face cracks into a sinister grin knowing she's in pain because of me.

I start down the winding drive, the woods surrounding the road on either side. The sun is low in the sky, casting the trees in a red orange hue. For as long as I have lived here, I'm still not used to the view. It's what drew me to this place. Dark, eerie, and full of endless places to hide corpses is always a bonus too.

Growing up, I had what most would probably call a shitty childhood, but to me, it was my life. I was raised surrounded by *mostly* heroin, but so many other drugs are involved when that shits around, and the random guys my mother would bring home.

I've always had to fend for myself, so when I lost my mother to an overdose at the age of eleven, it didn't change my life much more than the scenery. The only difference her death made for me was, I became completely alone. I never had her before, but her presence made me feel a little less lonely. But when she died? I lost every shred of any hope I had.

I bounced around foster homes for a few years until I finally got sick of being a pity party for people to take in for no other reason than to make themselves feel better and ran away. At the age of fourteen, being on the streets was fucking hard, I'm not gonna lie. I struggled with finding somewhere warm to sleep every night and finding food daily was a whole other disaster.

When I first went off on my own, I went days without a single bite of food, but over the weeks, I learned tips and tricks from simply observing the people around me and the area I was living in.

Once I got the hang of things, most of the food I ate was stolen from stores or it was shit I found in dumpsters outside of bakery shops or other restaurants. But the bakery shops always had not only the best food, but the freshest too.

I struggled with that lifestyle for about a year before I met my *now* boss. Leo was a big-time dealer on the streets back then and I still remember the day I met him. It was the one and only time I let someone do me a favor.

It's raining, but not the nice kind of rain, no. It's fucking pouring and forty degrees out. I'm walking around with my backpack, freezing my ass off while trying to find somewhere to sleep for the night. I make my way down a back alley, barely watching where I am going, the rain coming down in sheets, making it too hard to see clearly.

I run into two dumpsters, smacking my face against the side of one of them. Cursing, I shake my head and step back while rubbing where I know it's going to bruise. I see the dumpster lids open, overlapping each other and creating a small enclave which I crawl underneath as soon as I see it. The smell is repulsive, and I instantly gag the second I'm under the makeshift shelter, but I breathe through my mouth and fight the urge to vomit. It's the first dry place I found no one would see me, so I need to suck it the fuck up.

I wish people would mind their own business and stop trying to put me back into the system whenever they see me on the streets. I do fine on my own—I've always done completely fine. I want people to leave me alone and let me survive the only way I know how.

I hear a loud bang. I jerk, startled, and then duck into the shadows to avoid being seen even though it is virtually impossible to see a thing in this rain.

A man steps out of the shadows. Just steps out of the fucking shadows like you see the villains do in the movies. My first instinct is to cower at his dominating presence and the motherfucker can't even see me but I refuse to cower, whether I can be seen or not.

He must have seen me duck out of the rain because he walks right up to the dumpsters and crouches down, leaning inside of the shelter to keep his head out of the rain. If this guy thinks he can take advantage of me, he's got another thing coming. I pull my knife from my pocket and flip open the blade, hoping if he can't see it he can at least hear it open and know I'm not fucking around.

"What the fuck do you want?" I manage to keep my voice steady despite my anxiety, but I raise it slightly so I can be heard clearly over the rain.

"What are you doing out here kid?" the man asks.

"Trying to fucking sleep if you'd back off and leave me be," I snap, a natural reaction I have always had to people but he laughs, brushing off my tone.

"Hey, I'm not trying to bother ya. Just wondering why a kid your age is out here in this weather, alone, and trying to hide in the dumpsters. It's fuckin' cold out."

"Clearly I know how fucking cold it is. I don't have anywhere else to go and I'm exhausted. So, if you could fuck off, that'd be great." I keep the sarcasm in my voice, hoping he takes the fucking hint and leaves.

"I get it kid. I know you don't know me and you probably won't even listen—which is one hundred percent on you—but there is a pub around the corner. A friend of mine owns it and they're open all night. I'm sure we can find a booth for you to crash in. It's nothing great. In fact, it's actually pretty shitty, but it's better than freezing your ass off in here, eh?"

I contemplate his proposal for a second. I don't trust him. But then again, I don't trust a soul, not even my own. But he did say it is a pub, meaning I wouldn't be alone with whoever this guy is. Plus it will actually be fucking warm inside. I could warm up and maybe sleep for more than an hour at a time.

The man backs up and I move to stand to my full height, five foot eleven at the age of fourteen. My height has definitely helped me out while being a runaway. People don't tend to question someone my size with a beard too often, but it does happen, much to my fucking annoyance.

He turns around and walks down the alley, expecting me to follow, so I do, keeping myself a few paces behind him. He rounds the corner and pulls open a door with a sign hanging above that says, "Leo's Pub".

I walk through and heed the few people scattered about. "Rockstar" by Nickelback plays through the speakers at a surprisingly comfortable level. I'm not sure what time it is, but gathering the lack of people, it's either really early or really late.

The guy walks in behind me saying, "Go ahead and find somewhere to get comfortable. I'll be at the pub." He walks past me to the bar and takes a seat, ordering a whiskey.

Damn, I want one of those. It would definitely help me sleep.

CREEP

Pushing the thought away knowing it's not an option, I make my way to the corner of the room and take a seat in a booth. I rest my back against the wall so I can keep my eyes on everyone around me. I refuse to let my guard down one bit despite the fact a stranger is choosing to help a random street kid. Trusting people is how you get fucked over and hurt. I'm not stupid enough to make that decision again.

No one pays me any mind and because of it, I find myself slowly closing my eyes, succumbing to the exhaustion which has been begging to pull my body under.

I absently rub my arm where my poppy tattoo is at the thought of my mother and all the shit I went through because of her. I know heroin is derived from the latex found in its unripe seed capsule, but the poppy itself is still a representation of many things, especially for me.

It's a reminder to myself to never succumb to drugs or to that lifestyle. But, also, it's ironically in memory of my mother. I say ironically because a poppy was her favorite flower and yet she died from a heroin overdose.

We pull into her high school parking lot and I eventually pull into a space after looking for an open one for over ten minutes. I slam my door as I exit, then round the car to wait for her. We walk into the building together, and she's still strangely quiet. I wrap my arm around her shoulders, pulling her into me.

"Better wipe the grimace off your face, baby doll. I have no problem taking you into that bathroom and beating your ass so bloody, you won't be able to sit in the chair you need to be in to get your diploma. You think your ass hurts now?" I whisper, running my mouth along the shell of her ear. "That's nothing." She stiffens against me, her eyes roaming the room, but doesn't pull away. *Smart girl.*

Plastering on a fake smile, she tilts her head up to stare into my eyes. "Oh please, like you would do something like that in a public place, with all of these people."

Yep, scratch that. She's most definitely not a smart girl. I guess she's about to learn her lesson in underestimating me and thinking I give a single shit about anyone or even where the fuck we are.

I grip her shoulders harder against me and steer us towards the bathroom on the other side of the room. I feel her resistance as she pushes her heels into the floor, trying to halt my advance, but I'm fucking determined now.

"You've really gotta stop underestimating me, baby doll. You really think I give a shit about being in a high school? About being surrounded by people? That's your first fucking mistake. Second, you're about to see about how much I don't fucking care. As a matter of fact, let them hear your fucking screams. Go ahead. I want them to know who fucking owns you. Tell them who you're screaming for."

I shove the door to the unisex bathroom open. Pushing her in, I slam the door behind us and flick the lock. Facing her, I grab her shoulders and spin her around, shoving her face into the cold, white brick wall. I yank her dress up around her hips and rip a hole in her fishnets to give myself easier access to her underwear. I yank on her panties until I feel them give way. Bringing them up to my face, I see a wet spot gracing the middle of her panties and smirk. *Little fucking bitch is wet for me.* I feel my dick stretch against the zipper of my slacks and I groan.

CREEP

I shove her underwear in front of her face. "Look how wet you are for me, baby doll. Why's that?" I taunt, licking the back of her neck. "You're wet for me and you fucking love it. You may hate me, hell, you even hate yourself, but you can't make your body hate what I do to you. My little fucking masochist. *All. Mine.*" I shove her underwear in her mouth, causing a whimper to escape her lips before it's muffled.

I grab her hips, pulling them back against me until she's bent at a ninety degree angle, her face still pressed against the wall. I take a step back and admire the view. Her plump ass is still red and her fishnets crisscross over her cheeks. I push my fist into my mouth and bite on my knuckles. This girl does have a fantastic fucking ass.

Her ass still has welts across it from my lashings earlier and it makes me crack a grin around my fist. This is gonna hurt like a bitch. Without further ado, I swing my hand down across her ass, instantly leaving a bright red handprint, mixing with the others covering her ass. My hand tingles from the force.

She screams, though the sound is muffled greatly by her panties shoved in her mouth. I smack her ass two more times before stepping up right against her. The heat radiating from her ass seeps into my slacks and my dick jumps, desperate to be inside of her pussy.

Not yet, but soon.

So fucking soon.

I grab her hair and yank her head up until her entire back is pressed against my front. I snake my arm around her and shove it between her legs. I'm greeted instantly by wetness coating both of her thighs. I groan, my eyes rolling into the back of my head. I sweep my hand up through her wetness, coating my fingers. With my other, I yank the underwear from her mouth and shove my fingers covered in her arousal into her mouth.

"Fucking taste how wet you are for me baby. All I did was beat your ass like the naughty girl you are and you're dripping for me. *For me. For what I do to you.* Suck." She immediately wraps her lips around my fingers and sucks, hard.

"*Fuuuuck.*" A groan leaves my throat and my dick pushes against the zipper of my slacks to the point it's painful. Essa keeps sucking, her tongue swirling around the tips. I yank my fingers from her mouth and wipe my hand across her cheek, covering it in her own spit.

"I have fucking told you time and time again I don't fuck around, Essa. I have no problem teaching you a lesson, no matter where the hell we are." I pull her dress back down, skimming the tips of my fingers along her skin and spin her around. I lean down to grab her panties and shove them into my pocket.

"Let's go. I want to get this shit over with." With that, she walks ahead of me and out the door with her head held high, exuding confidence, but her cheeks are flushed and her legs shake slightly with every step she takes.

I follow her out and we make our way to the chairs in the center of the room. She takes a seat in her assigned 'Monroe' chair and I hand her the phone I promised I would.

"Don't be stupid with it. Do you understand me?" She grabs it, peering up at me when I don't let go.

"Yes, sir." She turns away but I don't miss the roll of her eyes as she says it.

Ever the defiant little girl.

I ignore her and move to the guest chairs, taking a seat where I can see Essa perfectly. I keep my eyes focused on her the entire time. Through her walking across the stage and after, when she's watching everyone else receive their diplomas. I notice after a while her parents didn't show up, probably too high to fucking move.

After everyone has received their diplomas, someone makes some stupid speech about how there are greater things to come, blah, blah, blah. *I'm fucking bored.*

Suddenly, everyone is screaming and there is confetti and hats flying in every direction. *Finally, it's fucking over.*

Amidst all the chaos, Essa makes her way over to me, diploma in hand and a scowl on her face.

"Can we please go now?" she clips out, her teeth clenched.

"Fuck yes, let's go." I walk out the doors, her fast on my heels. Unlocking the car, we both jump in. She lets out a deep breath and turns her head to gaze at me.

"Do you mind if I call Holley? She's been calling me all night and I don't want her to worry."

"Sure thing. You know not to be stupid about it." I quirk my brow at her, reiterating what I have told her probably a hundred fucking times by now. I feel like a broken record, even annoying myself at this point, but I never know when she's going to decide to listen and when she's going to be a defiant little brat so I have to stay on my toes.

"Yes, I'm well aware. I'm not stupid," she mutters as she dials her sister, putting the phone to her ear.

"That's fucking debatable," I retort and she glares at me but her sister must answer because the biggest smile stretches across her face.

MARIE ANN

Her eyes even crinkle slightly from the sheer force of it.

She begins yapping away to her sister as I pull out of the parking lot, heading back to my house. The sun has long set, my headlights casting shadows along the road as I drive.

"So Far Away" by Staind plays on the radio in the background and I turn it up, attempting to drown out the sound of her voice as I lose myself in the lyrics.

CHAPTER NINE
ESSA

We pull up outside of his house a little while later. I talked to Holley for the first ten-ish minutes of the drive, but she had to get off the phone because she apparently has to wake up early for work, but before she did, she had to tell me about her new boss and how nice and accommodating he's been. I've missed talking to her, but I'm glad she's happy—it's what she deserves.

He puts the car into park and we sit in silence. Normally silence is a comfort to me, but my brain is all over the place tonight and nerves wrack my body. It doesn't help every shift of my weight on the seat causes pain to shoot across my ass, reminding me I let this man spank me in a very public bathroom at my old fucking high school. *And* he fucking *whipped* me.

I fidget with my fingers as I feel heat crawl up my neck and onto my face when I remember what he did to me. It's a nervous habit I've developed over the years and I don't even notice when I do it most of the time. But tonight I'm staring directly into my lap to avoid Vincent's eyes boring into me. He reaches across the center console, gripping my hands in his to halt my movement.

"Would you fucking stop? It's annoying the hell out of me. You've been doing it sporadically since earlier. What the fuck do you have to be so nervous about?"

Is he really fucking serious asking me that right now? But I stay quiet, ignoring his question.

At first, I was fidgeting all night because I was nervous to see my parents at graduation. It's only been over a day since I've seen them, but honest to God it seems like a whole lifetime ago already. Knowing I would see Benjamin caused my nerves to skyrocket and not being able to cut all night has caused all of my feelings to build and now I feel them boiling over.

When Vincent gave me my things earlier and told me to get dressed, the first thing I did was search for the knife I have hidden in my bag but the motherfucker must have gone through it with a fine tooth comb because I couldn't find the damn thing. Anywhere. I guess he was serious when he said he didn't want me to cut myself.

I haven't the slightest damn clue as how to deal with emotions of any kind. The only time I truly feel anything anymore is when it's in relation to Holley. I feel her love and I have love for her. I make sure she knows and I try to show it as well as I can, but it's fuckin' hard sometimes. I have to fight with myself tooth and nail because it's been a long time since I've had to rely on myself to work through shit instead of going straight to cutting to solve my problems for me.

I fucking hate it.

But now we're back at his house and I'm annoyed with everything.

CREEP

For one, Ben and Sierra didn't even bother to make an appearance tonight. I kept my eyes peeled for them, but nope. Of course they didn't show and now I'm stuck with their drug dealer, but I'm out from underneath their roof so they're probably having the time of their life with no kids and no responsibilities—not that they made us ones to begin with. I can't help but wonder if things are going to change now with my visits to Vincent's. Ben was pretty pissed off about the whole situation and I know he's dying to take it out on me.

I exit the car and walk along the path leading to the front door, kicking small stones out of the way with the tip of my shoe. There are small lights along the edge of the walkway, illuminating the path and making it easier to see in the black of the night. Though, out here, there are no lights from the city to pollute the sky therefore I can see every star. The moon shines bright and heavy in the sky, illuminating everything around me, but still keeping everything dark enough to have a sinister feel to it.

Glancing up from the ground, I peer through the trees surrounding us for miles, their depth exceptional.

I halt my steps to stare into the woods, hypnotized and lost in my thoughts.

I wonder what it would be like to run through the trees, the wind rushing past me as I push my legs faster and deeper into the dirt, propelling myself forward. Every sense heightened with only your basic instinct to guide you.

Wolves are majestic animals. They're highly intelligent and loyal to a fault. They bond with their pack and take care of each other—even fighting to the death to protect one another if it comes to it. And a lot of the times it does.

I crave that type of love, that type of loyalty and I *need* that type of freedom. Sure, I have Holley and I know she loves me and would do anything for me, but let's be honest. Throughout all of the bullshit of our lives, she was kept in the dark about most of it—about basically fucking all of it. She hasn't a single fucking clue as to what has ever really gone on because I've always protected her from it all. Fighting with not only Ben, but myself too, because it was my choice to keep her out of it, but it doesn't mean it hurts any less.

When it comes down to it, I'm the only one who would die for her. Which I do, every single fucking day of my existence. Every day I'm breathing, every day my heart keeps on beating, I'm dying for her.

I take a deep breath and look to the front door. Vincent's standing right inside the threshold, staring at me and waiting for me to follow him into the house. He tilts his head to the side in question, but doesn't say a word. I glance back at the trees and launch myself towards them.

I take off running, my legs already burning from the exertion. I have no fucking idea what I am doing. All I know is it feels good to run, to feel *free*. The breeze rushes past my face as I pick up my pace, pushing my converse covered feet harder into the ground.

Once I make it to the thick foliage, a tree with deep red stains catches my eye because it sticks out like a sore thumb, even in this darkness. My steps falter, but I don't dare stop. *Curiosity killed the cat and all that nonsense.* My heart pounds against my ribcage. I feel like a wolf, running to catch their prey, only in my instance, I'm the prey running *from* the predator.

In the thick of the trees, it's harder to make out where I'm going.

CREEP

Their thick branches keep the moonlight from penetrating completely and I have to slow my pace or risk running smack into a fucking tree trunk. My chest is heaving and my lungs are screaming at me to slow down, but I can't. I've already made it this far.

I didn't know my intention when I took off, but now I'm out here, I know I have to fucking escape. I have to leave and find Holley. Once I'm with her, I can figure out where to go from there. But first things first, actually making it out of these fucking trees.

I dodge a few low hanging branches, keeping my pace steady. I don't even think to listen for the sound of footsteps—a grave mistake on my part—because without warning, my body is shoved forward and I nosedive to the ground. I let out a scream as my face hits the dirt, inhaling it in the process. Hands wrap around my upper arms as a knee digs into my spine. I cry out and I try to scream at him to let me up, but he's pushing me so far into the ground, I can't lift my head enough to speak. He leans down over me, his knee digging into my spine further.

"You think you can run away from me, baby doll? I know these woods like the back of my fucking hand. Where exactly did you think you would be able to run to out here, hm?" His voice almost a whisper, caressing along my skin and igniting chills, but I'm not fooled by the soft tone of his voice. He shifts his knee against my back, alleviating enough of the pressure I can speak.

I croak, spitting dirt from my mouth. "I wasn't trying to run from you, I swear. I just wanted to run through the trees. I don't know what came over me. I wanted to feel free and now that I say it out loud, I know how stupid it sounds. Please don't hurt me." Though what I'm saying is truthful, even I can sense the bullshit in my words. He chuckles darkly as he runs his finger along my face, smearing dirt and saliva across my cheek.

"You wanted to feel free, huh?" He leans down more, his front pressed against my back. His warmth seeps through our clothes, even in the chill of the night. Every time he touches me, his raging inferno heats my frigid soul—even as he has me pinned to the dirt.

Bringing his lips to the shell of my ear, his baritone voice caressing me, "You will never be fucking free, Essa. No matter where you go, no matter where you run to, I will fucking find you. You're *mine.*" He stands and pulls me alongside him. Before I can get my bearings straight, I'm slung over his shoulders. I let out a screech in surprise, but he turns and heads back to where I presume the house is without a word.

I dangle from his shoulders, acting like a sack of potatoes as he hauls me through the trees. I feel utterly defeated, not bothering to fight him at this point. I know he's going to punish me for running away when we get back inside and I don't even care. I've been fighting every fucking day and I'm exhausted, but more than that, what's the point? Holley's gone and I'm here with Vincent, exactly like my parents wanted. Therefore, I have no reason to keep trying. He's going to do what he wants to me and nothing I say or do will change that.

Vincent keeps an arm clasped around my waist, squeezing tighter the closer we get to the house. After walking for a few minutes, we break through the clearing and the house comes into sight. I lift my head from staring at his ass—*and what a nice ass it is*—to look at the house and see he left the door open to chase after me. I don't know why it brings a smile to my face, but it does. Any minor inconvenience to him is a win in my book, I guess.

Still smiling, I relax my neck again and let my head hang so I can resume my staring at his ass. His muscles flex with every step he takes and the slacks he's wearing showcase his ass perfectly. We walk through the door and Vincent kicks it shut behind us.

Without putting me down or slowing his pace, he walks us straight up the stairs to his bedroom which is down the hall from mine. When we reach his door, he pauses in front of it, not moving.

My first instinct is to ask him what the fuck he's doing, but I bite my tongue. I can feel his anger rolling off of him in waves and I know if I open my mouth right now, it won't do anything but worsen his mood and I'm not stupid enough to make my situation worse than it already is.

I'm most definitely stupid enough to do that.

After a minute of deafening silence passes, he opens the door and walks across the room to the bed. He flings me over his shoulder, throwing me down onto the bed. I flop like a fish on top of his mattress, a shriek leaving my mouth.

Without sparing me another glace, he turns around and shuts the door. Moving to the dresser across the room, he opens the top drawer and pulls out what seems to be handcuffs and… *are those chains? Fuck!*

Dread pools in the pit of my stomach and my hands feel clammy as anxiety swims in my bloodstream. He grabs my hands and clasps the cuffs around them quickly and efficiently. He pulls them above my head, stretching my arms at an incredibly painful angle. He wraps a chain around both wrists on top of the cuffs and then locks the chain to his bedpost with a fucking padlock.

The cuffs and chains are already biting into my skin, causing more discomfort, but I welcome the feeling. He moves away from me once he is satisfied my arms are secured. With nothing else to do being chained to a fucking bed, I take in his bedroom. He has me chained to a giant black four poster bed and on either side of the bed, there are two end tables. One of which has a lamp with a really ugly lamp shade, in my opinion.

The walls along the perimeter of his room are made of glass—like the rest of the house—but the interior walls are painted a dark gray keeping to the monochromatic color scheme he seems to have throughout the entire house.

I tilt my chin towards the ceiling, trying my hardest to look behind me but I can't see much other than I'm lying on a black silk covered pillow and a thick black silk blanket. They feel soft against my abused skin. My body automatically relaxes and my eyelids droop in exhaustion. I fight to stay awake by searching for Vincent, but he must have left the room because I can't find him. I lose the battle and sleep overtakes me.

CHAPTER TEN
VINCENT

I left the room after I tied her up to grab a few of my favorite knives and when I came back, she was sleeping. Fucking sleeping while I have her chained to my bed. The girl I've come to know would've never fallen asleep. She would be fighting me, kicking and screaming and the fact she's passed out on my bed right now is unusual.

This girl has brought out the best and worst sides of me more times in the last twenty-four hours than in my whole fucking life. I don't give a shit about anyone or anything, but she somehow manages to make a part of me feel empathetic and I can't fucking stand it. I don't give a shit about her or her sob story of a life. Which is exactly how I feel when she runs that pretty little mouth of hers. Her attitude is a fucking trigger to the monster in my head.

It's not like I have another personality. I'm fucking fine. It's only every time I feel my rage blazing through my blood, set to fucking explode, a different side of me comes out and takes over and I can't control it.

I noticed it began happening shortly before my mother OD'd and killed herself because that's when her "boyfriends" started trying to put their hands on me, coming into my room at night. Once it began, every time shit got exceedingly difficult, it's like he would show up and I'd suddenly have the power to fight back and any fear I had would disappear.

Whenever she brings that side of me out—which is a fucking lot for only recently having met her—I fight to keep it at bay because I know how fucking ruthless I can be and I don't wanna kill the fucking girl. But I'm fed up with the attitude she's been giving me and I think her meeting my fucking monster is exactly what she needs to straighten her ass out. I'm going to let loose and force myself to stop giving a shit about her.

I still can't believe the little bitch tried to run away from me. Meek little attempt as it was, it still pissed me the fuck off. I'm not used to my slaves being so disobedient and it's throwing me for a loop. You'd think she'd catch the fucking drift and just behave. She knows her attitude will only make things worse for her, so that's why I don't understand why she's making this so hard for herself.

Except I do understand.

I fought it at first, but the natural instinct we all have inside of us telling us to survive is one we take to heart every single time it rears, because as much as we think we want to die, very few actually have the balls to pull it off. I know because I was one of them and still to this day, I have no idea what the fuck happened.

There is a ninety-nine percent reliability on guns, meaning there is a chance you might hit a misfire in one of every three hundred thousand rounds give or take.

That night I was the one percent.

I stand at the glass staring into the woods, my eyes focused on a specific tree stained with blood. It's dreary and gloomy outside, as it has been for the last few days. The rain has been pounding down nonstop, washing any and every remnant of blood and brain matter away—much to my disappointment. I enjoyed being able to look outside and see the fresh blood, but I can't stop the fucking rain.

Walking to my bed, I sit and pull out my Glock, resting it against my thigh.

I've always wondered what death is like. What happens when our heart finally stops? Does everything go black and we no longer exist? Do we become ghosts and roam the earth in search of some sort of peace? Do we become stuck in another dimension, locked in a purgatory? Do we go up to what most call heaven and live in paradise? What about the ones who are a plague to this earth, like me? Do we go to hell and burn for eternity? Or do we get to have peace too?

So many questions and so little answers. I know if a place like hell exists, then it's where I'll end up. There is no retribution for things I've done and seen, but I don't regret a single decision I've made. There is no time for regrets in this life. You take the hand you were given and work with it. Whether it's one which sets you on the right path to do great things, or in my case, one which leads you down a long, winding, brutal road to hell, you roll with the punches. So that's what I have fucking done.

MARIE ANN

I murdered a man right outside of my house twenty minutes ago and his blood is still splattered across my skin from the close proximity. I run a hand over my face, the blood tugging against my skin as it dries, annoying me. As sardonic as it is, I generally prefer much bloodier methods than just pulling a trigger. Pulling a trigger is way too fucking easy and most of the time, the fuckers I have to kill deserve to die painfully and bloody.

I generally have free rein to do what I see fit because my boss doesn't give a shit how the task is done as long as it gets taken care of, but tonight, Leo told me it needed to be done quickly. No torturing, simply end it. I don't know why it needed to be quick, but I didn't argue and I didn't ask questions. I did what I was told—but I still had to put my own spin on it. I tied him up first to let him feel a little fear before I ended his fucking life.

I prefer to taunt my victims before I end their life, to make their fear skyrocket before I finish it, but tonight, the annoying piece of shit would not shut up and he fucked up my damn plans. He kept whining on and on about how sorry he was, blah, blah, blah. Same fucking story, different fucking day. I've heard it all before, but his incessant whining was really digging on my nerves, and before I even knew what I was doing, I lifted my hand and pulled the trigger. Blood and brain matter coating the tree he was tied to and splattering on me as well.

He finally shut the fuck up at least. I rolled my eyes and secured my gun back in my waistband, grabbing my knife in the process. I walked over to... I don't remember his name. I cut the rope and can't help chuckling as I watch his body flop to the ground like a fish.

Wrapping my arms underneath his, I drag him through the woods to where I have a hole already dug. Dragging him through the dirt, I toss his body in and grab the lighter fluid which is lying next to the hole. I douse him, emptying the entire bottle because why the fuck not.

I strike a match, throw it in the hole, and watch as flames shoot up and lick around his body. Another perk to living in the middle of fucking nowhere—body disposal is pretty fucking easy. I watch his body burn for a while, the flames majestic but the smell is fucking putrid.

Deciding I've had enough, and need to go clean up, I make my way back to the house. I can go back out tomorrow and fill the hole once he's done burning completely and only his bones remain.

Sitting on my bed after my shower, staring out of the window, I realize how seriously fucked up I am. And not like a normal fucked up, like truly fucked the fuck up. I'm sick in the head with these thoughts I have, but they are all I have ever known. My need to have power over everyone and everything around me stems from all of the bullshit my mother put me through, but I know I can't put all of my shit on her. I'm just a fucked up waste of space.

Shaking my head, I bring the gun up to my lips and shove it inside of my mouth. The metal clashes against my teeth, jarring me.

My heart rate kicks up, anxious of what my brain is telling me to do.

Pull the trigger.
Just squeeze it.
You know you want to.
Just do it.
End it all.

MARIE ANN

I put my finger against the trigger, not putting any pressure on it, but it's enough for my heart to hammer out of my chest. But my heart is the only part of me which is showing anything other than eerie calm. My hands aren't shaking, my breath is steady, and a sense of calm has washed over me.

Without thinking twice, I squeeze the trigger the rest of the way, finally ready.

But here the fuck I am.

I shake off the fog of my flashback, the images in my head too real for my liking. Grabbing the whip, I move to the side of the bed and glance down at her. She looks so fucking beautiful tied up in my bed, her dress riding up her thighs, teasing me with a view of her bare pussy. *On second thought...*

I drop the whip next to the bed—I know I'll be using it soon—and go back to my dresser, grabbing the vibrator I keep in there. *I think it's time to show this little brat how painful pleasure can be.*

I push her dress up so it lies over her hips, baring her to me. I clasp both legs and spread them as far as they'll go, giving me a better view of her folds. She shuffles a little from the movement, a small sigh leaving her lips.

I crawl up the foot of the bed, moving between her open legs and sitting between them. With one hand, I spread her apart with my fingers, exposing her clit, and with the other, I push the button to turn the vibrator on.

I bring it to her pussy and push down hard against her clit. I shoot my eyes to her face, not wanting to miss the look and flick the vibration to high. Essa's eyes fly open as she screams and tries to lurch

CREEP

her body away from me. I grip her hip hard enough to bruise, pushing her into the mattress as I move the vibrator across her pussy, back and forth.

Switching it up, I shift to an up and down motion which seems to be the jackpot because she attempts to bring her legs together. Fear and pleasure ring loud in her eyes.

Ah, the fear. It's exactly what I need to see right now.

Tears run down her face as she continues to struggle against the vibrations torturing her bundle of nerves. Fed up with holding her down, I drop the vibrator and get off the bed. A sigh of relief leaves her mouth in a whisper, thinking I'm backing off.

I chuckle. *Naive little girl.*

I grab another chain and seize her left leg. I wrap it around her ankle and tug it through the bed frame, repeating the same notion with her right. She's kicking and screaming, trying to fight me off, but all it does is make my dick throb.

I hate her fighting me just as much as I love it.

Once I finally lock it together with a padlock, I walk to the front of the bed and unbutton my slacks. I push my boxers down slightly and pull my dick out, the tip already leaking precum. I twist my hand up and down on my length, squeezing, while keeping my eyes locked with Essa's.

Her fucking eyes.

My dick throbs as I began to stroke it faster. I push my pants and boxers the rest of the way down my legs and let them drop to the floor. I climb on to the bed, moving until I hover above Essa's face. I feel my balls tightening with the need to come, so I slow my strokes, wanting to make this last. Her nipples are pebbled, easily visible through the fabric of her dress.

"Is my baby doll turned on right now?" I taunt, licking my lips. "You like the sight of my big cock don't you, baby." Her eyes are glued to my dick but she then quickly deviates her gaze and her cheeks flash red as she closes her eyes. Her blush trails from her high cheekbones, creeping down her neck and even onto her chest.

"It's okay, baby. You're just a little brat who acts all big and bad until there's a cock in her face and then she wants to act all shy. That shit ain't gonna fly with me." I lean over her with my dick hovering right above her mouth. Her chest heaves and the heat of her breath fanning across my dick causes more cum to leak from the tip. Groaning, I smack my dick across her face, hissing from the sting but loving it all the same. Pain and pleasure are two sides of the same line.

She shrieks and bares her teeth at me, struggling with her binds. "Get the fuck off of me, you piece of shit!"

There she is, my little fucking brat.

My cock aches with the need of a release, but I jump off of the bed, barely fighting the urge to come all over her fucking face. Right now is for making her feel the fucking pain she so desperately wants, the pain I so desperately need to give her.

Moving back to her legs, I notice she's managed to bring them together as best as she can with the way she's chained to the bed. I roll my eyes and easily spread them before moving between them again. When I gaze down at her pretty pussy, I see it's glistening, along with her thighs.

Without taking my eyes off of her pussy, I can't resist taunting her.

CREEP

"My little fucking bitch is so wet for me. You're my dirty little girl, you know that don't you? Fuck yeah, you do. You wanna know how I know?" I pick up the vibrator again and turn it on high, circling her nipples with it. I twirl it around, bringing her nipple to a peak beneath the fabric of her dress before moving onto the next and repeating the same notion.

I drag it down between her breasts and move it across her ribs. I trail it over her stomach, moving across to her pelvis where her skin is exposed. When I reach her bare pussy, I hover right above, teasing her. I bring it down just enough to make a split second of contact before pulling it up again. Her arms yank against her binds, the chains clanking against the metal bars they're wrapped around.

I reach between our legs and grab my cock to stroke it. It pulses and throbs as I gather the precum on my tip before sliding my hand back down. As I stroke myself, I push the vibrator to her clit. She screams, arching off of the bed.

"Please stop!" she wails, tears tracking down her face in fast trails.

"Like I was saying, I know you're my dirty girl because while I'm down here staring at your pretty little pussy, I can see you clenching at my words. Because you fucking love it." She screams again, and it's music to my fucking ears.

Her face is still flushed, from anger and arousal. *She's fucking beautiful.* I shove two fingers inside of her pussy, curling them upward before dragging them back out.

She screams at my intrusion. "Please, stop! Please fucking stop! I'll do anything but please don't do this." She whips her head side to side and continues to scream at the top of her lungs, begging me to stop, but of course I don't. I know she wants this, deep down inside. Her pussy wouldn't be dripping for me right now if she didn't. She feels like a fucking glove wrapped around my fingers, clenching so hard I swear I feel it in my dick.

Her thrashing kicks up tenfold and though the fear is evident in her eyes, her desire starts to cloud over. I can feel her pussy clenching harder around my fingers, her orgasm on its precipice. I thrust my fingers in and out, curling them to hit that place inside of her which has her thighs quivering. Right when I know she's about to tip the edge, I remove the vibrator and my fingers simultaneously.

She gasps at the sudden loss of ecstasy, even more tears running down her beautiful face. Her mascara mixes with her tears, leaving black smudges. *Exactly what I envisioned earlier and it's even more fucking perfect than I thought.*

She has her eyes and thighs clenched shut as best she can. I can tell she wants to say something, to keep begging for me to stop, but something has switched inside of her. She completely shuts down. The thrashing, screaming, all of it stops at the drop of a dime. The only thing that continues is the tears running down her face—only because she can't stop them.

Too bad for her, I don't give a shit. I shove my hand between her legs, not bothering to hold them open and push my fingers back into her. She breaks her stoic expression to cry out, but I welcome her screams, they feel like home to me.

If she thinks she can resist me, I'll show her just how much she won't be able to help herself or her reactions to me.

I put the vibrator back to her clit and switch it back on. I continue to push my fingers in and out of her aggressively. I'm sick of the mood swings from this girl. The constant back and forth is pissing me off and I take it out on her body. It's not long before I feel her clenching her inner walls and again, I yank my fingers from her along with the vibrator.

Whimpering, she shifts from side to side, aching to move away from me, but not uttering a single word in protest. She was fighting me the entire time even though I know she wanted this. Then she suddenly changes her entire attitude and becomes compliant? It doesn't make any sense but I don't care enough to think through her bullshit right now. She fucking wants me, whether she wants to admit it or not. She can hate me all she wants, but she can't deny the fact her body is desperate for me and what I can do to her, what I can give her. To shove my cock in her tight little pussy, ripping her to fucking shreds, and leaving nothing but a bloody fucking mess behind. I know this little brat has never been denied an orgasm before and I'm loving every minute of showing her just how painful something so pleasurable can be.

"You don't wanna beg me to stop, baby doll? Because I fucking love hearing it, but either way, it's not going to change a goddamn thing. You need to be taught a fucking lesson 'cause I'm sick of your shit." She yanks on her chains, anger seeping into her cloud of lust.

"Keep your fucking hands off of me or I swear to God, I'll…"

There's that fucking attitude I hate to love.

"You'll, what? What do you think you're going to do while tied to my bed and at my mercy?"

She stares me square in the eyes as she says, "I'll never be at anyone's mercy. One day I'll fucking ruin you." I laugh at her audacity. Bitch is tenacious, that's for sure.

"Sure thing, baby doll, you get right on it. In the meantime, I'll be here, *ruining you*. And might I mention, you look so good being ruined by me." I flip her over and shove her face into the mattress, tired of hearing her voice already.

The chains wrapped around her ankles twist harder, keeping her more trapped than before. I grab a pillow, and then lifting her hips, I shove it underneath her—keeping her waist elevated and her arms and legs pulled taut.

I admire her luscious ass pulled up into this position. I trace my finger down between her cheeks to her pussy. I spread my fingers through her juices, coating them before bringing them back to her ass. I spread her cheeks apart and push against her tight ring, circling it with my finger. She tenses underneath me as I push my finger into her. She cries out at the intrusion, begging me to stop. I laugh and yank my finger out of her. I have plans for that later, but not tonight. Tonight's about pain.

I lean down to grab the whip off the floor. Bringing it up, I smack it across her ass. With each lash, her screams worsen until they eventually die down to quiet sobs. The welts have long turned bloody and the blood trickles down her ass, trailing down her thighs, creating the most beautiful pattern across her creamy skin.

I need to see more of it.

I dash over to grab my knife out of my slacks and bring it down to her skin. I know she loves the pain of a blade, so I'm sure out of everything I've done tonight, she will probably enjoy this the most.

I stare at her ass as I try to find a place to cut her, but the whip has left no available room so I press the blade to right below her left ass cheek and I push down slightly, barely nicking the skin. A drop of blood forms at the tip, teasing me. For some reason, making her bleed because of my knife is a different feeling than her ass dripping blood from the whip.

It feels more *personal*.

Her body instinctively relaxes underneath me. I drag the blade across her upper thigh in a straight line, making a clean cut. Blood flows from the wound, running faster down her thighs, already beginning to drip onto the bed.

Essa cries out as I dip my head down and trace the wound with my tongue. My dick pulses as I taste her. Her blood dances along my tongue, the metallic taste zinging as I lick my lips before going back in for more.

She was made to fucking ruin me.

I push my tongue inside of her wound, ripping it open with my teeth I dig into her skin. More blood spills out and I lap at it all, wanting every drop of her inside of me. There is something about this little brat's blood which fucks with my head. I feel completely fucking euphoric—almost as if I'm high on it.

I take the knife to her other leg and make a mark identical to the left, doubling the blood covering her. Having my fill for the time being, I stand back and watch, fascinated.

Her chest rises and falls with slow, deep breaths, no doubt her way of working through the pain, but what I see at the apex of her thighs which has grabbed my attention. She is fucking *dripping*. Her arousal is mixing with her blood, smearing together and creating the ultimate concoction. *My own personal fucking nirvana.*

Unable to resist the temptation, I shove my tongue into her pussy from behind, her ass pushing against my face. I fuck her with my tongue as I run my hands along her ass and the backs of her thighs, spreading her blood all over her body.

She gasps, trying to squeeze her legs together but they won't stop shaking. Moans leave her mouth, sounding huskier and breathier by the minute. I run my tongue along her inner thigh, trailing through the blood and cum mixed together. I groan at the taste, the smell of her arousal overtaking my senses.

I trail my tongue back up, running it through her folds. She gasps the moment my tongue meets her clit, her legs about to buckle. *My little baby doll is about to come.*

I flick my tongue across her little bundle of nerves, working her up, and then I pull away. I grab my cock, line it up against her entrance, and slam into her to the hilt, her blood and cum making it easy to slide inside of her.

"Fuuuck. You have the tightest little pussy, baby. Fucking made for me." Gripping her hips, I slam into her, grinding against her ass before pulling back out. Moans are leaving her mouth with every stroke of my cock inside of her, telling me just how much she really fucking likes this.

"That's it, baby, let me hear how much you love fucking my cock, you little fucking tease. You aren't shit baby. Just a tight pussy for me to fuck." Her pussy clenches around me like a fucking vice. Her moans turn into screams and I feel my balls draw up with the need to come. I slow my pace, drawing it out, not wanting it to end quiet yet.

She whimpers as I slowly pull out, dragging the head of my cock along her walls before slamming back in. As I pull back, I notice the blood from her ass has smeared across my groin and onto my dick. A guttural growl leaves my chest and my pace instinctually kicks up.

I brutally slam into her, losing all sense of rhythm, but all it does is draw more screams. Heat shoots up my spine as I reach my hand between Essa's legs. I rub her clit vigorously, wanting her to finally let go and come. She's been a good girl thus far, she deserves it.

"Fucking come!" I bark out. My words tip her over the edge because she clenches her walls around me in a vice grip, screaming into the bed as her release racks her body. I push into her once more before I let go, pulsing inside of her. Blackness flicks at the edge of my vision, my eyes rolling into the back of my head.

I lay on top of her as I pant, attempting to catch my breath. After I come back down after losing my mind, I mutter, "Fuck, baby doll," as I slowly withdraw from her. As I pull out, I feel her pussy still pulsing.

I roll next to her and glance over to her. She has mascara smeared across her face, tears long since dried, creating a crazy trail of black and her lashes are clumped together. Her hair is a knotted mess against the side of her head and her dress somehow got torn throughout the whole ordeal, but I have never seen a girl look so fucking desirable.

Even though I just came, my dick grows hard again just staring at her. Her eyes are closed, and her chest rises and falls with even breathing. She must have fallen asleep—knocked out from everything I put her through.

Completely satiated, my eyes slowly drift shut.

CHAPTER ELEVEN
ESSA

The next morning, I wake in my own bed, completely covered and curled into a ball. When I realize I'm no longer bound by any restraints, I instantly stretch my limbs, pain and stiffness radiating throughout my entire body. Groaning, I roll onto my side carefully to avoid brushing my ass against the mattress and grab my iPod off of the stand.

I search through my playlist until I find "Ghost" by Badflower. Hitting the repeat button, I shove the earbuds in my ears and drop it to the bed next to me as I stare out of the window. Agonizing pain consumes me as flashbacks of last night pummel through my mind at a million miles a minute, each memory feeling like someone is hitting me over the head repeatedly.

I have no idea what the fuck came over me when I decided to stop fighting him. I hate Vincent with every fiber of my being. He took me to cover a debt and treats me like I'm some spoiled little brat who doesn't listen, expecting me to obey to his every command like I'm a fucking robot. But what's worse, is the fact I'm fucking attracted to him.

I imagine his tattoos covering his body, only enhancing his muscular, but lean, build.

His hand wrapped around my throat as he shoved me against the wall.

The scruff on his face burning against my neck as he whispered in my ear, his deep voice crawling across my skin like the smoothest, but strongest whiskey.

His veiny arms holding me down as he pounded into me, his cock hitting every fucking nerve inside of me.

His tongue swirling through my blood, igniting more heat in my core when I felt his muffled moans against my skin.

My face burns with the memories, liquidating my anger into something much more desirable. As deeply as I despise him, I fucking want him. I love how he makes me feel. Not only the pleasure he brings me, but how he knows to give me the pain I need.

But more than my anger for him, is my anger at my parents. I haven't talked to them, or even heard from them since I left, but I did speak to Holl last night after my graduation. It was nice to hear her voice after the shit I've been dealing with since she left—more bullshit than the usual. She told me she's enrolled in classes which start this fall and she's finally all settled in her apartment and starting her job at a coffee shop. I'm happy for her, I truly am, but I can't help the jealousy which pulls through my veins thinking about her being all the way in Rhode Island, away from all of this bullshit.

The true source of my anger lies with them though. They couldn't even fucking show up to my graduation—though I'm not fucking surprised. They are the reason behind every single bad thing that has ever happened in my fucking life. The drugs, abuse, fear, toxicity, *all of it. Because of them.* They threw me away like piece of fucking gum stuck to the bottom of their shoe—a mere inconvenience taken care of by ripping it off and throwing it away. They blame all of their problems on everyone else, never taking responsibility for a thing—even their own fucking children.

I throw myself out of bed—ignoring the fact I'm naked because I somehow lost my fucking clothes—the blood and dried cum coating my thighs makes my legs stick together as I walk to the chair in the corner of my room. I grab my bag that's sitting on the cushion and walk into the bathroom. I rummage through it for a few minutes before I remember he took my fucking knife. Heaving a sigh of frustration, I ransack the cupboards in search of something sharp enough to fucking cut. At this point, cutting is not something I do because I need it, but because it's a fucking habit. I've been doing it so long, it feels like second nature.

Feelings too much to deal with? Cut.

Don't feel well? Cut.

Have a headache? Cut.

Self-loathing? Cut.

Everything that happens, I use it as a reason to cut, to detach myself from it all. No feelings, equal no *real* pain—the emotional kind anyway.

I heave a sigh of relief when I find a razor stuffed in the back of the cupboard under the sink. With it in hand, I step into the giant shower and turn the knob to the hottest possible temperature, steam rising into the air. The second the water hits my skin, I hiss at the contact but welcome the sting. My ass is beyond raw from last night and the water running over it feels like flames licking against me.

I bring the razor to my arm, like always, when an idea hits me. I've always cut on my arm, my right to be exact, because it always had the easiest access for instances I needed the pain quickly. Because of it, I never thought to cut in other places, but Vincent taking his knife across my legs last night is giving me ideas.

I push the razor against the skin of my upper right inner thigh. With my head bent over, water drips down my face and into my eyes, distorting my vision. My eyes burn with the need to wipe the water from them and I try to ignore it but it's distracting me from the task at hand. I bring my hand up to wipe my eyes so I can see what the fuck I'm doing, but of course the hand I use is the very same one holding the razor, so in the process the small blades glide across my cheek bone, nicking me.

Blood drips down my cheek, falling to the shower floor. I regard the first drop splattering at my feet below me, mixing with the water and swirling down. The water begins to turn a murky pink color the longer I'm under the stream and I'm confused until I remember it's last night's blood. It slips down my body in bloody water droplets, disappearing down the drain.

I take the razor to my thigh again and began making nicks on my skin. The razor can't do much more other than nick me. The sting is better than nothing at all, but it's not enough. It's never fucking enough. When deep down inside you want to die, is anything ever truly enough? The answer is no, so you take what you can get to help yourself try to feel a little more alive, to want to live, if even for the day.

I continue to cut my leg, until every drop of water splattering against my thigh has me hissing in annoyance, bringing nothing but enough pain to keep me satiated.

Pain.

I fucking hate myself and I wanna die, but I don't have the balls to do it. I have one reason and one reason alone for fighting this shit. Holley. I hate her so much for it too, and my anger gets the best of me from time to time, but I also know it's not her fault. She never asked for this life, neither of us did. We got dealt a shitty ass hand and we're doing our best with what we were given. Make lemonade out of the lemons life gives you and all that bullshit. But that's exactly what it is—utter bullshit—because even if you are handed a shitty life, you make of it what you will. You can roll over and accept the beatings, or you can stand the fuck up and fight for your life. I know who I am. Yep, I'm the little bitch who rolls over, taking every beating and never fighting back. I'm a fucking coward.

Head against the shower wall, I drop the razor to my side and shift my legs until my knees are against my chest. I sit in that position until the water runs cold and shivers wrack my body.

I get dressed, leaving my wounds uncovered after cleaning them because the fabric of my clothes rubbing over them and my injured ass creates enough of a constant sting to keep me focused. I make my way to the kitchen, deliberately keeping my eyes peeled for Vincent, but I don't see him anywhere. The house is eerily quiet.

As I step into the kitchen, I see a carafe of coffee still hot from being made recently. Smiling because I get to have some much needed coffee, I pull open numerous cupboard doors until I come across the one stocked with glasses and coffee mugs. I fill a mug, adding my usual two teaspoons of sugar and a splash of half and half I find in the fridge. I bring it to my lips and eagerly take a sip of the steaming beverage, burning my tongue in the process. I am a major coffee addict but I never got to drink it because it was a luxury we couldn't afford.

As I drink my coffee while leaning against the counter, Vincent casually strolls into the room. Jeans grace his long legs and a tight black T-shirt stretches across his muscular chest. His hair is damp, indicating he recently showered. *He looks utterly fuckable.* I drag my eyes from my mug to his face and find him already staring at me.

"Mornin', baby doll. Sleep well?" He winks before turning around and grabbing a mug. I ignore him as he moves about the kitchen, preparing himself a cup of coffee, adding half and half to his. Cup in hand, he takes a seat on the stool right next to where I'm standing.

Rolling my eyes, I ask him if I'm allowed to go home yet. But if I'm being honest, I don't want to go home, but I also don't want to be here. It's a catch twenty-two because either way I'm fucked. *Literally.* I cringe, my body physically shuddering and nausea rolling in the pit of my stomach. He keeps his eyes locked on me as he takes a drink. I follow the movement as he swallows, his throat bobbing before he sets his mug down. I clear my throat as an indication for him to answer, but of course he ignores me.

"Are you going to give me an answer?" The impulse to snap at him is immense, but I'm surprisingly able to fight it.

"Baby, you're not going anywhere. You're mine now, or did you forget that? Because I can give you a reminder if it's needed." He grins.

"No, I do not need any reminders. I just want to go home." I turn away from him as I say it, my blatant lie apparent even to me.

Out of the corner of my eye, I see his brow quirk at what I said. "Do you really, though? Because I don't think you do, little girl. As much as you loathe me, you loathe your parents more. You'd rather deal with me and this situation then go back to your pathetic excuse of a life. Tell me I'm wrong."

My ability to fight the urge to talk back dwindles greatly as anger hits me like a punch in the gut. *How fucking dare he say shit about my life being pathetic.* Of course he's not wrong, but it still doesn't give him the right to talk about shit he knows nothing about.

Knowing I'm going to later regret the words I spew in anger, I can't help myself—*another brain to mouth malfunction.*

"You don't know what the fuck you're talking about. And besides, you don't have the right to say shit about my life when you have taken me as a payoff for a debt. If anyone is pathetic, it's you."

One second I'm sitting on my stool, coffee mug in hand, and the next I'm flying to the floor, my mug crashing to the ground somewhere behind me. My skull bounces off the floor and all the breath leaves my lungs.

Disoriented, I groan and roll to my side, attempting to sit up, but his hand wraps around my throat, shoving me back down to the floor.

CREEP

As I try to take a breath, his hand increases in pressure, crushing my larynx beneath his palm.

"How. Many. Fucking. Times. Do I have to tell you to watch your fucking mouth with me?" Vincent snarls in my face, the tip of his nose grazing mine. His pupils are dilated in anger and because they are such a dark brown, they seem almost black.

My heart falters, fear instantly coating my skin in a sheen of sweat. His eyes in this moment remind me of someone else's eyes. Black, demon eyes which belong to Ben. Eyes which bring flashbacks of memories I don't want to fucking own. Memories I wish I could light on fire and watch burn to nothing.

I lose myself to their power, getting sucked into the vortex of them. They fucking consume every part of me. My ears ring and my skin is icy cold to the touch and shivers wrack my body. I remember his hands crawling across my skin, making me feel dirty, disgusting. My heart squeezes in pain when I remember everything he has ever said to me, every threat he has ever made and vomit swirls in the pit of my stomach when I remember him shoving himself inside of me—utterly destroying every piece of me. My innocence, my blind faith in the stars, my hope for a new life, all gone in an instant.

I blink my eyes rapidly in a futile attempt to clear the haze which has come over me, but it's useless. All I can see are the memories. *So many fucking memories.*

Knowing I'm about to vomit—which happens every time this does—I turn my head to the side right as the bile shoots up my throat and onto the floor beside me. I wretch until there is nothing left and then I continue to dry heave. I hold onto my stomach in an attempt to ease the pain and hope it stops soon, but it's not likely. The vomiting has helped clear the fog surrounding me and I blink a few times as things come back to me. My ears stop ringing for the most part, but my heart continues to pound.

    I lay slumped on the floor in utter, to the core, exhaustion. My face lies less than a foot away from the vomit, but I can't bring myself to move, or to care for that matter. These episodes I have are always triggered by the littlest things and they leave me dazed and confused every single time.

    I forget all about Vincent until I feel his hand on my back. Instant heat shoots through me, but the fear overrides every other feeling, and I jerk away while whimpering, thoughts of Ben's hands on me still ripe in my mind.

    "Hey, it's just me, Vincent. What the hell happened to you?" he asks in what seems to be a sincere tone, but I have been fooled by manipulation far too many times in my life to let it trick me now.

    "Nothing. I'm fine." I manage to push myself off of the floor, wiping the back of my hand over my mouth to clear any leftover vomit on my lips. *I'll brush my teeth later, I have to clean up this mess first.* I set about looking around the kitchen for the things I'll need to clean up with. I find a mop with some cleaning solution and paper towels. I tuck the paper towels under my arm as I grab the garbage can and make my way over to the mess.

    The smell is putrid, and I wrinkle my nose in disgust. I continue to ignore Vincent as I wipe up the bile, tossing the paper towels into the garbage as I go. With it cleaned up, I go to the sink and fill the mop bucket with the cleaning solution and hot water, setting it onto the

CREEP

floor. Dunking the mop in, I go about mopping the entire area, wanting to be certain I don't miss a spot.

I fucking hate messes, they're chaotic. My life has enough chaos and I don't need more of it. Cleaning and organizing makes me feel better, more in control. I don't have control in, predominantly, every aspect of my life, so for things I have the ability to control, such as my pain and my ability to give it to myself, I need it. I thrive on it. It keeps me going and keeps me sane.

It also doesn't help growing up, the house always seemed as if a tornado blew through it. *Thank you tweaker parents.*

I believe it's where the beginning of it all started—way before the abuse did.

Now done with cleaning, I pick up all of the things I used, washing and rinsing them before putting them away in their rightful spots. Kneeling on the floor in front of the sink, I shift my eyes to Vincent's stoic form. He moved to the counter and is now leaning against it. When my eyes reach his, I falter before pushing myself into a standing position. Being on my knees while he's staring at me the way he is makes me feel awkward and small and it's intimidating.

I stealthily grab a knife from the knife block on the counter as I make my way out of the room. I'm cautious of his eyes on me as I grab it, but I'm not too worried. I'm used to sneaking things because it's what I always had to do growing up. I had to steal food from stores sometimes, or even sneak shit inside of the house.

I quickly glance behind me, but Vincent unexpectedly lets me leave without a word. I trudge up the stairs to my room, desperate for another shower to wash this stink off of myself, and if I'm being honest, to avoid Vincent. I have never had an episode in front of someone before, and I'm embarrassed, but more than that, I'm ashamed of myself. I don't need anyone knowing the shit I have been through, or even worse, feeling pity for me.

Locking my bedroom door behind me, I make my way to the shower, and step right in—clothes and all. I turn the knob all the way and let the ice cold water hit me. It feels like tiny pin needles across my skin, stinging in their wake.

I sink to the floor, thoroughly drained. Even my bones feel tired as I focus on the knife in my hand, twisting it around in my fingers, admiring how something so mundane as a kitchen knife used to prepare food can bring so much happiness to someone like me. You would never think staring at a random knife block on someone's kitchen counter, one of the knives inside of it was used to cut open someone's skin, their blood flowing all over it.

The bathroom door creaks open, lightly tapping the wall as it opens all the way. I don't even turn my head, already knowing who it is. *As if it would be anyone else.* I keep my head tilted down and away from him, wiping the water running into my eyes.

He doesn't make a noise, just standing quietly. But he doesn't have to say a word, his presence is domineering enough to the point it's suffocating me. It feels like he's right next to me in the shower, hovering and staring down at me. *Am I imagining this or...* I glance up in question and my cold gaze locks onto his fiery one. He's standing directly under the spray, his clothes becoming soaked and sticking to him like a second skin. I can't help but notice his defined muscles, seeming more explicit because of his wet clothing. I get pulled into his intense aura, everything around us falling away.

He squats down in front of me, the water now falling directly into my face, but I can't pull my eyes away from his. I'm frozen in place and my body is screaming at me to move, to blink the water away which is burning my eyes, but I can't.

He yanks the knife out of my closed fist, and the blade cuts across my palm. I don't know how my hand became wrapped around the blade, but I don't remember doing things sometimes when I get in this self-destructive mood. I hiss at the pain, but it brings a maniacal smile to my face.

"You're one twisted bitch, you know that don't you?" Vincent chuckles. I shrug my shoulders in response, too tired to verbally respond. He pinches my chin between his thumb and forefinger, pulling my face up to meet his.

"You best fucking answer me unless you want more of those across your beautiful skin." He lets go of my chin and runs his index finger across my exposed arm, trailing across my scars. My older ones, my newer ones, and my most recent ones. He tilts his head down until I feel his lips brush across them, lingering on one in particular. The one which almost killed me.

I still remember that night like it was yesterday...

I'm sitting in the bathtub, cold water running down across my back while my hair hangs in front of my face, shielding me from the light and blanketing me in darkness. He hurt me again tonight, for what feels like the millionth time. Every time he leaves, I tell myself, "tonight will be the last night" but it never is because I'm a fucking coward. I can't fucking stop him, and I'll never be able to stop him.

There is only one way to end this. One way to stop him once and for all.

A cold chill shivers down my spine as I bring the razor blade to my arm and cut down vertically. No hesitation, and no second fucking thoughts.

I need to end this.

I can't do it anymore.

Holley will be okay. I know Ben won't hurt her.

A sign of relief fills my lungs as things become hazy around me as warmth floods through me.

But what if he does?

The warmth turns to a blistering chill in a nanosecond. My arm has long since gone numb and it's now radiating through the rest of my body. My limbs feel like dead weight and a cold chill has broken out across my entire body as the panic sets in.

Goddamnit. I knew this was going to happen.

What the fuck did I do?

I attempt to sit up, my entire body sluggish, and grab a towel to wrap around the cut to slow the blood flow, but before I get the chance, everything goes black...

Shame eats at me when I think about what almost happened.

Of course I want to die. I think about it every single day, but I'm not allowed to be selfish. I have my sister who needs me to be strong, to survive for her, to live for her, and knowing I almost left her alone with those fiends eats away at me every day.

I watch as Vincent kisses my scar and all memories of the past fade instantly from his single touch. My blood warms the longer his mouth remains against my skin, heat swirling in the pit of my stomach but I remain frozen, unsure what his intentions are.

"This specific one seems to be the worst of all the scars covering you. You really tried to end it on this one, didn't you?" I watch as his tongue peaks through his lips, running along the raised skin, tracing it down the length of my arm. Heat pools in between my legs and goosebumps subsequently rise along my skin, following the path of his tongue.

"Answer me, Essa. Any other time I want you to shut the fuck up, you won't, but when I want you to answer me, you want to clam up? Speak."

I stammer over my words, the heat from his mouth on me jumbles them up in my brain. "Y-Yes." I manage to spit out. His mouth is fire against my icy skin. The water may be warm now, but it has no effect on my skin like his touch does.

"You clearly didn't do a good enough job." I swing my gaze to him with confusion and anger etched on my face and he's smirking at me, clearly trying to get a rise out of me.

"Don't talk about shit you know nothing about because like I've told you before, you know nothing about what I've been through." I attempt to spit venom into my words to get my point across, but his tongue running along my skin turns into his teeth grazing up and down and I lose my train of thought. More heat pools at my core and floods through my body. Confusion clouds my mind as my pussy begins to throb.

"What," I clear my throat, trying to clear it, while also attempting to gather my thoughts. "What are you doing?" I try to pull my arm away, but his grip on me turns to stone. He brings his brown eyes to mine, peering through me and straight into my soul.

It's an otherworldly experience feeling like someone can see straight through you to the depth of your soul. You feel naked, laid completely fucking bare to them.

Toxicity runs through my veins. His touch is venom in my bloodstream, slowing my heart and weakening my body. I'm paralyzed and it becomes difficult to breathe.

"I'm doing whatever the fuck I want. Now shut that pretty little mouth." I snap my mouth closed, not wanting him to stop whatever it is he is doing to hurt me. The result of his anger is not the kind of pain I want right now, but I like what he's doing to me far too much to ever admit it aloud, much less to myself.

I feel the sharp point of the knife push into my skin. My eyes snap open automatically at the sensation of pain.

"If you want to cut, if you *need* to cut, if you *need* the pain, you come to me and I will be the one to give it to you. Do you understand me? You are no longer allowed to bring this knife, or any other sharp object I will add," he quirks his brow to let me know he already knows what I'll try, "to your skin while you are in this house with me. That will be my fucking job. If you want to hurt yourself, I will do it for you. No ifs, ands, or buts about it. That's final." I swear I feel my jaw unhinge in my shock.

How dare he.

Rage boils through my bloodstream, every ounce of my lust gone. *Lust?* No. It was only confusion.

"Are you fucking kidding me? You think you have the right to tell me what I can and cannot do with my own fucking body? I don't know what sick fucking notion you have in your head about me, but let me tell you some—" I'm cut off by the blade dragging across my arm, leaving a trail of blood in its path as it bites through my skin.

"Well, would you look at that. It seems all I have to do to get you to finally shut the fuck up, is to cut you. I'll keep that in mind. Second, did you forget you're my fucking property? Your beautiful, scarred, and bloody body is mine to do whatever I fucking want with."

I vaguely hear his words as I stare at the cut he gave me, his voice muffled. It's longer than the ones I usually give myself—though not deeper. I always get lost in the moment and end up with short, deep, and mutilated cuts. It's almost like I'm in a frenzy and I completely lose myself when it happens.

But his is a much cleaner cut, and for some reason, even a fucking cut on *my* body, surrounded by dozens of others I did myself, his feels more like me than the rest. And I fucking hate it. I don't even know what it is, but I don't want to think about it right now either.

My eyes must have drifted closed because, without warning, I feel Vincent's lips press to mine in a desperate kiss, his tongue instantly seeking mine. I open up to him, tangling my tongue with his. The water continues to rain down on us as he moves back, pulling me with him. He shifts my legs on either side of him, but not before ripping my leggings down my legs. He grips my ass cheeks in both of his hands, grinding my body down on top of him. I have no idea what's going on, but all I do know is I'm so fucking lost in this moment and never want to leave. The pain, the pleasure, all of it mixing together creating the ultimate storm of chaos.

A moan escapes my lips as he trails his mouth down my neck, sinking his teeth in deep enough to pierce the skin. I hiss at the sting and then moan as it transforms into heat pooling at my center. My pussy throbs the more bite marks he leaves.

I bring my hands to his hair, tugging the strands in my fists while I continue to grind myself on his jean-clad cock.

He pulls his head from me, "You fucking want this, don't you, baby doll? You can try to lie to me all you want, but this," he cups my pussy, his fingers putting enough pressure on me, they almost tear through the delicate fabric of my panties.

"This can never fucking lie to me. Even though we're in the fucking shower right now, I can still tell how wet you are." He pushes harder against the material and they tear, allowing him the access to shove his fingers inside of me and for the first time, I moan instead of scream.

"You see how easily I pushed my way inside of you, baby? That's because you fucking love it." He continues to pump his fingers in and out of me and I rock my hips along with the movement of his hand. I tilt my head back, my hair falling down my back and brushing my tailbone. Vincent wraps my hair around his fist and tugs, my neck arching higher the harder he pulls.

"Keep your head like this, do you understand?" I don't answer him at first, lost in the moment, so he yanks my head, ripping strands of hair out. "I asked if you fucking understood?" He stops moving his hand inside me and it snaps me out of my reverie.

"Yes. I understand you." My words come out breathy, giving away how turned on I really am, but at this point, I'm way past caring. I want more of what he's giving me.

He lets go of my hair and begins moving his fingers again. "Good girl." He curls his fingers up, massaging my walls and hitting a spot which has my legs shaking. My pussy clamps around his fingers at his words, showing him just how fucked up I really am. At the angle my head is tilted at, it's hard to see a thing, especially with the water, but I still manage to see his smirk. I hate how hot his smile is. *Pure, sexy fucking evil.* His straight, perfectly white teeth, with literal fangs gracing his mouth. Fangs which have left bloody bite marks all over my body.

Pleasure pools in the pit of my stomach and heat spreads from the tips of my toes, upward. I think this is what the beginning of an orgasm feels like because when he fucked me last night was the first time I have ever felt anything like this. I rock my hips faster against his hand, my clit rubbing against his palm.

I feel the cold of the blade press against my exposed throat and I don't want to stop, but with the way it's pressed against me, I freeze. I'm all too aware of the fact all he has to do is push in at a certain angle and I'll bleed out in seconds. *But would it really be such a bad thing? Death brings peace, it brings nothingness.* I smile. The fear is still present, but pushed to the side at the thought of dying.

"I wonder what I'm going to do now, baby doll. With this blade pressed to your throat, there are so many options. Your neck stretched taut as it is would make slitting your throat much more difficult, but definitely not impossible. All I would have to do is put in a little more effort and it would sink into your skin like hot butter. Slicing you up and making you bleed all over is what I'm thinking about right now though. I can see it now. Your blood running down your beautifully fucked up body, flooding the shower floor beneath us and turning everything the most beautiful shade of red."

I dare to defy him by bringing my head down to look him in the eyes. The blade digs deeper into my skin, but I push against it. "Do your worst, baby." The fire in his eyes at my words should have me worried, but I'm not. I don't care if he kills me. I am so fucking tired of fighting this battle every day.

What's the point? Holley is off at college, free from our parents. And yeah, Ben can threaten her all he wants, but he wouldn't ever hurt her, I don't think. All of his anger has always been directed towards me. Besides, Holley was always only a fucking excuse for me to be a coward. I have always been too afraid to fight back, scared of what would happen if I ever did break free.

Ben's abuse is all I have ever known and I have always been too terrified to know what would happen if everything changed. Would things get better or, god forbid, get worse? If I would've had the courage to speak up, would Holley and I have ended up in a foster home with even shittier parents? Foster parents who would have abused us both, or worse, her instead of me.

It was a chance I never would have taken, therefore, I remained a coward and stayed hidden in the shadows with my secrets. Secrets I kept from everyone. I never made friends at school and I only remained at school long enough for the classes I needed to be in. Then I would ditch.

The whole school thing always seemed so mundane and unimportant to me. There were always much bigger things I had to deal with, but Holley adored school. It was her escape away from home which I can understand. It's why she graduated with honors and got a full ride to college. She's going to do amazing things with her life, and how I know my death won't affect her any longer.

I'm ready to give up, to let what happens, happen. I'm ready to stop fighting—I think—and to give in to what feels good.

Vincent pushes the blade into my throat, dragging it from the back of my neck, and following the curve, stopping right as he reaches the center of my throat. I feel the blood running down, following the curves of my body before it splatters to the shower floor beneath us. The cut isn't deep enough to need stitches, but deep enough to continuously bleed.

"Did you know red is my favorite color? I'm sure you can guess why." He chuckles as he leans forward and runs his tongue along the cut. It stings, but it soon turns to more when he begins to rub his thumb against my clit in small circles.

He did say he liked to give pleasure with pain.

A moan pushes past my lips and my legs begin to shake. It's too much all at once and I don't know how to handle it. The sensations consume me. I never knew pain could feel like this but I realize now, I'm quickly becoming addicted.

Vincent continues to lap at my blood while I circle my hips in motion with his hand. He groans against my throat, the noise vibrating through me and shooting straight to my pussy. It is the sexiest fucking noise I have ever heard and wanting to hear it again, I grind myself harder against him. His teeth clamp down on my wound and I shriek.

"What the fuck," I pant. "Are we doing?" I blurt the words the second they come to me. I'm so fucking confused but my words instantly snap him out of whatever the hell it is we are doing because he suddenly growls as he shoves me off of him and my head smacks the shower wall from the force. I watch as he storms out of the shower, clothes soaked and dripping while clinging to every muscle.

He stops when he reaches the doorway separating my now bedroom and bathroom. His back is rigid and his hands are clenched into fists at his sides. I watch him in silent confusion, not knowing what to say, or even what to do. We stay like that for what could be minutes, or hours. I'm not sure, time ceases to exist. The water has long run out of heat and now the freezing water is running over me, but I don't move because I don't care.

Vincent rolls his shoulders and tilts his head to the side as he turns towards me. The look masking his face causes the fear I should have been feeling earlier to crawl back inside of me stronger than ever. His entire demeanor has done a complete one-eighty.

The fire I saw in him minutes ago is now gone—in its place is his monstrous side, so detached. Soulless. Familiar.

He walks towards me, again. Every step calculated, and every move measured. He bends down and cups my chin in his hand, his touch surprisingly gentle despite the fire burning in his eyes.

"It doesn't matter what we were doing, I'm going to fucking ruin you." He leans his head back slightly as he lobs a wad of spit straight into my face. I gasp when I feel the warm saliva trail down my face, some of it slipping into my mouth.

That motherfucker just spit in my fucking face.

Seething, I shove away from him. I leave the spit clinging to my face, fueling my anger. I throw my fist towards his face and it connects with his chin. His head snaps to the side but his body remains unmoving. He slowly turns his head back to me, a manic smile plastered across his face.

He shoves me so fast and hard, I stumble backwards and land with a thud on the shower floor. Mortification sets in and my tears fall, despite me constantly swiping them away. Vincent laughs as he crouches in front of me again, bringing his hand to my face. I jerk away from him, a learned reaction, and it makes him grin as he swipes a finger through my tears and then licks his finger.

"Mmm, your tears taste good baby. I plan on giving myself the opportunity to taste them more often, I haven't done it enough. But shit is about to change. You've gotten a little too fucking comfortable here already." He stands and walks out of the room.

Turning before he exists, he adds, "Oh, by the way, I took your phone while you were asleep. You won't get it back for a while. Naughty girls don't get to keep fun things and you'll have to be a good girl to get it back. But I'll be sure to text your sister occasionally so she doesn't worry and do something stupid." He leaves, slamming the door behind him.

Every time my anger consumes me, it's not long after it dissipates and the despair living inside of me devours me once more. I try with everything in me to fight the tears I feel burning my eyes, but I can't. I'm not strong enough.

Sobs wrack my body, wails leaving my mouth without my permission. I am feeling so many things at once, I don't know how to handle them. Well, I do, but the fucker took the knife with him so I'm stuck trying to deal with this shit without it. And I don't know how to do it—hence how my cutting began. I've never been able to deal with shit before, much less now.

    I sit for God knows how long, crying and screaming everything out. My pain, my confusion, my situation, my fucking life, everything. I'm so fucking confused. I hate Vincent with everything inside of me. He's a cruel and callous man who reminds me way too much of Ben. So why is it that what happened a mere hour ago turned me on? I was about to ride his dick, a primal instinct over taking me, because I was *that* desperate for what he was doing to me. The pain and pleasure combination consumed every part of me, stripping me of all rational thought.

    Now I feel utterly disgusted with myself. How could I ever allow myself to feel anything other than disgust and animosity towards him? *Because you're a little fucking tease, a little fucking whore like Ben always said you were.*

    Screaming in frustration, I stand and shut the water off. My cuts from Vincent are still bleeding but I don't give a shit to even bother cleaning them at this point.

    I walk to the mirror and stare at my reflection. Water droplets cover the glass and run down, creating streaks in the condensation. Lifeless eyes stare back at me, void of any emotion. My skin looks ghastly and my hair is in knots, tangled at the base of my neck, probably from Vin—never mind. I don't want to say his name, let alone think of it.

    Before I register what I'm doing, I throw my fist out—the same fist I punched him with—and smash it into the mirror. Shards fly in all directions as I watch my soulless reflection shatter, matching how I already feel inside. I feel around for a piece of glass, never taking my eyes off of my broken, reflected ones. My hand wraps around a piece and I grip it tightly, the glass cutting into my palm.

I am so fucking tired of this shit. Of feeling hopeless, worthless, like a fucking creep. Yes, we all have demons. We all have shadows that chase us in circles, begging to drag us into the dark with them. Most people can fight them, push them away without much effort. But me? They fucking consume me. My demons dance along right next to me, controlling everything I do and every move I make. They're my constant companion. The creep living inside of me—inside of my head—is never going anywhere and I learned to accept it a long time ago.

We've long been friends, my darkness and me, but it has long since devoured me, leaving nothing left of the real Essa Monroe. I don't know who that is anymore, nor do I care to.

Every version of myself has been weak, but at least with my creep calling the shots, I no longer give a shit.

I bring the glass to my arm and start to carve, curving the glass with the letters, twisting and turning it when I need to, to get the letters just right. Five big, bold letters reside on my arm, bloody and gruesome, their edges jagged, but the word still clearly visible.

There. Now everyone will know who and what the fuck you are.

Smiling, I drop the glass and walk to my bed collapsing face first onto the mattress, exhaustion pulling me under.

CHAPTER TWELVE
VINCENT

I got lost in the moment with her *again*. Watching her bring a knife to her skin—knowing what she was going to do—something came over me and I lost all sense of reason. I need to be the one to hurt her and bring her pain, but I can't keep losing my control with her. She's going to be my fucking ruin, my fucking demise, and she's going to demolish everything in my life.

I groan in frustration as I lie in bed, staring up at the high ceiling. I blindly reach across to my bedside table and smack my hand around until I find the remote to the sound system. Without caring to choose a song, I hit play. "Send The Pain Below" by Chevelle blasts through the speakers but it's not loud enough so I turn it up as loud as it will go and toss the remote on the bed next to me.

Memories from mere hours ago flood my mind. The need to hurt her seeped into my blood, begging me to sink the blade in a little deeper. To watch her bleed out in front of me, the life draining from her little by little. But the moment those little moans escaped her lips, giving away how much she wanted me, I snapped.

She's so fucking addictive. Her broken and beautifully tragic soul lures my raging inferno of one out of its depths, and together they merge into something savage, ravenous. It wreaks havoc on both of our minds, and both of our souls. And when we come out of it? Neither one of us remains the same.

I trace my tattoo, thinking about my mother and her addiction. I swore to myself I would never touch the shit, or any drug in fact, but I'm slowly beginning to realize now, addiction is about much more than a simple fucking drug. An addiction can be so much more. Take Essa for example. I know she's addicted to hurting herself. She does it not only because she wants to, but because she *needs* to. And the fucking moment I drew blood on her, I *knew* she was going to fuck me up.

Because now I've had a taste, her blood and her fucking *pain* is what I need and the more I get, the more I crave. Her screams and her moans. Her fighting and her fucking attitude. All of it is becoming a fucking addiction and as much as I tell myself I don't want her, I know it's a fucking lie.

Her blood is a beacon, begging for me to set it free, to let it flow. And plus the way she fucking tastes? *Fuck.* My dick hardens, desperate to taste the metallic zing of her blood again. I grasp my cock in my fist, stroking at a fast pace.

In my head, all I hear are her moans for me. All I see is her blood covering her skin. All I feel are my fingers in her tight, wet pussy which grips me so fucking tight. I pump harder, the need to come coursing through my body. Stroking two more times, I groan as I spill across my stomach.

Fuck, she's even fucking with my goddamn dick. After wiping the cum off of my stomach, I roll to my side and stare out the window until I see the sun rising over the trees, turning the night into day, the dark to light.

I'm leaning against the door frame leading into my game room and staring at the pole which goes from floor to ceiling. When I bought this house, I had this installed myself. My previous fuck toys would *love* to dance for me and who am I to deny myself a good time. I originally came in here to play a game of pool to distract myself but since I walked in the door, all I can think about is Essa sliding up and down the pole for me, shaking that fucking ass of hers. Of course she'd fight it the whole way, but that's only part of the fun—her acting like she doesn't want me.

Sounds coming from the kitchen break my train of thought. I make my way to where I know Essa is, my mind already made up. When I walk into the kitchen, I see her fighting with my coffee machine, attempting to make herself a cup. She is wearing a pair of light gray sweatpants and some sort of band hoodie. Bring Me The Horizon I think. Her hair is thrown up on the top of her head, looking like a birds nest. She's flipping through the manual for the coffee machine, trying to figure out how to even turn the damn thing on. A burst of laughter escapes my mouth and her eyes swing over to mine, the noise startling her. Embarrassment flushes her face, but soon after it's replaced with the ever occurring anger she seems to have for me.

"What the fuck are you laughing at?" She sneers while holding my gaze.

I heard her crying and screaming last night after I left. I shut the door to her room behind me and leaned against it, sliding down until my ass met the floor. My clothes were soaked and sticking to my skin, pissing me off, but I couldn't leave when I heard the first sound of her cries. They broke through the barrier of the door and swarmed around me like bees. Each scream stinging me, becoming worse the longer they continued, until I felt as wounded as her. I wanted nothing more than to bust through the door and hold her in my arms, to stop her screams, but I couldn't do that. I couldn't let her know she has a hold over me. It would've ensued more chaos between the two of us and we're already set to implode. Then I heard the glass shatter and my heart stopped along with her screams.

"Just let me do it. I don't want you breaking my shit. It's expensive."

She scoffs. "Yeah, like you actually give a shit about what it costs. Look around. You live in a fucking glass house and you have top of the line everything. Money clearly isn't an issue for you." Rolling her eyes, she opens the cupboard and grabs a mug.

"Grab one for me too, brat."

"Yes, sir." She mocks as she reaches up again and grabs another for me. I'm about to make a comment about her calling me sir, but as she reaches her arm up, her sleeve slides up her arm and I notice a bandage covering her forearm. A bandage she didn't have before. Her sleeve drops back into place when she sets the mugs on the counter.

"What the fuck is that?" I start the coffee machine and grab the arm in question, and yank her to me. She collides into my body, her chest against mine. I feel her nipples harden at the contact.

"Is it cold in here, baby doll?" I tease.

"Oh, fuck off you asshole." She tries to pull herself away from me, but I wrap my arms around her waist and firmly hold her in place. I push her sleeve up her arm and rip the bandage away, revealing what's underneath. The word CREEP is cut into her skin in all bold, capital letters. I'm honestly fucking baffled but my interest is piqued.

She continues to struggle in my hold, but now I've seen what it says, I let her go. She stumbles away and yanks her sleeve down as if I didn't just see what was underneath it. She leans against the counter, feigning confidence, but doing the worst job of it. Her chest rises and falls rapidly as she clenches her fists into balls. I know why she does it too. She digs her nails into her palms, giving herself merely enough pain to stay centered and to stay calm. Yeah, I know this girl and what makes her tick.

"Care to explain what *that* is?" I gesture to her arm in question. She turns her head away from me, staring out the window into the mass expanse of trees, trees apparently both of us love staring at.

"I've always had sort of an obsession with wolves. I admire them, envy them. Their loyalty to one another and to their pack. They would die without a second thought to protect each other. Have you ever had that kind of loyalty? That kind of love? No? Yeah, me either." She chuckles, but it's not a happy one, more manic sounding. I choose to remain silent, waiting to see if she makes her point.

"You wanna know why? Because a creep like me doesn't get to

CREEP

have the good of others, doesn't get to experience those things because I don't deserve it. My demons have become me and the person I used to be is long gone. I honestly don't even think she existed to begin with. I have always barely managed going through the motions. Living, breathing, fucking *surviving*. So here I am, a creep emerging from the shadows, out to obliterate everyone in its path."

I'm stunned at the words leaving her mouth. How something so in depth just left her mouth astounds me. I knew she has had a rough life, a life much worse than most people can even think of, but what she said has me thinking about my own demon living inside of me. Festering, begging to be released *by her*...

Essa and I both remain unmoving as we stand in silence, our thoughts permeating the air around us. We're much more alike than I ever would have imagined. Our shitty parents, our shitty childhoods, having to grow up alone, all while fighting this *thing* inside of our heads. Our similarities are astounding to me.

The coffee machine beeps when it's brewed, snapping us both out of our reverie. I move to pour two cups of coffee while Essa grabs the half and half out of the fridge and then over to the cupboard to get the sugar. She takes a mug from me without a single glance and goes about making hers how she prefers it. When she's done, she hands me the half and half without question and then returns it to the fridge when I'm done with it. It's a little unsettling how she has already derived how I take my coffee, but I don't think much into it.

"Well damn, little girl. You're much smarter than I ever pegged you to be. I'm pleasantly surprised." I take a sip of my coffee as I move over to one of the stools and take a seat. I raise my cup to Essa in gesture for her to take a seat too. She rolls her eyes—ever defiant—and takes a seat in the stool directly in front of mine. We both sit in silence while drinking our coffee, and staring out into the woods.

The sky is a dark gray and the clouds coating the sky are releasing a constant fine mist, smattering against the glass, distorting the view. But even so, it's still breathtaking. It's why I bought this place. I'm constantly surrounded by the one thing that makes me feel so at home. The trees seem never ending and full of secrets. At least, I know my woods are full of secrets; and bodies—another benefit of living out here. It makes it pretty damn easy to get rid of somebody. Also, their screams can't be heard. I can tear someone limb from limb, cut them into tiny little pieces, and not one single soul will ever hear their demise. It's fucking perfect.

The silence encompassing us is surprisingly comfortable despite our mutual loathing. We are both clearly lost in our thoughts, or completely lost in our fucking minds. I glance over to her out of the corner of my eye and observe her. She's staring blankly at nothing in particular. Her pale green eyes are lacking their usual fiery depth and her body is slumped over, her elbow resting on the counter in front of her. For some reason, I miss seeing the fire in her eyes and the attitude she gives me at every turn.

"Do you have a staring problem or what?" she bites out as she clenches her jaw, but her eyes remain blank, lacking their usual spark.

"Yeah, baby, I do. You're my problem." I smirk and she balks at me, life momentarily returning to her impassive demeanor.

"What the fuck do you mean I'm your *problem?* I haven't done a fucking thing today, let alone anything to have pissed you off, so fuck off." She huffs as she moves to jump off of the stool. I reach out my hand, quickly wrapping it around her throat.

"There's that fucking attitude. My dick was missing it." I lick my lips, my dick already hard as a rock. *Fucker really did miss her attitude.* I squeeze until I know I'm constricting her air flow, her pulse racing against my hand.

"You know, I've got an idea of how we can spend a few hours today." I shoot her a wink as I drag her into a standing position with me, abandoning our coffee.

I let go of her throat and push her in front of me. I guide her in the direction of my game room, my excitement growing the closer we get. Once we reach the door, I open it and shove her inside, slamming it behind me. She tumbles to the floor but quickly gets to her feet. The look on her face is fucking magnificent. Her anger flushes her cheeks a brilliant red.

It's lighter than the color of her blood, but addictive all the same.

She walks up to me, getting right in my face, seething. This girl's mood swings change from hot to cold in two seconds flat. "Oh, you look mad, baby doll. My bad." I chuckle as I put my hands up in mock surrender. I sure as hell don't see it coming when she cocks her fist back and sucker punches me right in the jaw, throwing me slightly off balance from the force and my utter surprise.

If this bitch hits me one more time...

"Damn, baby, you got me good." I laugh maniacally. Something just snapped inside of me. *No, not something, someone. My fucking monster is begging to come out and play with this little bitch and today, I don't fight it. At all.*

MARIE ANN

I reach my arms out to grab Essa, but she escapes my hold and runs around to the back of my billiards table, standing in a stance which would suggest she's going to run if I get close enough. The bitch is fucking crazy going from punching me in the face one second to running away from me in the next.

She must have an eye for monsters.

"Come here, baby doll. It's time to playyyyy!" I cackle as I dart to her. She squeals as she runs in the opposite direction. I stop and we lock eyes. She's on the opposite side of the table from me. Leaning from side to side in debate of which way to run, depending on me. I lurch to my left so she automatically moves to her left.

We go round in circles a few times, her chest heaving. I remain perfectly calm on the outside, but on the inside, my heart is pounding with excitement. What she doesn't know is I could've grabbed her from the start, but I love a little cat and mouse game. Making her think she can escape me, when in reality she's fucking trapped, forever in my grasp.

I leap onto the table and launch across, grabbing her arm. I easily yank her up onto the table with me. "Wanna play, baby doll?" I whisper. I grip her cheeks between my fingers, forcing her to look into my eyes. Her pupils dilate in fear when she stares into my own. *Fuck, that look makes me so fucking hard for her.*

"Fuck, baby. You wanna know how hard the fear in your eyes makes me?" I grab her hand and yank it to my jean covered dick, forcing her to feel how hard I am for her. She tries to pull her arm back, but it only serves to make me tighten my grip on her and force her hand to move up and down on my length.

CREEP

"Mmm. Yep. Time to have some fucking fun." I shove her away from me and leap off the table, moving to sit in the oversized stuffed chair in the center of the room. I actually fucking hate this chair, hence why I never should've allowed some dumbass interior designer to design everything in my house. But if I'm being honest, I couldn't be bothered to do it, even now.

The chair sits directly in front of the pole which takes up the center of the room. I love watching my slaves dance for me, working their bodies in extraordinary ways all in the name of pleasuring me, of making me happy.

Yes, that's what Essa needs to do, my little fucking tease.

Not glancing to where I know she still stands, I bark out at her, "Get the fuck over here, baby doll." I keep my gaze turned away from her, purposely acting indifferent and listening as she quietly jumps from the billiards table. She makes her way to me slow as hell on purpose. She may be complying with me right now, but the deviant little bitch still has to act out in some way. One would think with the wounds covering her ass and upper thighs, she'd get the fucking clue to stop being a disobedient little bitch, but of course she doesn't. She still has to be a brat.

I bite my tongue as I swallow the words of anger I was about to spit out. Because as much as I hate to love her little acts of defiance, I need her to listen to me right now. I need to let her think she has some semblance of control.

All part of the plan. In order to fuck someone's mind, you have to make it seem like their idea.

She finally stands in front of me, her fingers twisting together with her nerves yet again. I grab her hands, halting them.

"Stop. No need to be nervous, baby. This is gonna be fuckin' fun, for me *and* for you if you'd drop your nervousness." She glares and snatches her hands from mine. Leaning back, I grab the crystal decanter filled with bourbon from the side table and pour myself two fingers of my favorite whiskey. I take a drink and savor the flavor as it burns its way down my throat.

I lean back again, folding my hands behind my head and spreading my legs, getting comfortable. My mask of indifference slips over my face like a veil, hiding any emotions she could possibly read from me. I've noticed when she's around, I slip—which I should never fucking do—and let the mask fall away but no more of that shit. I'm done with her control over my subconscious. *Amongst other things.*

"Strip." I demand.

"Strip?" she blurts. "Why the fuck do I have to strip?"

Sighing, I roll my eyes. "Do you not see the pole behind you baby? What the fuck do you think it's there for? I can't very well have you dancing on that pole, rolling your body to music in those fucking sweatpants. And as hot as you do look right now, your clothes don't fit the vibe. Besides, I want them off. So. Fucking. Strip."

She stares at me, flummoxed, as she fiddles with her fingers again. She shifts from foot to foot, clearly uncomfortable. I give her a few extra seconds before I step in. I grab the remote to the surround sound, pushing play on the song I got ready while I was in here earlier. "Porn Star Dancing" by My Darkest Days blares through the speakers, shattering the silence suffocating the room. A bellow of a laugh escapes my mouth when I catch Essa's expression to my music choice.

CREEP

I keep laughing and it does nothing but piss her off more, but I'm getting tired of waiting so I stand, putting myself right in front of her. She tilts her head up to stare into my eyes, ever the brat. All of the women I have been with knew not to look up at me unless I gave them permission. I don't have labels on what I like in my sex life. I don't call myself a dominant, a sadist, none of that shit. I merely like what I like and I make sure all of my partners are aware. Believe it or not, but Essa is the first woman I've been with that didn't start as consensual. And I say start because it sure as fuck is now. She can't deny how bad she wants me.

Most of the women were only quick fucks and the ones that weren't, let me use them anyway I wanted. But with her, for some fucking reason, I just don't give a shit. I'll take what I want and leave her absolutely fucking ruined afterwards.

I bring my hands to the hem of her sweatshirt and rip it off of her before she can protest. I'm pleasantly surprised to find her completely naked beneath, her small but perky tits jiggling as her chest rises and falls in rapid succession. I bring my hand up to her breast and run the tip of my finger over her right nipple, tracing around it in circles, never quite giving it the attention she requires.

The word she carved into her arm catches my attention, and as fucked up as it is, it turns me on. Seeing how badly she hurt herself, how desperate she is for pain, turns my cock to stone.

I bring my gaze to hers as I continue to taunt her. "Take your pants off. Now." I bark out, but she doesn't fucking move. *Of course she doesn't because heaven fucking forbid the little bitch listens. I just want to watch her fucking dance for me.*

Glaring at her, I pinch her nipple between my fingers, and it almost turns white from the pressure of my fingers, all of the blood leaving. "I said to *take your fucking pants off. Now.*" The pain of my fingers must be enough to motivate her because she brings her own hands to the waistband of her sweats and pushes them down. They fall, pooling at her feet as she carefully steps out of them, trying to avoid putting any more pressure on the nipple I'm abusing.

Smirking, which is something I constantly seem to be doing when she's around, I let go and her blood flows back to her nipple. A strangled moan leaves her lips as she absently rubs life back into her breast. My cock throbs, straining against the zipper of my jeans painfully as the tip leaks precum. Little does she know what her touching herself does to me. I drag my finger from her nipples down across her ribs, tracing each individual one easily because they protrude from her skin.

The song repeats as it ends because I have it on a loop and it reminds me to get my fucking head back in it because as soon as I watch her sweet little ass dance for me, the sooner I can fuck her within an inch of her life—literally.

Moving from her ribs, I circle my long fingers around her upper bicep and drag her to the pole, pushing her into it. She stumbles from the force of my shove so she has no choice but to grab the pole to catch herself.

"That's it, baby. Wrap those hands around the pole, and then your legs. Fucking dance for me." I take a seat again, sitting how I was before, my stance relaxed, or at least as relaxed as it can be with my nine inch cock making himself very well known. Adjusting myself through my jeans, I keep my eyes glued to her. She has her back turned still, so my eyes land on her peachy fucking ass. She's wearing a black pair of cheeky underwear. They cover most of her ass, but leave the bottoms of her cheeks out, still giving me a perfect fucking view, so I'm not complaining.

I mock clearing my throat to get her attention. "I said, wrap your fucking legs around the pole, baby. Now."

"I don't know how to fucking dance." She bites out as she turns around to face me, giving me a direct view of her tits. She doesn't even bother to cover herself when she catches me blatantly staring at her. I have the sudden urge to do something irrational like cut off her fucking nipple and then sew it back on, just so I can leave another permanent scar on her body. One which insures she will never fucking forget me. Not that I would let her, but still.

"It's not hard. Just fucking do it already. I'm fucking done waiting." My words seem to have had some effect on her because in the next second, she's on the floor, arms wrapped around her knees and tears streaming down her face.

What the fuck?

Shooting up from the chair, I move to her and put my hand on hers as I ask what's wrong, but the second my hand makes contact with her, she screams and jumps away from me. What she's going through right now is vastly similar to earlier, only less extensive. But my touch seemed to be the bucket of ice cold water she needed because the fog clears from her eyes and she seems to be back in the present.

"You finally gonna tell me what's happening, baby doll?" I inquire, genuinely curious. I'm sure it's some form of PTSD or something along those lines, but now it's happened a second time and she still refuses to tell me what's going on. I'm going to snap.

"None of your fucking business. Let's get this over with so I can go to fucking bed and be done with all of this."

"You'll never be done with me, baby doll. Don't fucking forget it." I remind her as I take my seat again for the third fucking time, more than ready to finally get this show on the road. If she wants to act like the last five minutes never happened, then so be it for me to stop her. I don't give a fuck about her.

Sure, keep telling yourself that.

My fingers dig into the arms of the chair, the material digging under my blunt fingernails.

Essa wraps her hands around the pole and slowly twirls herself around it, trying to get a feel for it. I sit quietly as I watch her, waiting to see if she'll ride it like she was trying to ride my dick last night.

Fuck.

I grab the remote and turn the music volume all of the way up, blasting the song throughout the room.

She continues to twirl herself around the pole, her confidence quickly growing as she loses herself to the music. I can't help but to watch her, transfixed on every move. She rolls her body along the pole and there is sweat beading across her skin. My tongue begs to lick it off of her as I pound into her tight little pussy while my knife digs into her breasts, blood slipping between the both of us, causing our bodies to slide together effortlessly. I reach down and adjust myself in my pants again, not caring to be discreet about it. In fact, I hope she fucking sees. I want her to know what this is doing to me.

CREEP

The song begins for what is probably the twentieth time, I'm not sure as I've lost count, but suddenly, Essa jumps off of the pole and her tits sway slightly as she lands on the floor. Sweat covers her body and she glistens under the lights. I lick my lips as I drag my eyes down her body. She walks straight to me and stands before me with confidence oozing from her pores.

Let's see how long this lasts before she crawls back into her shell.

She leans down and puts her hands on the armrests—right above where my fists are still clenched—her face right in front of mine. "Was it good enough for you, sir?" Her words dripped in sarcasm as she flips me a cocky grin.

I run my tongue along my lower lip. "Yeah, baby doll. It was *all right*. I mean, I've definitely seen better, but for a beginner, you weren't bad." I knew my insult would piss her off and boy was I right. She leans away from me and lurches her arm out, slapping me across my face. I knew what she was going to do even as I said the words. I fucking love to piss her off. Her feisty attitude is the biggest turn on, especially when she even surprises herself with what she does.

My face stings and I feel giddy with murder on my mind. But before I get the chance, the little bitch takes off running, even abandoning her clothes in her haste to escape me. I tear my fingers from the armrests and I slowly rise, stretching to my full six foot four frame. I guess my baby doll wants to play another game of cat and mouse—and so soon too.

I grab the remote and push the off button. Silence sounds through the room causing the thoughts in my head to scream louder than normal with nothing to drown them out. Throwing it into the chair, I make my way toward the stairs, knowing for a fact I heard her run in that direction. I know this house like the back of my hand, every creak of the boards, every echo, all of it.

I go to her room first and check the door, finding it unlocked. Well, there's one of two options as to where she would have ran to, which only leaves one...

Moving down the hall to my own room, I turn the knob and the fucker doesn't budge. *Of fucking course she chose my room. She does every little fucking thing she can to piss me off every chance she gets.*

She probably did it because she knew her being in my room would guarantee to piss me off more. My little baby doll loves to bring my fucking bad side out. And my bad side loves to be brought out. She knows it will never end well for her, yet she continues to do it anyway.

Makes sense if you don't think about it.

Exasperated, I pound on the door. "Essa. Open my fucking door." But of course there is no fucking answer. I tried to give her a chance, but she fucked up. What she doesn't know is I keep an extra key to my room on my key ring, which just so happens to be downstairs.

I grab them and come back to my door, shoving the key into the slot and twisting it until I hear the click of the knob. I saunter into the room as I say, "I gave you a chance, baby. Remember when I fucking hurt you, it's your own fault for being so damn stupid." As if I haven't already been surprised enough by her endeavors tonight, I still don't see it coming when something round and cold presses against my temple. I hear a resounding click, the sound echoing through the room. *The all too familiar feel of the barrel of a gun against my skin.*

A smirk pulls at my lips as I slowly turn my head to where I know her to be. The barrel digs into my temple the more I turn. She's standing on a small table near my door, slightly hunched over as she holds the gun against me. *If only she knew the memories that flood my brain at the feel of a gun against my head again. Not exactly shit I want to relive. It only reminds me of my cowardice. I never want to be that weak, ever again.*

"What are you gonna do with that, hm? Shoot me? Go a—fucking—head. I dare you." I taunt her. "Pull the fucking trigger, Essa. Do it. Fucking. Do. It. You know you want to." She locks her eyes onto mine, an internal battle raging behind those pale greens.

My breath stutters along with my heart when I hear the click of the trigger as she squeezes. The silence surrounding us is deafening as we both stand with our eyes locked on one another. Her radiate fear, but mine are full of fucking fury.

She pulled the fucking trigger with the gun to my head. The little fucking bitch actually pulled the trigger.

With my eyes still locked on hers, each second ticking by feels like a year. I watch as her face pales, any ounce of confidence she had leaving her body in an instant. I wrap my fingers around the barrel, slowly pulling it away from my head. She doesn't even fight me as she seems frozen in place. Probably from fear is my guess because the look on my face right now is one close to murderous.

Because I feel fucking murderous. I want to slice open her fucking neck and watch that pretty face of hers drain of all life.

I take a deep breath, my eyes rolling to the back of my head as I try to contain my anger. But *fuck it*. She doesn't deserve my calm. She deserves my fucking *rage*.

MARIE ANN

I toss the gun across the room, hearing a clunk as it smacks against the wall. I grab Essa around her throat and pick her up. She dangles in front of me like a fucking rag doll, my hand wrapped around her throat the only thing keeping her up. Her legs sway below her, but her hands wrap around my own, clawing at me in an attempt to get me to release her.

Grinning, I watch her face turn red from lack of oxygen and I have no desire to release her. Her nails tear the skin from my hands and arms, but the sting is nothing compared to the utter fucking rage I feel boiling through my blood. My hold on her tightens more by the second, adding gasoline to my internal inferno the more I feel her windpipe being crushed beneath my palm.

I lower her feet to the floor, but keep my hold on her as I drag her to my bed and toss her on top of it. The second I release her, she coughs and sputters as oxygen fills her lungs again. She brings one of her hands to her throat, running her fingers across her pulse as she heaves.

"Aw, what's wrong, baby doll. Neck hurt?" I grin as I tease her, thousands of ideas running rampant in my head, consuming me.

"Please let me go." She manages to spit out, her voice barely audible. "I won't do anything like that again. I made a mistake. Please, just let me go," she begs with tears running down her face in tandem with her words. She swipes at them as quickly as they fall, but it's pointless with how fast they're falling.

"Oh you're damn right it was a mistake. You think you can pull a fucking gun on me let alone pull the fucking trigger? There isn't a single person I have let live for pulling some shit like that. You think just because you're my fuck toy, I'll treat you any different? You fucked up big time, baby doll, and you're about to see just how fucking bad." I glare at her, "And don't you dare fucking move." I turn from her and go to my drawer which holds my restraints. Without thinking twice, I grab a packet filled with zip ties.

There isn't going to be much thinking twice going on tonight.

I grab her right arm and drag it to the bedpost and after wrapping the zip tie around it, I tie it to the bedpost. I pull it as tight it will go, the band already deeply digging into her skin. I move to her left and do the same thing, double checking to make sure she can't move either, but I already knew she couldn't. Moving to the foot of the bed, I pull her legs taut and bend her ankles so her toes point towards me. I need a little more room to tie her ankles because even though she's not short, she's still not tall enough to reach from the head of my bed to the foot.

Keeping her ankles bent, I zip tie them to the bed. "Bet you're regretting your decision now, huh, baby doll?" With every zip tie I add, my blood sings in excitement.

CHAPTER THIRTEEN
ESSA

I'm fucking zip tied to his bed and he's standing at my feet, staring at me like I'm his last meal. *Or maybe he's mine?* Either way, I'm fucking screwed. I honestly don't know what was going through my head when I slapped him and then ran. I ran straight past my room and right into his, thinking he wouldn't think to look for me in here, but I underestimated him which is something I'm not used to dealing with.

I began digging through his drawers and of course the first one I open is one filled with what seemed to be numerous sex toys. But, they were terrifying so I quickly closed the drawer, careful not to make a noise. I then opened the rest, but came up empty. I didn't know I was searching for something specific until I came across the gun in his nightstand drawer, then something switched inside of me. I picked it up, and my hands shook. I'd never held a gun before in my life, but surely it wasn't too hard. Aim and shoot, right?

But I was so, *so very wrong.*

His words after he made me dance for him pissed me off. The

things he says and does are giving me fucking whiplash. He fucking demands me to strip and dance on a pole for him and it's honestly not terrible compared to other things he's done so far. But then I start to have *another* panic attack because of those three fucking words he muttered. I don't give a shit who he is, I don't need anyone seeing me go through shit. But then he touched me and his touch was like fire burning through the icy fog in my mind, instantly snapping me out of it.

    I danced on for him, getting lost in the same song playing on repeat. "Porn Star Dancing" by My Darkest Days. I've listened to it a lot, so when Vincent played it, I instantly recognized it. Though I know I'm not the best dancer, losing myself in the music and simply letting loose felt cathartic. But then his ass had to go and say "It was *all right*" and every ounce of freedom and happiness I was feeling abruptly dissipated.

    Now here I lie, naked and tied to his fucking bed *again* while he leers at me with murder in his eyes. And I wouldn't put it past him either. I know for a fact he is more than capable of murder. I mean, *come on,* he has a house in the middle of fucking nowhere, surrounded by miles of trees and with his job description? Yeah, no doubt in my mind.

    The morning after my first night here, when I was staring out my window into the woods, a particular tree caught my eye. At first, I didn't have the slightest clue why, so I continued to stare at it for a while. But then it hit me like a punch in the fucking gut. The tree was stained red. A deep, blood red. And I'm pretty sure it wasn't an animal's blood that caused a stain like that in the *middle* of the tree.

MARIE ANN

Knowing what he's capable of isn't what scares me though. It's not knowing what he's thinking at any given moment. One minute he's a malicious monster and the next he completely shuts down and brings this mask of indifference over his face. He is hot and cold and back and forth so many times it's dizzying.

I close my eyes, fear taking hold of my body. My nails dig into my palms, only adding to the bite of the zip tie in my wrist, but right now I need all of the pain I can give myself. I know this is going to be bad.

CHAPTER FOURTEEN
ESSA

"Open your fucking eyes and watch me as I fucking hurt you. You don't get the reprieve of not fucking watching," he barks out the moment he notices my eyes were shut. I open them instantly and pin my stare at him. If he's going to make me watch, then at least I can enjoy the view beforehand, because damn is it a view.

He has no shirt on and his abs are glistening with sweat. His anger is so intense, it's radiating through his body. White Calvin Klein boxer briefs peek out of the waistband of his low hanging jeans. Jeans which cling to his iron clad thighs, the muscles flexing as he leans from one foot to the other. In the midst of being lost in my thoughts, he must've taken his clothes off and I'm not sure how to feel about it.

Don't get me wrong, I fucking love the view, but why do I have to love it? I'm supposed to hate him, but in moments like these, he makes it really fucking hard. Especially when I can gawk at his tattoo covered body, but when he's in this kind of mood, he takes what he wants with no hesitation.

MARIE ANN

I lay stretched to the max, completely fucking naked and right now, as I watch him run his eyes over every single fucking inch of my body, I regret not grabbing my clothes in my haste earlier. At least with clothes on right now, I would feel slightly better. And slightly is better than nothing at all. But it's too late now. Though, now that I really think about it, I don't think me having clothes on would stop him from doing what he's about to do. They would be a mere inconvenience he could rid himself of in a split second.

The heat of his gaze burns my skin and I squirm, my own heating despite my best efforts to remain unaffected. I can hate this man as much as I want, but he does things my body fucking loves. *No, not only loves, but fucking craves.* The self-hatred I feel because of him is insurmountable but I have a feeling it's about to hit an all-time high.

His index finger drags from the tip of my big toe, down my foot to my ankle and continues to move up. Once he reaches the apex of my thighs which are spread wide for him to see my glistening pussy, *the traitorous bitch,* he brushes his knuckle along my clit and then quickly moves back down my other leg. When he reaches my foot, he replaces his finger with his knife and then repeats the same actions. Except this time when he reaches the apex of my thighs, he presses the blade against my folds. The tip digs painfully into my clit and I cry out, but the pain is also eliciting something more. *Pleasure.*

I'm so fucking confused with myself and my reactions to him. The only person to have ever touched me in a sexual way was my own fucking "father", so clearly it's never been a pleasurable experience. But with Vincent, the way he touches me and the things he makes me feel, disconcerts me. Because I hate him. *But I don't.* I don't know what I feel and the only way I know to make it all go away hasn't been working like it always has.

The feeling of pain only makes me want him more now that I know what he's capable of. Because I know, and my body knows he can bring me the pain I want, the pain I fucking *need*, better than I ever could. He knows how to deliver it in such a way that while, yes, obviously it fucking hurts, it feels so damn good. I'm becoming addicted to the things he makes me feel. I am a junkie at heart, after all. Literally, it runs in my DNA.

He pushes the tip in further and I feel as it breaks the skin open, blood dripping through my folds. Tears fall as I struggle against my binds, though I know it's fruitless. I'm not escaping this. I fucked up and he's getting his revenge on me and on my body in the worst fucking way imaginable.

I keep my eyes locked on his every move as he roams his eyes over my body, his knife following the path they take. He pushes down harder against random spots, nicking me in places while others are cut open deeply. Blood covers my body as the wounds multiply by the minute, his movements becoming more frantic as he continues. His chest rises and falls rapidly and sweat coats his skin.

My screams eventually turn into silent sobs. After what feels like the hundredth cut he makes against my skin, he moves away from me. He brings the blade of the knife to his mouth and with his eyes locked on mine, he runs his tongue from the base all the way to the top, sucking the tip into his mouth. I watch, transfixed, as he cleans my blood off of his knife.

Pain is radiating all over my body making it hard for me to focus.

I can no longer feel any of my limbs, my binds cutting off circulation. I glace up to make sure they're still attached because I really wouldn't be surprised if Vincent ended up sawing my limbs off—that's just how fucking twisted he is—especially right now. My skin is already bruising and my fingers are a blue-ish white color from the lack of blood flow.

My vision begins to blur as I try to hold his gaze, but I lose my battle and my eyes flutter closed.

My eyelids feel like they weigh a hundred pounds as I try to peel them open. My body is weightless, though I still feel the mattress beneath me. I manage to pry my eyes open but it's not for more than two seconds before Vincent is shoving himself inside of me. I scream out at his intrusion, but more from surprise than pain because it doesn't hurt. I was expecting to feel the usual ripping fire throughout my body, but it didn't happen. No, my body was ready for him even though I was un—fucking—concious.

And fuck does it feel good.

My eyes impulsively shut again at the sensations tormenting my body. Vincent must have cut the zip ties on my ankles because I can feel the pins and needles sensation of blood trying to flow back into them as he grabs my upper thighs and pushes them apart, opening myself up to him more.

A moan escapes my mouth in a hushed breath as he pushes inside of me again. His palm lands across my face and my eyes snap open at the brutal sting across my cheek.

"Keep your fucking eyes open, baby," he spits out as he grabs my hips and lifts them into the air. I watch as he slowly pulls out, his thick girth hitting every nerve ending inside of me, eliciting the most incredible feeling.

When he pulls all of the way out with the head of his cock hovering at my opening, he yanks my hips toward him and impales me on his cock. I scream at not only his ruthlessness, but the brutal force at which my arms pull against my bindings. Every cut across my skin stings with every movement, eliciting massive amounts of pain which intermixes with the pleasure I'm feeling, creating the most explicit ecstasy.

My screams spur him on as he pounds into me, the tip of his dick hitting my cervix with every thrust. The blood from all of my wounds runs freely, coating us both and causing our bodies to slip against each other. He wraps one hand around my throat and the other finds a particularly deep wound he placed over my ribs. He digs his fingers into the wound as he tilts his hips up, dragging along my walls as he pulls back out. Sweat drips from his forehead and onto my face. I dart my tongue out to lick it off of my upper lip. His eyes follow my movement and darken with desire. The monster that came over him, the one that cut my body in a hundred different places in every which way is slowly dissipating. His anger is turning into what I can only assume to be lust.

While he's still aggressive with me, his hand squeezing my throat until I can't do more than wheeze and his fingers digging into my wound, he stopped solely bringing me pain and now he's giving me immense pleasure too. He moves his hand from the gash to in between our bodies and begins to rub my clit is slow, leisurely circles, a substantial contrast to the way he's fucking my pussy with raw abandon.

The threshold between the pain and pleasure becomes too much to bear and my legs begin to shake, my orgasm overtaking my body. Lightning shoots through my clit and I scream out from the intensity. My pussy pulsates, squeezing his cock as I lose my mind. My body feels hot and tingly all over as my vision goes black and I swear I see stars.

When I come to, my entire body sated, I glance up to Vincent hovering above me. He's wearing a slight smirk and for the first time, I'm close enough to notice the slight dimples that pop up with his smile. They're quite adorable, but they do nothing to soften his sharp features, instead adding to them. I don't know how it's even possible, but with Vincent, I'm not surprised. Of course he'd find a way to make something adorable look intimidatingly hot.

He stops his lazy strokes until he just rests inside of me. I can feel my walls squeezing around him, still pulsing from my orgasm. I wriggle underneath him, desperate for him to move again.

He flicks his tongue along the seam of my lips. "You see how fucking *good* pain can feel, baby doll?" He smashes his lips against mine before I have the opportunity to respond. His tongue tangles with my own and he begins to move inside of me again, his pace slow at first but it speeds up quickly. Before long, he's pounding into me with ruthless abandon and he jerks his head back because keeping our mouths sealed becomes impossible.

His hand around my throat tightens again, not enough to cut off my oxygen flow, but enough to have my pussy clenching with the need to come, *again*. With every thrust, my clit rubs against Vincent's pelvis, bringing me closer to the edge. He must see because he begins grinding against me once he fills me to the brink. I peel my eyes open and bring them to the junction of our bodies, feeling the overwhelming need to watch.

Vincent already has his gaze locked on our bodies as he pulls out and slams back in while tilting his hips at the last second so the tip of his cock hits my cervix again. I cry out in pain which instantly turns into a moan. Sweat dripping from his forehead continues to drip onto my body, mixing with the blood covering us both. His muscles bunch and flex with each thrust and we both watch our bodies move together as we slowly come apart.

My next orgasm hits me out of nowhere, consuming me. I attempt to scream, but nothing comes out as my body begins to shake, every sensation too much to handle. As I ride through the high, I feel as Vincent buries himself to the hilt and moans out his release, his dick throbbing inside of me. He rests his head at the junction of my neck and shoulder, sinking his teeth into my skin as he groans.

We lie for what seems like hours with him resting his full body weight on top of me while I lay helpless beneath him. My body is beyond lax and I could stay like this all night for all I care. Pain maintains its presence throughout my body and my arms scream for relief, but it only heightens the bliss I feel. Vincent has brought out a side of me I never knew existed.

He peels himself from me, our skin actually sticking together from the blood. He leans back, resting his ass on his heels as he sits in between my spread legs. I feel his release trickling down my thighs and his eyes follow the movement. Hunger flashes through them at the sight and he drags his fingers through it, coating them. He brings his digits to my mouth and attempts to shove them in but I clench my jaw, fighting his advance, but it's no use. He uses his other hand to pry my jaw apart and then shoves his fingers in, demanding I suck them.

So I do.

I keep my eyes locked on his as I wrap my tongue around his index and middle fingers and suck, hollowing my cheeks from the suction. In my peripheral, I see his dick hardening again.

Huh, I didn't think that could happen again so fast, but it's not like I'm experienced when it comes to this shit, anyway.

He abruptly yanks his fingers from my mouth and it makes a loud popping noise. He leans to the side and grabs his knife he must have dropped earlier. Leaning his torso across me, he shoves the tip of the blade underneath the band around my wrist, struggling to get it all of the way underneath with how tight it is. Once he does, he cuts it and frees my arm and it falls limply to my side. I attempt to move it, but the pain which automatically shoots through my arm is enough to bring tears to my eyes.

Fuck, this is gonna suck.

He quickly releases my other arm and lets it flop to my side much like the other. I don't even try to move them, lying like a limp noodle on the bed. I want to cover myself from his wandering eyes, but I know it's not something I can even attempt at this moment, so I don't even try. Though I do bring my thighs together to give myself some semblance of privacy, but because he's still resting between them, his body blocks my attempt.

Speaking for the first time since I woke up, I clear my hoarse throat. "Can you please move. I want to leave." My voice comes out sounding rough and low, probably from my screams. He laughs. A full on belly laugh, hunching over and grabbing his stomach. I blink at him, flabbergasted. *What the fuck is he laughing about? I don't understand what's so damn funny.*

Irritation crawls along my skin, replacing the high of my orgasm and because of it, I suddenly feel the pain coursing through my body. Well, I felt it before, but now it feels immensely different. There is nothing good about this pain now. *No. Now it just fucking hurts.* And it serves to make me even more fucking angry with him. He had to take away the shit that felt good by opening his stupid fucking mouth.

"What the fuck is so funny?" I spew as much anger into my words as I can manage. My dignity is dwindling by the second, and his laughter only makes it worse.

"You," he replies casually once he gets his laughter under control.

"Me?" I ask ridiculously, which serves to make him start his laughing fit again. I'm so confused it's not even funny. I'm lying here in agony from dozens of cuts because of this man because of the anger he was exuding not more than an hour-ish ago and now? Now he's laughing his ass off like I've told the world's funniest joke.

There now seems to be another thing I don't understand about this man. But do I really know anything about him to begin with? The answer is no because I fucking met him a couple of days ago. And why am I even attempting to know anything about him. He's a piece of shit who likes to hurt me, like Ben. He goes from hot to cold so fast I'm getting whiplash. He goes from acting like he cares to almost fucking killing me. I don't understand him and because of it, I'm also beginning to accept it.

He is something I can't control. He is something I don't need to control. In fact, since I've known him, he has actually been the one to pull me out of my head. He's been the one to give me such a pain and pleasure clash I detonate into oblivion.

He was fucking me like a wild animal, bringing me more pleasure than I ever could have imagined existed, and now he's acting crazy by laughing maniacally for no reason. I swear to fucking God, or whatever higher up exists, I have fucking whiplash.

His laughter dies down and he jumps off of the bed. He grabs his boxers and pulls them up his legs, his thighs bulging with the movement. Now that he's no longer between me, I sit up and yank the blanket over my body, feeling self-conscious. The material of the silky blanket feels like water running over me. Blissful but stinging. The white band of his boxers turns a muddy red color from the blood covering his skin, but he doesn't seem to care.

"You can leave now, baby doll. I'm done with you." He throws out at me as he pulls his jeans on and buttons them. *Isn't he going to shower?* But apparently I must have said it out loud without realizing or he can read fucking minds because he answers my thoughts.

"Nah, baby doll. I love your fucking blood on me, which is new to me but I'm rolling with it. It would be a waste to cut your beautiful body up like that and then just wash it all off." He gestures his arm toward my body and I didn't before, but now I take the time to look at myself. My eyes bug out of my fucking head at the sight.

What in the actual fuck did he do to me? I look like a butchered pig. I'm not too far off on that statement either. Rolling my eyes, I continue to take in my mutilated body. I'm sure most of these are going to leave scars. Not big ones, as he cut cleanly, but scars, nonetheless. I surmise my scars on the outside will match the inside now.

I glance down at my arm where the word CREEP is etched into my skin. Though it makes out a word, it's no different than the scars already covering my skin. Every cut I have given myself I have always kept to one spot on my arm which was easily covered by my hoodie or even a long sleeved shirt, but now? Now no matter what I wear, these will be easily visible which I'm sure was part of his plan. I have cuts from my neck down to my fucking ankles. They're spread about so there aren't any right next to each other, again serving his purpose to make them hard to cover, to fucking mark me as his.

I haven't the slightest clue as to how I will explain these to Holley, but I do have a long while before I'll have to deal with it so I have time to think of an excuse she'll hopefully buy. But even now I'm pretty fucking doubtful about it.

My gaze is snapped to Vincent as he casually strolls right out of the fucking room, not sparing another glance in my general direction. Irritation crawls up my spine. How the fuck can he do something like this to me and then leave after telling me he's fucking *done* with me. Well I definitely don't want to stay in his room a second longer. I don't know how I manage it, but I make it to the edge of the bed. I rest my ass on the edge of the bed, my feet dangling off as I gather the strength to move the rest of the way off.

MARIE ANN

Pain radiates over every crevice in my body. I shove my fists into the mattress and push myself into a standing position. Blood rushes to my head and I topple to the floor in a dizzy spell. My vision swims as a black cloud comes over my head. I lie slumped on the floor as I take deep breath after deep breath to prepare myself enough to move. It's going to take everything in me to do this, but that's the thing. I can fucking do it. Even though this is some of the worst pain I have ever been in, it's still *nothing* compared to the pain Ben put me through my entire life.

Once my vision is clear, I grit my teeth and grip the bloody blanket covering the bed, using it as leverage to pull myself up. Once I'm stable on my feet, I stand to my full height and take another deep breath, hissing. Every—fucking—thing hurts. Even fucking breathing hurts. The healing from this is going to take me so long, I already know. I gingerly take my first step. My teeth feel like they are going to snap right out of my mouth with the pressure I'm exerting on them. I take one step after another, slowly but carefully making my way across the room. Sweat trails down my naked back and the blood covering my body is sticking and only getting worse the longer it continues to ooze. It runs down my legs in trails, slowly drying and clinging to the hair covering my legs.

In what is probably ten minutes, I eventually make it to the door of his room. Using the frame, I push myself through and stumble into the hallway. I begin the long trek to my room. The only fucking safe place I have—for the time being. It takes me close to twenty minutes to make it to my bedroom door. My body is shaking with the exertion and sweat covers my entire body. The sweat seeps into the cuts causing

CREEP

them to sting even more than they already do.

Even though I want to collapse onto my bed and pass out, I know I need to wash this sweat and blood off of me or I won't be able to sleep. I've never been able to sleep being dirty. Not even when Ben raped me for the first time—and that was the most pain I have ever been in. I still managed to take a fucking shower then, and I fucking can now.

I stagger into the bathroom and fall into the shower. I somehow manage to reach up high enough to turn the knob to some degree of warmth before completely collapsing onto the floor of the shower. The water rains down over me as I lie curled into a ball. The water stings but feels good at the same time. I watch through squinted eyes as all of the blood covering me washes down the drain next to my face. It swirls around and around in never ending circles.

CHAPTER FIFTEEN
ESSA

    I lay in bed for days, only getting up long enough to use the restroom when I can no longer hold it. I don't even bother to take a shower. I simply don't give a shit. Every day Vincent brings food to my room, but it remains untouched. For some reason I can't fathom, he's left me alone. I haven't seen, let alone talked to him going on six days now.

    On the third day of me remaining in my room, he set the usual tray of food outside of my door. He knocked—per usual—but then something slid underneath the door before I heard his footsteps retreating. I waited until I heard him walking down the stairs before I forced myself to get up and move to the door. I didn't bother to open it—I didn't give a shit about the food. But what I did give a shit about was the phone lying on the floor with a piece of paper taped to it. My phone. I reach down, gritting my teeth but remaining silent. I tear off the paper and read it.

    Essa. I'm choosing to let you go through whatever the fuck it is

CREEP

you're going through, but just know I'm losing my patience and will force you to come to me eventually. Until then, baby doll, here's your piece of shit phone. You can talk to your sister but don't be fucking stupid.

He takes every jab he can at me, apparently even including my fucking phone. It's nothing fancy, but it's still a fucking phone. I took his dumb little note and tossed it into the garbage along with the fucks I give.

Now, it's been three days and I haven't heard a word from him since. He's left the house every day to go work—I'm assuming—and every time before he does, he comes up to my room and fucking locks it from the outside so I can't escape. Though I'm still in pain, I tried the door every fucking time, but it wouldn't budge a millimeter. Clearly whatever the fuck he put on my door was strong because I even tried ramming the door down using my nightstand.

I gave up on my endeavor to escape and now I lie here, listening to song over fucking song, many of them on repeat. I haven't even felt the need to fucking cut—the pain radiating all over my body enough to keep me satiated, for now. "Take It Out On Me" by Thousand Foot Krutch blares through my earbuds as I lean against the glass window, staring out into the night.

The sun set a few hours ago and I've remained in the same spot. My head pressed against the glass and my back leaning against the wall behind me. My ass has been numb for so long, it doesn't even feel like I have one anymore. Vincent left this morning and I haven't heard a peep in the house since. Not like I give a shit whether he's around or not.

MARIE ANN

It makes no sense to me. This whole arrangement was supposed to be temporary, but here I am, over a fucking week later and still in his house. He hasn't brought up taking me back home and frankly, I haven't even asked. As much as I don't want to be here, I most definitely don't want to be there. I already know the second Ben gets me alone, he'll in all probability end up killing me in a fit of rage because I'm sure he's pissed he hasn't gotten to "see" me.

I talked to Holley a little bit ago and I asked her if our parents have contacted her at all, just to be on the safe side. She assured me they haven't and they don't even have her number. She didn't want them to have a way to contact her. Which I understand one hundred percent. Hell, they don't even have the number to my phone.

I'm snapped out of my thoughts when I see a shadow emerge from amongst the trees. My blood freezes in my veins at the same time my heart stops. Even with the moonlight shining down, it's still nearly impossible to make out the shadowy figure moving around. I slink back into my room, hiding myself from the view of the window. I crawl underneath my bed and hide myself behind the blankets hanging off of the side. They hide my form, but still give me the ability to see out of the window.

I keep my eyes fixed on the figure moving about. Awareness creeps into my consciousness the longer I stare, but fear overrides my senses and refuses to let me connect the dots. I lose sight of the figure and it makes me panic even worse than being able to see him. I shoot out from underneath the bed and rush to the window, my hands smacking onto the glass as I catch myself from tumbling forward.

Time physically slows as I turn my head two notches to the left

CREEP

and my eyes lock on the figure. Recognition seeps into my veins right as apprehension does. Two coexisting feelings swirling around in my head, confusing the hell out of me.

Vincent's eyes remain locked on mine even through the distance. He takes deliberate steps out of the shadows, revealing his form to me. My eyes widen as I take him in. From his black hoodie down to his dirty, gray sweatpants. His white Nike shoes are stained with dirt and mud and when my eyes shoot back up to his face, I watch in a trance as he brings his hands to his hood and flicks it off of his head.

Once his body is completely free from the shadows, the moonlight shines down on him. But he's not what has my attention anymore.
It's the blood stains on his hands. On his clothes. All. Over. Him. My eyes widen with fear as I begin to back up. He flicks the corner of his mouth up in a grin as he brings his index finger to his mouth, making a "shh" motion before winking and submerging himself back into the shadows—completely disappearing.

My heart pounds in my chest as I continue to back up until I catch my leg on the corner of my bed, tripping over it and falling backwards. I don't even attempt to get up. I scooch my ass to the chair in the furthest corner of my room and hide in the corner. My body begins to shake and I'm fucking terrified. I've seen him covered in blood before, but it was my own blood. And it was happening to me. Watching him walk out of the trees covered in what I know to be someone else's blood has me tripping the fuck out. I knew he had probably murdered people before, but seeing it myself, *actually fucking knowing it is a whole different story.*

What the fuck did I get involved in?

CHAPTER SIXTEEN
VINCENT

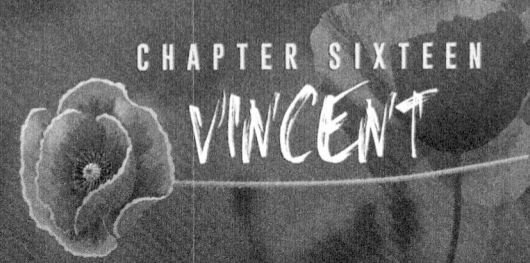

I chuckle as I step back into the tree line, out of Essa's line of sight. Watching the color drain from her face as she saw me emerge from the shadows. Lately she's been in a funk and has locked herself in her room. I decided to let her be, mainly because I've had shit I've had to deal with which involves me leaving the house and it's a lot easier to lock her ass up when she won't leave her fucking room.

Leo called me this morning to let me know I had some shit I had to take care of. Meaning, *someone* to take care of. It was simple, practically boring, and I'm slightly disappointed in the lack of a fight from my little friend hanging from the tree in the distance. This particular whore had decided to be a dumb bitch and attempt to steal from one of our many dealers littering the streets. She clearly failed and I'm sure, at this point, she's greatly regretting her decision.

Grabbing her was easy enough. All I did was come up to her while she was working, pretending to be a John and she walked right into my car. Easy as pie. From there, with one swift punch to her

CREEP

I knocked her ass out and brought her here. Now, she's tied to a tree bleeding out.

In the middle of my task, I caught a glimpse of Essa out of the corner of my eye. She was leaning against her window, staring out into the woods with a blank expression on her face. As always, she distracted me and I gravitated towards her.

She didn't see me until I was close to the tree's edge because she suddenly perked up when she saw, what I'm assuming to be, was my shadow. But when I actually brought my body into the moonlight and she caught a glimpse of what I looked like, *fuck*. The fear which came over her was so tangible, I can still fucking taste it on my lips. The way her entire body locked up, frozen like a statue.

Then she panicked and began backing away, as if it would fucking help. She knows she can't run from me. I fucking *own her*. My dick is already hard in my sweats and it tents against the stretchy material. Not ideal for cutting someone up, but it is what it is.

Now that I'm back at the task at hand, I don't feel as giddy to continue. Once I caught sight of Essa again, the want to kill, the *need* to kill has diminished greatly. Now all I want to do is play with my little toy. Groaning, I bring my knife to this bitch's throat and quickly slash across, from left to right, ending her pain and suffering. She gurgles, choking on her own blood until eventually, she goes silent. Her cold eyes stare at the ground below, empty.

Irritated, I cut the rope tying her up and toss her limp body into the hole. With the same ritual as always, I douse her in lighter fluid and strike a match. I watch as her body becomes engulfed in flames and then make my way back to the house. Fucking little bitch is always

MARIE ANN

ruining my plans. I've been itching for a fucking job and today Leo gave me exactly what I needed. Then here comes her little ass ruining it just by fucking existing.

My irritation grows into full blown anger the closer I get to the house, the closer I get to *her*. She's had her little ass locked in her room for days, of her own free will. But that's about to fucking change. I decided to let her be, but now I'm fucking over it. I don't need to convenience her, or give her a single fucking thing to help her out. *What the fuck is wrong with me?* She's here to make my life easier, to do whatever the fuck I say. Not the other way around.

Stomping up the stairs leading to the front door, I yank my keys out of my pocket. The blood on my hands causes them to slip and fall to the wooden stairs beneath me. I bellow out in anger, swiping them off of the wood and shoving them into the lock. Once I have the door open, I slam it shut behind me, the reverberation of the door sounding through the entire house. The blood covering my hands covers the door handle and my keys, basically every—fucking—thing I touch. Usually, I'm more diligent and meticulous about cleaning up, but tonight, I'm fucking slipping.

My skin crawls, itchy to run upstairs and storm into her room. To show her who the fuck is in charge. So that's exactly what I do. I make a beeline for the stairs, keys in hand. As I approach them, I quiet my steps as much as possible in effort to see if I can hear any movement from Essa's room, but it's eerily silent.

I round the corner and find her bedroom key on my keyring. After struggling with it slipping between my fingers, I finally manage to get the fucker in the keyhole and unlock it. I shove the door open with

CREEP

brute force and stride into her room. Her lights are off and the room is almost pitch black. The moonlight outside shines *just* bright enough I can make out the shadows of things in the room, like her bed and the chair so I avoid bumping into those.

I close the door behind me, the soft click resounding through the room. I creep forward, inch by fucking inch, straining my eyes as I search for Essa. I make it across her entire room without so much as an inkling of her presence, which is fucking odd. I know she has to be here somewhere. There's no way she could have escaped. I push her bathroom door open and pause as I listen to it slowly creek open. I step in and flick on the light, instantly coming up with nothing. *She's not in here. What the fuck!*

I run my fingers through my hair, gripping the strands and yanking. I fucking love this cat and mouse game she likes to play, but now that I can't find her, my excitement is now quickly turning to anger again. *And maybe fear...*

Fucking little bitch is going to be in for a treat when I find her.

Turning back around, I make my way to the chair in the corner of her room. The same one I sat in as I watched her sleep the first night she was here. It already seems like a lifetime ago and it wasn't more than a couple weeks. She's fucking everything up.

I lean back and pull a pack of cigarettes out of my pocket. I push one between my lips and strike a match, lighting it. I wave the match to blow out the flame and set it down on the stand next to me. I take a long drag and exhale through my nose. The smoke swirling in my lungs feels like a breath of fresh air, allowing the fog in my mind to clear. Ironic speaking I'm smoking a fucking cancer stick, but it is what it is.

I take a few more drags before pulling it away from my face. I glance down and notice the blood on my hand has transferred to the cigarette, but I don't even fucking care. Right as the thought crosses my mind, I see the tiniest movement out of the corner of my eye. The blanket on the bed twitches slightly before settling again. I quickly divert my eyes and bring my hand back up to my mouth to hide my smirk. The little bitch actually hid under the bed like a fucking child. I can't believe I didn't think to look there to begin with.

Eager to get my hands on her, or rather around her fucking throat, I stub the smoke in the ashtray and push to my feet. I crank my neck from side to side and crack my knuckles. All a fucking show for Essa. I want her little ass to be afraid of me. I *need* her to fear me. Because that glimpse of lust she gets in her eyes, as much as I fucking crave it, I can't see it. I can't fucking have it. It's too much. Her fear though? That I will take gallons of, daily.

I walk to the edge of the bed where I saw the blanket move and bending to one knee, I ever so slowly lift the bottom of the blanket enough to give her a glimpse of my hand. I suddenly yank it the rest of the way up and shove my face underneath the bed frame and scream, "Boo!"

She screams bloody murder as she crawls to the furthest corner away from me, but before she gets too far, I jerk my hand out and wrap it around her ankle. I drag her to me as she kicks and screams the whole time. I laugh and yank her out from underneath the bed.

"Where do you think you're goin', baby doll?" I chuckle as I reach for her arm too.

CREEP

"Pl—please let m—me go," she stammers. Her face is as white as a sheet of paper and I can feel her pulse racing from here. I yank her arm up until she's in a sitting position and turn her to face me.

"Tsk tsk baby. You know that'll never happen." I drag my bloody finger across her cheek, digging my blunt nail into her skin. When I pull my hand away, I view the trail of blood I left on her and it brings a sinister smirk to my face. I fucking love seeing her covered in blood and there's something about it being the blood of the whore I just killed that has my dick turning to stone.

She struggles in my hold again, and I swiftly reach my arm out and slap her across the face hard. Her head snaps to the side, red instantly blossoming across the entire left side of her face. I grasp her chin and yank her face towards mine. The heat of her face radiates into my hand and it makes me feel slightly better.

"Stop fucking fighting me you little bitch. Or I'm going to fucking kill you. Just like I killed that whore who's burning in a dirt hole right now." Like a glass of ice cold water running over her skin, she stops fighting me and melts into the floor, no longer holding herself up. I let her fall as I watch her. She curls into a ball, wrapping her hands around her knees, but that won't fucking do. No, not at all.

I rise to my full height and gaze down at her. "Get the fuck up. On your knees."

Without question, she rises until she's resting on her knees in front of me. Her head is bowed, looking at the floor and her arms hang limply by her sides. She may not even know it, but she's acting the obedient slave she already should have been. *Better late than never.*

Pushing my sweats down, they fall to the floor and I step out of them, kicking them to the side. My cock is tenting against the fabric of my black Calvin Klein boxers. I grip the waistband and waste no time pushing them down my thighs so they fall to the floor beneath me. Kicking them to the side, I stand in front of Essa. My cock just out far enough if she were to purse her lips in the slightest gesture, they would brush against the head of my cock.

Anticipation rolls through me of what I'm about to do. Since the first moment I met this girl, I've thought about shoving my cock so far down her throat she can't breathe.

"Open your fucking mouth." I tilt my head to look down as Essa as I make the command. I want to see her obedience as she obliges my every whim. She falters slightly before slowly opening her mouth. I glance down at my dick, grasping it in my hand as I glance back to her.

"I think you'll need to open up a bit wider, doll." Her closed eyes spring open and automatically zero in on my dick right in front of her face. Her eyes widen as she takes me in and I crack a cocky smile. Gulping, she opens her mouth as wide as she can and her hot breath fans across the head of my dick. Precum leaks from the tip and I shudder as my dick twitches. When I open my eyes, I see Essa has closed hers.

"Open your fucking eyes," I bark out and she snaps them back open, locking her eyes on mine. Without warning, I grab the back of her head and shove my cock between her lips, pushing myself to the back of her throat and then I keep going until I feel her gag around me. I pull out enough to let her catch a breath—because she's going to need it—and then I thrust forward. I grip both sides of her head and fuck her face as hard as I can. Every thrust into her mouth, she gags aggressively, her throat squeezing my cock in a vice grip. I groan, my eyes rolling into the back of my head.

I slow my pace, wanting the moment to last. Tears are welling in her eyes and running down her face in fast trails. Saliva drips from her mouth and runs down her chin before dripping onto the floor beneath us. I've never seen someone look so fucking hot choking on a dick before. I wish I had my phone on me right now, I'd take a fucking picture of this.

Surprisingly, her eyes stay on mine for the most part. There are a few times when they flutter close from the force of her gagging, but still, I'm pleasantly surprised. But it's her fucking stare that's causing me to drift so close to the edge of coming already. I loosen my hold on her head a bit and when I do, I feel her begin to bob her head over my length. Shock falls over my face at the fact she's actually participating and not fucking fighting this. She bobs her head once more and swirls her tongue around my tip once she comes back up for air. She releases my length with a resounding pop and peers up at me again. I stare at her, my face impassive and she quirks her brow in return. Apparently her feistiness is making a comeback.

She leans forward and darts her tongue out, trailing it along my cock. She traces one of the thick veins, running her tongue along it a few times. I can't help the shudder running through me at the feel of her mouth on me, the feel of her actually enjoying this. I barely catch as she smirks slightly before enveloping me in her hot mouth again. She sucks with brute force, working her mouth up and down.

I feel my balls seize up and tingles shoot through my spine. I instinctually grab onto her face again and begin to move faster as my release begins to move through me. I pump my hips two more times and bury myself into the back of her throat right as I feel the white hot tingle shoot through my body. My cum jets into her mouth and I slowly gyrate my hips against her face as my cock pulses. She swallows greedily around me, every swallow squeezing my cock.

I slowly pull out of her mouth and she has the fucking audacity to suction her mouth around me as I do. My dick twitches in effort to get hard again. I yank myself out of her mouth and snake my long fingers around her bicep. I yank her to her feet in front of me, putting my face right into hers. Our noses smash together and our breath mingles. Her chest is heaving with her trying to catch her breath from what just happened and mine is heaving because I fucking hate craving her and what she does to me.

I lick my lips as I say, "Listen here, baby doll. Enough of the fucking games. You're done keeping yourself locked in this fucking room and you're done with the fucking attitude. You're going to do as you're told and that's that. I'm sure you realize by now, your life will go so much fucking smoother if you simply *behave*. So be a good girl for me."

She clenches her jaw, but remains silent. I run my eyes over her features, searching for something, but I don't know what. I can't focus on shit with this blood smeared across her face and in her hair. It's too fucking hot. She needs to be cleaned up.

"No objections?" I pause for all of two seconds before continuing, "Good. You need to go get cleaned up. This blood all over you is distracting me and it's fucking late." I turn her around and smack her ass, pushing her toward the bathroom. She doesn't even flinch as she saunters to the shower, her ass swaying slightly from the way she walks.

I reach down to grab my boxers off of the floor when, through the crack of the door, I catch sight of Essa stripping and lose it. I saunter into her bathroom right as I hear the shower turn on. As I'm pushing open the door, I catch the last bit of Essa's legs disappearing into the shower. With a one track mind, I move over to the shower and fling the glass door open.

Essa whirls around and gawks at me. She flings her arms across her chest and turns the lower half of her body away from me like I haven't already seen it, or fucking touched it. Or made it fucking come so goddamn hard she was seeing stars. *Yeah, right.*

I step into the shower and close the door behind me. Essa takes a step backwards and to counter her, I step forward until she is pressed against the tiled wall. She fumbles slightly and I reach my arms out to steady her—a reaction I don't realize I make—until she falls against my chest. My arms automatically wrap around her waist as she rests her head against me and my hands run across the smooth expanse of her back.

Alarm bells sound through my head. Screaming at me to push her and walk the fuck away. I'm almost tempted. *Almost.* But the feel of her skin against mine, the feel of her heart beating against me is just what I need right now. So I ignore my instinct of self-preservation and continue to hold her. To live in this moment for the time being.

I grip her waist and haul her into my arms. She impulsively wraps her legs around my waist and lays her hands on my shoulders. She smashes her lips to mine, her tongue probing against my lips in a desperate attempt to gain entry. I oblige and open my mouth, tangling my tongue with hers. She sucks on my tongue and bites down hard before sucking again. The metallic taste of copper fills my mouth from the sting of her bite. She moans and shudders against me and I feel my cock beginning to harden again.

This crazy little bitch makes me constantly desperate for more. Her little surprises and hot and cold attitude fucks me up, but makes my dick hard. If her pussy wasn't so goddamn good, I would've taken her back to her junkie parents the same fucking night I brought her here because of the shit she pulled. But even then, when she was virtually a fucking stranger, something about her drew me in.

She begins rocking her hips against me as she runs her fingers through my hair. Our naked flesh rubs together in delicious ways. I reach my hand between us and grasp my cock in my hand. I rub it between her pussy lips before shoving myself inside of her. She screams and throws her head back as I shove her back against the shower wall. I wrap my hand around her throat and latch my teeth to the skin of her neck. Biting down as hard as I can, I rut into her ruthlessly.

Her screams echo throughout the shower, but I don't slow down. Her nails claw into the skin of my back, leaving a bloody, mutilated mess behind, but I don't slow down. Her pussy clamps around my cock and I feel the need to come tingling down my spine, but I don't slow down. This is a fast, hard fuck. One we both need. Moving my hand from her throat, I reach between us and rub her clit vigorously until she screams out in ecstasy. I follow right behind her and grunt as I sink my teeth into her skin. Her blood trickles out and I lap it up as I slow my breathing.

I pull out of her and set her feet on the floor of the shower below us. She drops her arms from around me and bends her head to the ground to stare at the floor.

"Look at my baby doll acting all submissive already. I'm diggin' it, baby." I compliment her. She quirks her lip but remains unmoving. I step away from her to wash myself off before stepping out of the shower. I dry off and move to the bedroom to grab my clothes. Once I have them on, I head downstairs, leaving her to shower alone and gather her thoughts.

CHAPTER SEVENTEEN
ESSA

Two months. It's been two fucking months since Vincent forced me to move in with him and honestly? I've had it worse. Ever since I decided to give up and submit to him, things haven't been too bad. I mean, he's still a complete fucking asshole who continues to treat me like shit, but he also makes it good for me, so at least I have something to look forward to. We seem to have a routine down. Basically, he tells me to do something and if I do it without an attitude, I get rewarded in orgasms.

Though every time he leaves the house, he still locks me in my bedroom until he returns. Not that I blame him I guess, but it still fucking sucks. So here I lie, blaring "Chop Suey!" by System of A Down through my earbuds, waiting for him to return home so I can be let out and make him his dinner.

Yep, that's another thing I do for him now is fucking cook his meals. But I don't mind it too much because I also get to eat whatever I make. Vincent is one of those rich people who always has tons of food

CREEP

in his fridge so the possibilities are endless.

Right as I turn my music off, I hear the familiar crunch of gravel as his car pulls through the driveway before slowing to a stop. Speak of the devil and he shall appear. I stay where I am. I know he'll let me out as soon as he walks in the door and sure enough he does. The front door slams and he comes thundering up the stairs. The keys jingle as he shoves them in the lock then my door creaks open. He stands in the doorway, leaning against the door frame.

"How was your day, baby doll?" I wrap the cord of my earbuds around my iPod as I answer him.

"It was as good as it could've been, I guess."

"You guess?"

"Yeah." I deadpan as I shift across my bed, bringing my ass to the edge to sit with my legs dangling over.

"Care to elaborate?" he deadpans right back.

"No, it's okay." I chirp. "I don't want to get in trouble." Vincent strides over to where I'm sitting on the edge of the bed and kneels in front of me, between my legs. Seeing him nestled between my legs has uncomfortable feelings swirling in the pit of my stomach. I instinctively push my thighs together in an attempt to dull the ache which has now settled between them, but of course with Vincent's body taking up residence between my legs, he feels them squeeze together, making him smirk—a knowing look in his eyes.

"Baby doll. Fucking spit it out. You've never been one to bite your tongue." He laughs out, but speaks the truth. I sigh and slightly shake my head, not wanting his punishments. It's been two fucking months since I've taken any sort of blade to my skin. But that doesn't mean I haven't *been* cut.

Vincent kept true to his word and whenever I felt the overwhelming urge, I told him and he would do it for me without question. Sometimes he would be happy to, and others he seemed upset by it, but either way he obliged.

Scars now cover a massive expanse of my body. Many of them from the night he cut me open, mutilating my skin because he lost himself. He lost control and now my body proves it. Not that I care, because I truly don't. What's another scar? I was already covered in them from not only myself, but from Ben's abuse as well. Except now when I look at these scars, they don't bring instant self-loathing and self-hatred to the forefront of my mind. As fucked up as it sounds, they kind of turn me on. And I know they sure as fuck turn Vincent on.

"Okay, fine. I'm just tired of being locked up every time you leave. I've been here with you for over two months now and I haven't disobeyed you in almost as long. I guess I don't understand why you're still locking me in my room." I hurl the words from my mouth before I lose the courage to say them.

Vincent runs his index finger back and forth across his top lip while he remains crouched in front of me, thinking. After a few long, agonizing minutes, he stands to his full height, dragging me up with him. He wraps his hand around my throat and squeezes. Not enough to the point where I can't breathe, but restricting enough so if he holds me long enough, my head starts to swim deliciously, creating the best fucking high. One I've become utterly addicted to.

"All right, baby. Next time I leave, I'll leave you out. *Only* because you've been such a good girl. But remember, I've got cameras in every room of the house, including your own. So, if you do anything stupid, I'll see it right away and speed my ass home to beat yours. Got it?" He clasps my neck tighter for emphasis as the last words leave his mouth.

"Yes, sir." I nod my head slightly. He rolls his eyes at my sarcasm but doesn't say anything else. He pushes his lips against mine before pulling away.

"Come on. Let's head downstairs, I'm fuckin' starving and I need my girl to feed me." He smacks my ass before heading out of the room and down the stairs, to the kitchen. I move to follow after him, but halt in my tracks the moment his words register in my head.

My girl.

What the hell is that supposed to mean?

CHAPTER EIGHTEEN
ESSA

True to his word, when Vincent left for work the next day, he didn't make the usual trip upstairs to lock me in. No, he actually called me downstairs to kiss him goodbye and then out the door he went. After I watched him begin the drive down the long and winding driveway, I went and poured myself a cup of coffee.

Now I'm sitting at the kitchen island sipping the steaming beverage while I contemplate what to do with my day. Before, when I would be locked up, my only option really was to listen to music and talk to Holley occasionally, but now the possibilities are endless.

Of course my first thought is to escape, but I know it won't be that easy. For one, there's a security alarm on the door he only ever sets when he leaves the house for work. For one I do not know the passcode to, so if I were to open the door right now, the blaring alarms would sound and he would be notified immediately along with the local authorities. And the authorities are exactly who we *don't* need to be here, so that's out.

CREEP

As much as my life is better because of him, it's also so much worse. Yeah, I don't have Ben and Sierra near me and I also don't have Ben putting his hands on me, but it doesn't mean Vincent doesn't do the same. Most of the time, sex between us is consensual and I enjoy it greatly, but on occasion he still takes it from me. And it makes it all the more confusing because even when he does do that, it doesn't hurt like it did when Ben would do it. My body is always ready for Vincent's abuse and I don't know why. That's what makes it so much worse.

At least with Ben I knew I loathed him. I fucking despised him and those feelings were easy for me to work with. But with Vincent, not so much. Even when I hate him and the things he does to me, my body has a completely different reaction and confuses the hell out of me. I truly don't know what I feel toward him, but it sure as hell isn't pure hatred anymore.

It's... more.

Another thing I could do is call Holley and tell her everything. He's not here and he wouldn't hear a word I say, but I question it. I don't want her to up and leave her life behind for me. It's not fair, especially because she got out and away from our parents. And if I'm being honest, so did I.

I haven't seen Ben or Sierra since the day I left. They haven't tried to call Vincent as far as I know and I know Holley hasn't talked to them. So, the fact Ben scared me into doing this to protect Holley irks me. I should've trusted my gut and *believed* he was full of shit then I could've avoided this whole fucking situation. But it's too late now.

I'll give Holl a call later. My irritation is too high and I know if I talk to her right now, she'll pick up on it and I really don't want to have to lie to her—*again*.

Not knowing what else to do with my newfound freedom, I decide to explore the house. I haven't gotten the opportunity to since I've had Vincent up my ass twenty-four seven. Starting downstairs, I make my way through the open area. There's not much to see down here I haven't already because it's one big room, but I still look anyway. I open all the drawers and snoop inside. I don't know exactly what I'm searching for, if anything at all. I suppose I'm merely curious and I'm looking for more information about him.

I've been living with him for months now. He's been inside of me and I still barely know a damn thing about him, other than the fact he's a drug dealer and he likes to hurt me. In the grand scheme of things, that's not really a lot to know about someone you're fucking—if you can even call it that. I don't even know at this point. I'm barely going through the motions and living day by day.

Finding nothing in the kitchen or living area, I move on to the game room. I haven't been here since the day I danced for him and the second I open the door, the memory floods my brain. My panic attack, my dancing, his expression, and then the look which passed over his face as I smacked him before it turned murderous. I shiver as I shake off those thoughts, not wanting to relive them. There's pain, and then there's what he did to me that night.

Skipping the middle of the room where the pool table and stripper pole is, I walk around the perimeter. A massive television takes up most of one wall while the others are blank. No pictures, nothing resembling it's a place where someone hangs out doing, I don't know, fun things?

Massive floor to ceiling bookshelves run along the walls that

CREEP

aren't made of glass. I run my fingers along the spines as I walk past, skimming the titles of a few. He has thousands of books. So many, I could never possibly dream of reading them all. I'm not a big reader, music was always my go to escape, but I can appreciate them.

My eyes zero in on a book, the spine catching my eye. I bring my index finger to the top of the spine and tilt it down and out before grabbing onto the book, diligent not to crease the corners. The book is a goldish yellow color and it says *The Odyssey* by Homer. I've heard of it before, but have never read it. I flip through the pages and it confuses me enough to the point where I get a headache and put it back on the shelf.

My frustration begins to grow the longer I go without finding a single thing. It's not like I expected to find much, but this is fucking ridiculous. I stomp my way up the stairs, every thundering step echoes through the house. Once I make it to the top, the deafening sound of silence greets me. The silence is so high pitched, my ears ring. I turn around and glance down. My gaze peeks through the gaps of the stairs, giving me the ability to see straight through. My eyes land on the remote for the surround sound speakers I've seen Vincent use a hundred times. I fly down them to grab it and hit play. "The High Road" by Three Days Grace blares through the speakers, but I hit the volume up button until it won't let me turn it up any louder.

Satisfied, I toss the remote on the stand and go back upstairs. I turn down the other hallway, the one opposite of mine and Vincent's bedrooms. The first door I walk to is the one at the end of the hall. When I jiggle the handle to turn the knob, it doesn't budge. *Ding ding ding! We have a winner!*

MARIE ANN

I stand there for a few messing with the handle, but it doesn't budge. I run down the stairs and sprint into the kitchen. I grab a butter knife and run back upstairs. The butter knife is flimsy enough I can wiggle it between the latch of the door and the door frame itself. After trying to wedge it just right for the last twenty-ish minutes, I finally get it and the door clicks open, swinging backwards.

I heave out a sigh of relief before stuffing the butter knife in my back pocket. I stand to my feet and cautiously walk into the room. I know Vincent said he has cameras throughout the house, but I'm not so sure. I've never seen any before so I'm choosing to remain optimistic about it and if I get caught? Well, I guess I know about how bad it can get.

I feel around on the right side of the wall just inside the room, and my hand catches on the light switch and I flick it up. The light floods the room, bringing everything to light.

Bingo.

It's his fucking office. There's a massive wooden desk located in the back center of the room with the glass wall behind him, but it's covered by massive black out curtains which work really fucking well because I can't even tell it's mid-morning outside right now. More floor to ceiling bookshelves line the wall made of what seems to be the same wood his desk is made out of. A black leather chair rests behind his desk and a few typical desk things are laying on top, but other than that, even this room remains bare. I'm not even surprised at this point.

Moving to the desk, I take a seat in the chair. My body sinks into the leather and I groan at how comfortable it is. I could fucking sleep in this thing. Forcing myself to get up, I began yanking on drawers.

CREEP

None of them are locked, and I began sifting through papers, careful to put everything back exactly as I found it. I have a feeling Vincent is one of those people who would notice something like that and I don't need him questioning anything.

Once I reach the bottom drawer, I pull it open and find only a single manilla envelope. Carefully pulling the top tab open, I grip the papers and pull them out slowly. I run my eyes over the top, but the only thing the top paper says is the name Vincent Lee Anthony in big bold letters. With my curiosity piqued, I meticulously place the paper on the desk before looking back at the stack in my hand. The next has a bunch of numbers scribbled here and there. Which is what I assume to be bank numbers and money transfers, but I wouldn't have a clue. I've never seen a bank statement in my entire life.

But I do know what a balance of something looks like and from the looks of this, it seems to be many money transfers into an offshore account with the account holder name being Vincent Lee Anthony. Transfers of money from at least two hundred thousand dollars and up. My eyes bulge out of my fucking head the further down the paper I get. And it continues. I flip through six pieces of paper before I reach the last one. The last page has an ending account balance on it and when my eyes land on the number, the paper falls to the floor.

I scramble to pick it up, somehow managing to keep my wits about enough to gather them all and rush to the printer. Paranoid out of my mind, I keep skirting my eyes all over the place, terrified I'm going to be caught. I'm wary not to mess with the papers too much as I make a copy of each one. After they all print, I slide the original papers back into the envelope and put it back in the drawer.

MARIE ANN

I rush from the room and shut the door behind me. I turn the knob and push against it to be sure it's locked and then make a mad dash to my room. I pull my bed out from the wall enough to squeeze myself in. I roll the papers into the tiniest roll I can manage and shove them into the gap behind the headboard. I never would've noticed it if I weren't tied to my fucking bed for an entire day.

I quickly push my bed back and then flop on top of it. My heart is still racing and I place my hand over my chest to feel it. A grin cracks across my face as I begin to feel elated.

I fucking did it.

I found something I can use against this motherfucker.

I can finally be free.

I crawl into bed as the music blaring through the house continues. The song playing now is "Fragile Minds" by Silent Theory and that's the last thing I think about before I shut my eyes, the taste of freedom resting on the tip of my tongue.

CHAPTER NINETEEN
VINCENT

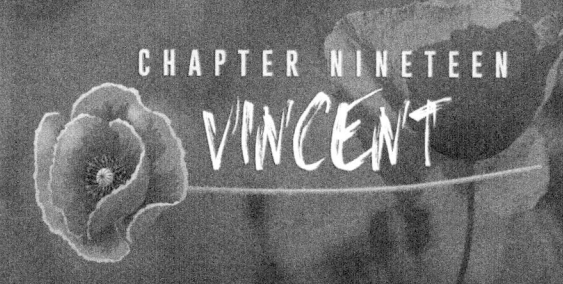

Unease has eaten at me all day long. I left Essa to roam free today when I left the house, something I never planned on doing, but I know she won't be able to step foot outside of the house or even open the fucking door. I have a security system in place I've been using. I never had much use for it before, but now I'm glad I have it.

Last night when she brought up she was tired of being locked up and reminded me she's been good, I thought about it. She has been good ever since I threatened to kill her.

I told her yesterday I have cameras in every room of the house, but that was a straight up fucking lie. I don't have a single camera, only because, like the security system, I never needed them. I live in the middle of nowhere and no one even knows where I live—aside from Leo. I hope she believes me and keeps her ass in line.

I've been sitting at the fucking pub all goddamn day, wasting time waiting for Leo to get back from a run. He went with the usual crew to make sure things run smoothly with this new supplier. I offered to go with because I need something to fucking do, but of course he brushed me off and told me to hang out at the pub and relax. As if I need any more fucking downtime.

So here I am, on my fifth fucking bourbon and it's only two p.m. I'm attempting to drown my sorrows, but much to my fucking luck, it's not working. My mind keeps racing, Essa consuming every thought I have and it's driving me insane. I've only known her for two fucking months. *Two months.* And yet somehow in that miniscule timeframe, she's managed to crawl under my skin. I knew from the very beginning she was different, but this is something else entirely.

Whenever I'm away from her, at work, getting groceries, hell even outside doing fucking yardwork, *I miss her.* I fucking miss her and it's eating me alive. I've never felt like this towards anyone in my entire life. Not even my own mother. But Essa? Fuck, I'm a goner. My blood aches for hers. My nonexistent soul rises from the deepest depths inside of me, crawling back into the light. My fucking monster now goes into hiding, only coming out to play when I allow him to.

Everything has done a complete one eighty and I'm still dizzy.

I've been struggling with how to handle my situation with her because it's not exactly ideal. I love it, but I also know I can't keep her ass locked in my house forever. Furthermore, I don't want her to leave. I need to come up with some sort of plan as soon as possible.

Slamming back the rest of my drink, I lean my back against the counter of the pub. I rest my arms behind me and glance around the very same pub that saved my fucking life. Well, not the place itself but the man who owns it. I've come to find this place a comfort to me. It was a safe place when nothing in my life was remotely that way and still to this day I am forever grateful to Leo. I owe him my fucking life, therefore I do everything in my power to make his easier in every way. Hence why I take jobs he no longer wants to do. Not that I mind. He knows I enjoy it.

For a Thursday afternoon, it's pretty busy. Almost every booth is full and there are a few people scattered amongst the stools along the bar. About three years ago, Leo decided to build on to his rundown pub and set up a kitchen while also remodeling the place a bit. It took about a year, but it's been up and running for two years now and busier than ever. Now that it doesn't look like a shit hole, many people stop by and even bring their families. The food may be greasy pub food, but it's fucking good, nonetheless.

I turn around and signal to Andy, the bartender, to get me another drink and also a burger with fries. I haven't eaten anything since the dinner Essa made the night before. She made this chicken pasta shit with broccoli or whatever the fuck. I have no idea what she called it, but it was delicious. My stomach rumbles when I think about it and Andy sets my refilled glass back in front of me.

I'm not exactly drunk, but I'm not sober either. My head feels light and my body sways slightly on the stool. I should probably slow down before I wind up too drunk to drive. I toss back the shot and push the glass away, shaking my head at Andy as he goes to refill it.

"No man, I'm good."

"You sure? You don't look too good."

I rub the back of my neck as I contemplate my answer. I'm not exactly close with the kid, but he wouldn't be here if Leo didn't trust him. Deciding to go with my gut, I get a few things off my chest.

"I'm not. I've got this bitch back home I picked up a few months ago and fuck man. She's under my skin and it's eating me alive." I keep my gaze locked on the slightly sticky counter below and rub my neck again. I have a fucking headache from all of this goddamn thinking—the alcohol doing the exact opposite of helping.

Andy whistles before grabbing the rag and wiping down the counters—not that it helps, they're always sticky.

"Damn man. What the fuck? You're the fucking Monster dude—that's what they all call you anyway. Ruthless, merciless, fucking cold. And you're telling me some girl has gotten under your skin? I need to write this down, let me grab my pen."

I growl as I turn my head, irritated, but he's fucking right. I don't even know who I am anymore. I'm still ruthless and merciless at work and with Essa. But cold? Fuck, not anymore. She ignites this fire inside of me that blazes so fucking hot we both get burned.

The clatter of a plate being set down in front of me snaps me out of my reverie. Andy walks away, leaving me to eat in peace. Shaking my head, I grab my burger and scarf it down.

I disarm the beeping security system the moment I step through the door. The smell of grilled meat wafts through the air and my mouth waters. Essa can fucking *cook* that's for sure. Which also surprised the hell out of me. We haven't talked much about her life growing up, but I do know she didn't eat much, and when she did, it was always cheap food. So the fact she can cook as well as she does was a pleasant surprise. One I utilize often.

Slamming the door behind me, I drop my keys to the table by the door and make my way to the kitchen. "Life is Beautiful" by Sixx:A.M. blares through the surround sound and a smirk pops up on my face. She really does have great taste in music for only being eighteen. Most teenagers only like shitty mainstream shit, which I'll admit, some of it is good, but nothing beats rock.

I trip over my feet when my eyes land on Essa. Her back is to me as she stirs something in a pot on the stove, but it's not what she's doing that has my attention, it's what she's *wearing*. She's in one of *my* white T-shirts and that's *it*. No underwear, no bra, nothing and the light from the sun shining through the windows makes it very easy to see. Saliva pools in my mouth and my dick turns to stone in my jeans. She looks fucking edible.

Her hips sway back and forth to the beat of the music and her hair swishes along her lower back. She turns around to grab a box off of the kitchen island behind her when she sees me. She gasps and her hand flies to her chest.

"Jesus fucking Christ you scared the shit out of me, Vin." She chuckles as she turns back around, but it doesn't meet her eyes.

"Vin? That's new."

"Uh, yeah, I guess it is. I don't know. It kind of came out. I'm sorry." She keeps her back turned but her head falls down so she's staring at the counter. I move until my front is flush against her back. I push her hair to one side and wrap my arms around her waist, pulling her tighter against me. I run my lips across the back of her neck and goosebumps follow the trail of my lips. She shivers slightly in my arms as her breathing begins to accelerate. I lift my hands up under the hem of my T-shirt, running my fingers back and forth across the uneven expanse of her skin.

"Fuck, baby doll. I missed you." I latch onto the side of her neck and suck. I know it will leave a mark, but that's the point. I love marking her skin. I sink my teeth into her flesh and she cries out. Blood flows into my mouth and I suck until no more comes out. Satisfied with the metallic taste of her blood resting on my tongue, my craving satisfied for now, I pull away slightly and tilt her chin up until her eyes meet mine.

"Baby, you can call me whatever the fuck you want. Vin is fine by me. Don't start getting all whiny on me." I pull away and smack her ass as I move to take a seat on a stool. With a smirk playing on her lips she turns back around to continue cooking.

"Hurry up and feed your man, baby doll. I'm fuckin' starving."

"For food or for me?" she quips back.

"Well, when you put it like that…" I launch from the stool and round the island. I flick the burner off, then fling her over my shoulder and onto the island. She squeals out when her bare ass hits the marble but I drown the noise with a kiss. I push her onto the counter until she lies back fully. I grab the hem of the shirt and pull it up to her neck, revealing her body to me.

Sex between us has become somewhat carefree. I don't always have to bring her pain and I don't always have to force her. This is uncharted territory for me, but I'm enjoying it, and trying not to think too much into what it could mean.

Essa's body writhes beneath me, and I wrap my hand around her throat like I always do and squeeze with enough pressure to get her attention.

"Lie still, baby doll. It's time for Daddy to eat his dinner." I know if I would've said something like that when I first met her, it would've sent her in a tailspin, but now she squirms harder. She's blossoming into the perfect little toy.

I nip, suck, and fuck every inch of her pussy with my tongue until her thighs crush my head and she screams out my name.

Dinner was fucking served.

CHAPTER TWENTY
VINCENT

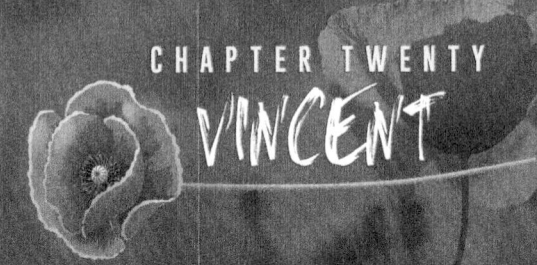

After I made Essa come all over my face, she finished dinner up and now we're sitting and eating at the table like a fucking couple or something. The dialogue between us has been short, back and forth bullshit like her asking how my day was and whatnot. I can't focus on a single thing she is saying because she won't stop fidgeting with her fingers and my fucking eye twitches in irritation. So many things—and not good ones—are popping into my head as to why she could be so nervous around me again.

She did something stupid, like try to run away.

She called the cops.

She went through my things.

She found ammo and loaded the fucking gun.

Every thought is pulling me under more, fucking drowning me. I can't focus so I ask her straight up what her problem is. I can't take it anymore.

Her eyes dart to mine and she physically pales.

CREEP

Side note, never take her to fucking gamble. Her poker face is shit.

I quirk my brow in question, but keep my mask in place as I wait for her to answer me. I'm tired of the bullshit and she knows she better not lie to me. It's been too fucking long since I've gotten to mutilate her pretty fucking skin.

"I—it's nothing," she stammers before pushing her chair away from the table and grabbing her plate. She walks to the sink and places her plate in the basin. She rests her hands on the edge of the counter and bows her head. I sit and watch her come undone, transfixed by her every move. Her shoulders move up and down slightly with her even breathing. The fact her chest isn't heaving is a good sign to me. She's a shit liar.

"What is this?" she whispers, but doesn't move an inch. I turn my body to get out of my chair but stop. *What the fuck is this?*

It's a good question. One I definitely don't know the answer to anymore. Shit is awfully more complicated than I ever could have imagined it to be.

"I mean. We're fucking on a daily basis. You go to work every day and I stay home. I cook, I clean, I suck your fucking cock. What the fuck is this?" She whirls around and tears are streaming from her eyes. She doesn't bother to wipe them away. She stands tall and crosses her arms over her chest, waiting for my answer.

Her confidence, her fucking strength, is so goddamn beautiful it stuns me. I've always been able to appreciate a woman's beauty—it's hard not to—but with Essa, it's different.

I don't just see her physical beauty. I feel like I can see into her fucking soul—much like how I know she can see into mine. I know she can sense the monster inside of me. The monster that itches and crawls its way through my mind, begging to be released until my strength dwindles and I let him. She knows what my monster is capable of. She's seen it firsthand. The night she saw me outside of her window covered in blood, I know she knew what I was doing, but now she's seen it for herself.

I glance down at her legs. Her scars are healed but still pink from being so new. She has over one hundred cuts littering her body because of me. I cut her so many fucking times, my hand ached. My monster came out to fucking play and he didn't disappoint. But they don't seem to bother Essa like I thought they would, like I *hoped* they would. No, every time she sees them, she smiles. And that's the creep she has living inside of her.

A creep and a monster—two sides of the very same coin.

Staring at her scars doesn't help my already hard cock. They turn me the fuck on and I'm damn sure she knows it too. There is something about her bearing a permanent mark from me that brings out the most possessive side of me and I go mad with desire.

I stalk up to her, prowling like a predator does to its prey. She steels her spine, and narrows her eyes.. Wrapping my hand around her throat, I push my thumb into the underside of her chin and tilt it up until she can look me directly in the eyes.

"I don't know what the fuck we're doing, baby doll. I haven't the slightest fucking clue. You and me? We're two insanely fucked up individuals who have found solace in one another, as fucked up as it is. You're one crazy fucking bitch who loves to hurt herself to feel better, to make all of the demons retreat back into the shadows. And I'm a savage bastard who craves the fucking pain I can give you."

I watch as Essa's eyes widen and she takes a shaky breath before glancing down at her fingers. "It wasn't supposed to be like this. This wasn't supposed to work, but here we are. You need what you need the same as I and somehow, some fucking way, we found that in each other. Now, I'm not saying I love you or any dumb shit like that. I don't even like you. But for some twisted reason, I crave you.

I crave your pain.

I crave your blood.

I crave your screams.

I crave your skin against mine.

We're fucked up, but it's just who we are. I don't have an exact answer because I can't give you one. It is what it is."

My hand against her throat allows me to feel her pulse racing underneath her neck. A neck which would be so easy for me to snap like a fucking twig.

Her throat bobs as she plasters a fake ass smile across her face.

"Okay."

"Okay...?" I question and drop my hold on her. It's not exactly the response I was expecting, but she nods her head anyway. She turns away from me and walks up the stairs. And I let her.

Why do I feel like I just gave this girl a piece of me and she fucking threw it right back?

CHAPTER TWENTY-ONE
ESSA

"The Offering" by Sleep Token blares in my ears as I try to calm my racing heart. My palms are still sweaty so I wipe them across my bedspread, again.

Fuck. Vincent spilled out so much shit down there and I completely panicked. I didn't know what else to do so I put on my best poker face and practically ran up the fucking stairs so I could be alone. I put on my music right away to help calm down and to hopefully give me some comfort since I can't fucking cut.

I itch at my arm where "CREEP" is still healing on my skin. The need to cut seeps into my veins like I knew it would and I dig my nails in deeper. The tiniest beads of blood pop up where my nails tore my skin. It's nowhere near good enough, but the slight burn will have to do for now.

I close my eyes as I let the music carry me away—if only for a little while.

CREEP

It's now Friday morning and I'm still lying in bed even though it's after ten a.m. I hear Vincent downstairs doing whatever the fuck he's doing. Ever since I rushed up here last night, he's left me alone, surprisingly.

After he told me I wasn't allowed to do it anymore, I was expecting him to stomp up here, chasing after me, but I'm more than relieved he didn't. I need to fucking think but my mind won't process a damn thing. It's running round and round in circles, swirling like a fucking hurricane.

"Heavier" by Slaves plays on my iPod as I twirl the cord to my earbuds around my fingers. Vincent's words from last night ring loud and clear in my head. Even my fucking music can't block them out.

"But for some twisted reason, I crave you."

I don't know why, but it's the main thing that's sticking with me. Guilt has long seeped into my pores and has now sunk deep into my bones. It eats away at me the more I lie here, but I fight it. I don't need to feel guilty. He took me as a fucking trade for money. *Me. A human fucking being.*

He hurt me.

He still hurts me.

He's not a good man.

I need to be free.

I repeat those four things over and over in my head, hoping like hell they fucking stick because this guilt is making me nauseous. The only time I have ever felt like this was when I tried to kill myself. I have never been so selfish in my life, but this is a lot like it, or at least it feels similar.

I'm putting Holley's life on the line and risking everything with these papers I have stuffed in my headboard because if Vincent were to ever find them, or somehow find out I have possession of them, he would kill me and then nothing would stop my father from going after Holley.

I don't exactly know why I copied the papers. They seemed important and at the time, gave me a sense of freedom I needed. A back up plan—or maybe a plan in general because I don't fucking have one to begin with.

All I know is I need to get out of here. I've been getting far too comfortable in a situation which is anything but. I'm starting to feel things for this man I *definitely* shouldn't be. It's not right and it is fucked up on so many levels. And that's where he was right. We are two insanely fucked up individuals who have found solace in one another.

As much as I hate him, he's not wrong. I crave the pain he gives me as much as he loves to dish it out and it's why this is so complicated. I don't really have it that bad here, now anyway, but solace is something I don't want to keep, something I don't want possession of.

At the beginning it was rough, really fucking rough, but now it's okay. I haven't seen Ben and Sierra in months and I get to talk to Holley every day. I can eat whenever I want and I pretty much get to do whatever I feel like doing.

It certainly doesn't help my decision making Vincent is really fucking good in bed. I never thought sex was something I would ever want, let alone crave, but he has awoken something inside of me I don't want to part from.

Passion.

Desire.

Pleasure.

Pleasure with pain.

Pain has always been my go to escape from reality. Whatever went wrong or whatever was too much to handle, the simple fix has always been a blade to my skin. A few angry swipes and I would be rocked out in blissful agony. It's my system. Always has been and probably always will be. But Vincent has shown me a different way to slay my demons.

With pain and sex.

My mind has become a muddled mess and I can't tell which way is up and which way is down anymore. All I know is I'm fucking struggling to stay afloat more than I ever have before.

Vincent fucked everything up with what he said earlier. I was perfectly content living in blissful ignorance, but then he had to go and run his fucking mouth ruining everything, and causing every single question that has been stuffed in the back of my head to come screaming to the forefront of my mind, blindsiding me.

As if on cue, "I ALWAYS WANTED TO LEAVE" by The Plot In You plays next and I feel the weight of every decision come crashing down upon me.

I know what I have to do, but *fuck.*

This is going to hurt.

I pick up my phone and hit the redial button.

CHAPTER TWENTY-TWO
VINCENT

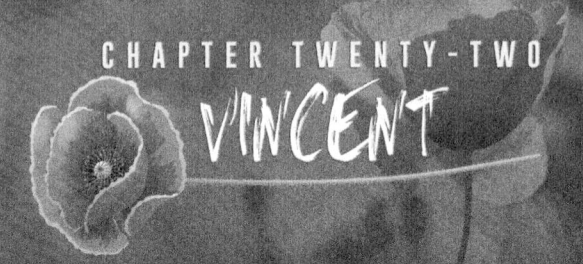

I'm so fucking idiotic.

Seriously.

What in the hell was going through my head that made me blurt out a bunch of almost sappy shit, like I actually give a shit about this girl. But everything I said was true as much as it physically pains me to say it—and I do mean physically. I sit at this kitchen stool clutching my chest and attempting to rub the ache away, but it's fucking useless.

This girl came into my life kicking and screaming—literally—and now she's gone and thrown everything for a fucking loop. She's damaged, broken, and straight up fucking ruined. Everything I am.

Our souls have emerged from the deepest depths of our hells to find one another. And found one another they have.

I have always been a soulless creature. A monster lingering in the darkest shadows, waiting for the right moment to strike.

I was content with everything in my life. I have a nice fucking house, someone I care about who I know will always have my back—

Leo, all the money I could ever want. I don't struggle anymore, and I never have to stress about mundane shit. I have everything I ever wanted from back when I was living on the streets. From rags to riches they say, though you'd never know it with me. I may have money but I'm not one of those money hungry goons who feels the need to flaunt it in everyone's face.

Now? Now I feel a piece of myself I have always thought was missing, has returned. But I don't fucking like it. In fact, I loathe it. I never asked to fucking feel. I never asked to fucking care.

I need something to take this shit away.

I'm feeling things I have never felt before. No, it's definitely not love, but it's something. And something is better than the nothing I have always felt.

...Right?

It's been three hours. Three fucking hours since Essa darted upstairs and I'm barely holding on by a thread. My conflicting feelings and thoughts have long since passed and now anger has taken their place, and the longer she remains up there, the worse it gets. I swirl the bourbon around in the glass as I attempt to restrain myself. Other than getting up to grab a bottle of my favorite bourbon, Woodford Reserve, and a glass, my ass has remained seated in the same fucking stool.

I told her little ass she wasn't allowed to pull shit like this again, but of course she didn't listen. I was beginning to think after these last couple of months, she had actually burned it into her brain she was to *fucking* listen, but she loves to surprise me. It's an Essa specialty.

Well, I'm fucking tired of the one being surprised. It's about high time the roles become reversed and she's the one getting the surprise of a lifetime.

I toss back the rest of my drink and slam the glass against the counter. The amount of force I use is enough for it to shatter. Glass shards fly everywhere and a few bigger pieces of glass remain intact at the base of the glass cut into my hand. I glance down when I notice blood dripping onto the counter and there are gashes that are a few inches across and deep, but my anger keeps me from feeling a fucking thing.

In fact, it only adds gasoline to my already raging fire. I clench and unclench my fist a few times. The gash spills more blood onto the counter, and a small puddle begins to form. The heat of the wound seeps into me and for a split second, I remember what it was like. Taking anything remotely sharp to my skin to take away the cold, the hunger pangs, the utter loneliness.

I grip the stool I was sitting on moments ago and hurl it across the room with a roar. It lands with a crash against the glass wall and for a moment, I think the glass will shatter. Much to my disappointment it remains intact.

I feel an insatiable need to break something.

And I know just what to break.

"Wake up, baby doll. Guess what time it is?" I chuckle as I watch Essa's beautiful green eyes flutter open as I toss her down onto my bed. At first, she takes a quick glance around the room before bringing her eyes back to mine, confusion ringing loud and clear. She doesn't say a word, apparently choosing to remain silent.

Either way, I don't fucking care.

She sits up slightly but struggles a bit with her hands bound together and resting against her stomach. I tied her hands together while she was asleep in her own room before I moved her. The red rope digs into her skin just enough she already has indentations from it, which I catch a flash of as she twists her wrists a few times, most likely testing the strength of the knot. As if she doesn't know I don't fucking around when it comes to my bondage.

She's my fucking slave and the little bitch needs a reminder.

I take a drag from the cigarette which rests between my teeth as I keep my eyes trained on Essa. She drives me fucking crazy.

She rests her back against the headboard to my bed and focuses right on me with a look of pure boredom across her face. *Well, it seems like I'm going to have to fix that.*

I take one last puff and smash the cigarette in the marble ashtray that's on the stand. An evil fucking thought crosses my mind on how to punish her and it's fucking brilliant, but it's something I've never done before—surprisingly. I've done a lot of fucking shit in my life, but this particular one never crossed my mind until now. As I said before, this bitch drives me fucking mad. I guess we're about to see just how fucking mad that is.

I walk over to my dresser and pull out another bundle of rope and bring it over to Essa. I feel giddy with excitement and there's even pep in my step as I make my way to her. Her eyes narrow the closer I get.

Without a word, I unwrap the rope and then step up onto the bed. With my feet planted on either side of her, I bring the rope up to the bars I have across the top of my canopy bed. A bed I had custom made in iron which was assembled right here in my bedroom because the materials made it too heavy to move even in larger pieces.

The rounded bars running across the top have come in handy quite a few times, but I've never used them for something like this. Now, I'm fucking thankful to myself for this brilliant idea.

Chuckling to myself—probably sounding like a maniac—I continue to tie a knot on one end of the rope, tugging hard against it a few times to make sure it won't budge. I need this to go perfectly or else I'll fucking kill her.

Not that killing her wouldn't be a good idea right about now.

Once I'm happy with the knot, I take a step back and drop to my knees in front of her. I reach my hand out and grip the back of her neck, hauling her to me. Her bound hands land against my abdomen with a thud as she falls against me, unable to hold herself up.

She uses her head to push off of me slightly as I also lean back. I hold the rope in both of my hands and begin to wrap it around her throat. Before I even make it around one time, Essa jerks her entire body to the side and crashes to the floor. Her movement causes me to fall a split second after her, but not before she's already attempting to get up. She's a little too late when my body comes crashing down on top of hers, pushing her even further into the ground.

"Where do you think you're goin', baby doll?" With my chest to her back, I can feel every intake of breath and every exhale, too. And right now, her chest is heaving. Either because she's terrified—as she should be—or because I'm lying on top of her. In either case, both are completely warranted.

I push myself up and run my fingers through my hair before reaching down and grabbing a fistful of Essa's hair. I launch her to her feet from my grip on her and she cries out, tears immediately springing from her eyes.

I yank her back against me again and wrap my arm around her slim waist, but it's definitely not as slim as it was when I first met her. I suppose having the ability to eat whenever you're hungry helps.

I dig my fingers into the skin of her right hip and she whimpers, rolling her head to the side as I run my nose along her collarbone.

"Essa, baby, haven't you fucking learned by now?" She doesn't answer me, but instead rubs her wrists together. I grab her hands and halt her endeavor to hurt herself. I know what she's aiming to achieve, but I won't allow her a reprieve.

Holding her bound hands in one of mine, I grab the rope that is still somehow around her neck and wrap it around one more time. I spin her around and throw her over my shoulder as I crawl back onto the bed. I stand exactly how I was minutes ago and pull her from my shoulder, making sure to slide her body across mine. Every curve of her runs across mine on her way down my body and I groan as my cock twitches, desperate to be inside of her.

I've become too fucking used to everything with her. Mainly, the everyday mundane shit like eating together, talking about the fucking weather occasionally, little tidbits about ourselves and the fucking sex.

MARIE ANN

Fuck me, the fucking sex.

Every goddamn day I get to have her tight little pussy wrapped around my cock and now he's like a fiend searching for his next fix. It's a problem I'm finding considerably hard to ignore because when I came up here, my only plan was to hurt her, to remind her of her fucking place, but now all I want is to fuck her senseless and call it a night.

I didn't realize my eyes had closed until I feel the rope slipping through my fingers ever so slightly. My eyes snap open and I catch Essa attempting to unwrap the rope from her throat.

Goddamn her for fucking with my head, again.

Before I even register a damn thing, my palm is connecting with the side of her cheek. She stumbles and I yank on the rope to right her. She cries out as she brings her bound hands to her face. Tears run down her face in fast trails, but all they serve to do is turn me on even more.

I run my tongue along her cheek, catching every tear that falls and collecting them on my tongue. The salty flavor of them has me groaning and grabbing my cock through my pants to ease the ache. Groaning in frustration, I pull away from her and wrap my arm around her waist. I lift her up slightly, until her feet no longer touch the mattress and bring the rope to the bars above us. I pull it taut and tie another knot, but this one is a slip knot in case I need to release it quickly. I don't wanna fucking kill her.

Or do I?

With the second knot tied, I slowly drop Essa and now she hangs from my bed frame with rope tied around her neck. Her toes dig into the mattress just enough that if she continues to hold herself up, she won't have any issues breathing. It's when she gets fucking tired that the fun will really begin.

I jump off of the bed and walk over to where my pack of cigarettes lays and pull one out. I bring it to my lips and roll it around between my teeth as I twist the lighter around my fingers.

So many options, such little time.

I flick the lighter and watch the glow of the flame flicker. I bring it to the tip of the cigarette, then remove it when the tip glows red. I inhale the tobacco while tilting my head back to stare at the ceiling, letting the nicotine flow through my lungs. I can hear Essa's whispered whimpers as she struggles to stay upright already. I chuckle darkly as I lower my head to bring my gaze back to her.

"What the fuck you whining for, baby doll? This is all on you. You knew better and yet you continued to disobey me. You know what shit is not allowed—which is why I'm surprised you even pulled this stunt to begin with.

But alas, here we are, back to the fucking beginning. If you thought that was bad, you're gonna *really* hate what's about to happen." Essa screams and tries to pull the rope from around her neck, but her bound hands make it virtually impossible.

I finish my smoke and put it out before making my way back to her. I hop up onto the bed and stand in front of her. Though she's clearly vulnerable in the position she's in, she still makes an effort to jut her chin out to feign confidence. I roll my eyes and grip her chin between my fingers before smashing my lips to hers, unable to resist her any longer.

My fucking craving for her is beginning to overtake all of my senses. When I see her, I feel mad with possession.

She's mine.

When I touch her, my skin burns, yet cools at the same time. It's almost like her cold soul cools my inferno.

She's mine.

When I fucking kiss her. Fuck. Ever since that first goddamn kiss. My first kiss. She irrevocably changed me.

She's fucking mine.

And now I'm gonna show her just how fucking mine she is.

I pull the knife I always keep on me out of my pocket and flick it open. The sound echoes through the room and makes me realize how quiet it is. Essa's cries have stopped and now all I hear is the sound of our breathing, hers more labored.

The moment her eyes land on the knife in my hand, they light up with what could either be excitement or fear, but knowing my baby doll, it's probably both. Shaking my head, I bring the tip of the blade to the tip of her nose and push it in slightly while also bringing my own face closer to hers until both of our noses touch the knife.

"You ready for this, baby?" I ponder. I know she's not, but she doesn't have a choice anyway. It makes me think of the saying don't play with your food, because whoever said that was a fucking moron. Playing with your food before you eat it makes it all the more delicious.

Her lip quivers and she wobbles from side to side a bit as she struggles to remain upright. The pressure of the rope around her neck is increasing the more she struggles. I step back and lean down, putting the blade against the tip of her big toe on her left foot. Wasting no time, I push in and drag up from her toe, across her foot and up onto her shin. I continue to travel up while digging the blade in deeper the higher I get because the more blood I see flowing, the more excited I get. But seeing it also tempts me to taste it and I've never been one to deny myself of anything I want, so I lean my head down and run my tongue along the top of her foot and halfway up her shin. I would continue, but that's when Essa gets the bright idea to fight back and she boldly lifts her left leg to kick me in the face. Unlucky for her, I see it coming and smack her leg away from me. She loses her balance and falls to the side but the rope around her neck keeps her from falling completely.

She flails around as panic begins to consume her. She brings her bound hands to her neck, attempting to pull the rope away but she can't reach the slip knot—I made sure of that and I can't help but to stand here and watch it all unfold. I'm utterly fascinated by her entire state of hysteria. I know I should probably help her, but it's not long before she begins to lightly wheeze as she attempts to draw oxygen in, that I finally step up to her and lift her from the bed.

The second the pressure is released from around her throat, she coughs so fucking hard her entire body shakes with the force of it. After her fit is over, I place her back on the bed, ensuring her toes are touching the mattress and then I release her.

"Might wanna stay on those toes unless you wanna fucking strangle yourself," I point out as I bring the knife back to her knee where I left off earlier, not giving her any more time to recover. I push the blade back into her skin and watch as the sharpness splits her skin open, her blood flowing out easily and onto the bed beneath us.

MARIE ANN

I make my way up her body until I make it to her mid—thigh before stopping. The only clothing covering her is a lonely T-shirt that I slip my knife behind and easily cut away from her body. It falls to the bed in heaps of shredded cotton which I kick to the side. I don't need anything getting in my way.

Now she is completely naked in front of me, I pause. Her body is fucking delicious and I can feel myself wavering again, but I force my eyes to close and allow the rage to come back to the forefront of my mind. I can't feel things for her right now. I don't want to because hurting her is what I *need* in this moment.

I dig the tip of the knife into her pebbled nipple, beads of blood forming and clinging to the blade. Essa cries out and arches her back, in pain and in pleasure. Two sides of the same fucking coin, much like her and I. It was such a pleasant surprise to find out how much Essa loves pain, even more so when I found her cutting herself in my bathroom on her very first night here. It changed the entire course of our relationship—if you can even call it one.

Knowing she loved pain as much as I loved to hurt others, shifted something inside of me. Like a puzzle piece falling into its rightful place. The edges fit perfectly and once it's there, it's like it was never missing to begin with.

That's what meeting Essa was like for me. She's the missing piece to my puzzle I never knew I needed. She fits with me so much more than I ever would have thought. Not only because of her love for pain, but because of who she is as a person and how her childhood shaped her into who she is now.

But it still doesn't deter me from what I have to do. I may feel things for her and I may not want to *actually* kill her anymore, but it doesn't change the fact that this is something I need to do. It's something we both need—I'm merely taking it a little further than usual.

Essa's eyes drop down to the blade I have now moved to the other nipple and she whimpers as I dig the tip in. I swipe it across her nipple and create a little slash the size of a papercut. Not a lot of damage, but enough to sting and irritate you. I lean my head down and lap at her nipple, sucking it into my mouth before releasing it with a pop.

Her legs shake and she struggles even harder with keeping herself up. I smirk as I use my other hand to trail it down her abdomen to the apex of her thighs.

"Let's see how wet you are for me, baby doll." I work my hand between her clenched thighs and run my index finger through her folds. I can feel the moisture gathered there, but when I pull my hand away, it glistens with her arousal. A rumbling growl leaves my throat when I can visibly see how fucking turned on she is.

I knew she loved pain, but fuck. This wasn't the goddamn plan. She wasn't supposed to love it. This was only supposed to be about pain—about putting her in her place.

Seeing how fucking aroused she is throws me off kilter and I come to feel impatient. Desperate with the need to be inside her, to fill her and hear as she screams my fucking name.

Bringing my hand back to the apex of her thighs, my fingers run through her folds, gathering her wetness, until they land on her clit. I begin to circle my fingers over her sensitive nub until she's arching her back and attempting to move her legs wider so I can have better access, though it's hard when she has to remain on the tips of her toes to remain upright.

I bring the knife back up to her skin and lightly run it up and down the valley of her chest, the blade touching her just enough to give the sensation of a light, feathery touch. She shudders as goosebumps pop up along her skin. I abruptly shove my fingers inside of her and she shouts at the unexpected intrusion, though she was more than prepared. I can hear how wet she is as I begin to move my fingers in and out of her pussy, her walls clamping around my fingers with every withdrawal, desperate to keep me inside of her.

Low moans escape her mouth the faster I move my fingers. I scissor them, stretching her walls while also curling them upward to hit that magic spot inside of her which always has her going crazy with need. It's not long before she's panting and a sheen of sweat beads across her skin. I remove my fingers and bring them up to my lips. I suck them until they're clean, savoring the taste of her before shoving them back inside of her.

The moment I do, I also bring the knife to the left side of her neck and slash across, leaving a long horizontal line from the back of her neck all the way to the front near the center of her throat. It wasn't a deep cut, but enough to get more blood flowing between us

She groans at the pain, but her pussy clamps like a vise on my fingers at the same time and that's fucking *it*. I snap.

I shove the knife into my back pocket, undo the button on my jeans, and slide the zipper down. I push them down enough to free my cock and then grip Essa's waist and lift her into the air. She wraps her legs around me and I grip my cock as she hovers above me. She slowly sinks down on top of me, but I don't want any of that slow shit. Our fucking has always been hard, fast, and full of fucking desperation. I don't need to savor a single moment, so I fuck like the animal I truly am.

Long, hard, and fucking brutal.

I shove her down onto me until the tip of my cock hits her cervix. She screams out at the pain and I groan. "Fuucckk."

I wrap her hair around one fist as I hold onto her with my other hand in a bruising hold. I piston my hips as she begins to grind against my cock at the same time. Every rotation of her hips to every thrust of mine has my own fucking legs shaking with the need to come. I bite my lip as I fight back the urge, not yet ready for this to end.

Essa must see because she smashes her lips to mine and her own teeth sink into my bottom lip. My cock pulses as my blood floods both of our mouths and we both moan. I yank her head back with my grip on her hair and she releases my lip. Tilting her head back further, I bring my mouth to the side of her neck and lick the wound that's still oozing blood. Trails of it run down her neck, onto her shoulder, and down her arm and between her breasts.

She looks so fucking beautiful covered in blood.

I lap at every drop I can reach, but in this position, it's not enough. I sink my teeth into the wound and she screams out. Her orgasm hits her full force as her pussy pulses around me and her screams permeate through the room. Her orgasm triggers my own and I shout my release as I pump into her two more times before spilling inside of her. Her tight pussy milks my cock for every last drop as she ever so slowly grinds against me.

MARIE ANN

I release my teeth from her neck and tilt my head back to gaze at her.

So many thoughts.

So many feelings.

All so fucking confusing.

She quirks the corner of her mouth up in a pathetic attempt at a smile, but I can see the exhaustion dominating her expression. Without removing my eyes from hers, I reach my arm up and pull the slip not. The rope falls from above us and the rope around her neck loosens. I slip from inside of her, shuddering as the chill of the room hits my wet cock and tuck myself back inside of my jeans.

Essa flops to the bed beneath us and begins to slowly work the rope away from her. As she unwinds the last portion and tosses it across the room, I can see the black and blue bruising already forming against her beautifully pale skin. My dick jumps in my jeans at the sight.

I fucking love marking her.

I jump off of the bed and grab my pack of Marlboro's, pulling one out and lighting it. I sit in the chair next to my bed and take a puff as I watch Essa fall right to sleep. No hesitation, nothing. She must've been fucking exhausted because she doesn't sleep much as it is and when she does, it usually takes her forever to actually pass out.

I sit for a while, chain smoking the rest of my pack before getting up and carrying Essa to her own room. I have too many conflicting feelings I need to deal with right now and having her in the same room as me makes them exceptionally worse.

I lie her down on her bed and watch as her lids flutter for a moment before stilling again. She seems peaceful for once, and for some reason, it's a look I want to see on her face when she's actually conscious. Shaking my head, I exit her room and shut the door behind me with a soft click.

Once in my room again, I pick everything up before undressing and flopping down on my mattress face first. I can resume these torturous thoughts in the morning.

CHAPTER TWENTY-THREE
ESSA

I wake the next morning with an insatiable need to piss. I run to the bathroom and relieve the pressure in my bladder. When I go to wipe, I hiss at the pain. My entire vagina feels bruised and utterly fucking abused. I loved it just as much as I hated it—the same as always. He knows how to bring out the sick and twisted parts of myself better than anyone.

Once I finish on the toilet, I move to the sink to wash my hands and gasp as I catch my reflection in the mirror. My entire neck is black and blue, with the worst of it centered at where the rope was tied around me. I move my hand to touch it, but the second my fingertips make contact with the skin, tears leak from my eyes from the pain. It hurts so fucking bad and that's not even mentioning everything else that hurts.

The cut along my neck, the teeth marks, the cut up my foot and my leg, my abused nipples. I'm brutalized all over, physically and mentally. I don't know why I willingly let him do this to me. Except maybe I do. The pain along with the pleasure is so fucking intense individually, but together? It's fucking nirvana. I get lost in the ecstasy of it all and it consumes me.

But the next fucking day I regret it all when I can barely move more than an inch without wanting to scream out in pain. Pain keeps me centered and whole, but this kind of pain is the consuming kind. You can't think of anything else other than the agony running through your body and how you'd do anything and everything to be rid of it.

Well, almost anything.

I will never stoop to the same level as my parents. As much as I need an escape, I swore to myself a long time ago I would never go there. I have never tasted alcohol in my life, I have never done a single drug, none of it. And I don't want to either.

Forcing those thoughts from my head, I jump into the shower, hoping when I wash all of this blood and filth off of me, the water will also somehow manage to wash the pain away too.

It didn't work.

I'm rummaging through the fridge, searching for something to eat, but don't find anything I'm in the mood for. I spin and slam the fridge shut, coming face to face with a—dare I say—happy looking Vincent.

"I've got an idea of something for us to do today, baby doll. Get your shoes on and let's go."

"But I'm hungry," I argue.

"Shut up. You can eat later. Let's go." He grips my upper arm and drags me to the front door, not giving me a choice. Rolling my eyes, I slip my Converse on before we step outside. I make my way to the car, but Vincent heads in the opposite direction. My steps falter for a moment as I watch him walk towards the woods surrounding us.

Confusion clouds my mind as I watch him step into the tree line, stopping right next to the red-stained tree before turning around to face me with an evil glint to his eyes.

He fucking stopped right there on purpose.

"Come on, baby, this way." He gestures behind him all willy-nilly. I grunt in annoyance, but begin to follow him anyway. *What choice do I have?*

Once he sees me trailing him, he turns back around and begins making his way through the trees. He ducks and swerves around low hanging branches as we march further into their depth. It's abundantly clear he knows where to move and when, most likely having traveled this very path a time or two. I don't want to know why, so I keep my mouth shut and let him lead the way.

The sun shines bright through the gaps in the tree branches above us, highlighting the ground in random spots. It's late August and you can tell with the sun beating down on top of us, even with the trees blocking most of it. It's only around mid-morning and the breeze slightly blowing keeps me comfortable as we traipse through the dirt. Overall, it's a beautiful fucking day out.

We walk in silence for I don't even know how long before he breaks it by turning his head back to glance at me as he continues to walk forward, not missing a step or slowing down at all.

"I found this spot about a year after I bought this place. I stumbled upon it by accident, but ever since then, I come here at least once a week. It's my happy place." He murmurs the last statement, probably because he didn't want me to hear it, but I did anyway.

I'm about to ask him what he means, but before I do, we step out into a break in the trees—right into the middle of a field of poppies. My breath catches in my lungs as I stare out at the small, but plentiful field of red-orange flowers. It's fucking stunning and I'm in awe. I don't move forward because if I were to, I'd walk right into them and ruin them. So I remain still, the same as Vincent.

He stands right beside me as we both gaze forward, staring out into the field. It's almost a perfect circle, surrounded entirely by trees. A little piece of paradise in the middle of hell.

Fitting for a man like Vincent.

I glance over and up at him, for some reason wanting to see the look on his face. He says this is his happy place and I want to see if it's true. Vincent may be the master of the poker face, but lately, he's becoming more comfortable around me and he lets his mask slip from its place more and more often. Whether it's intentional or not, I'm not sure.

His face remains stoic as he stares forward, but I can see the calm in his eyes, the utter peace he feels being here. His arms hang limply by his sides and for some unknown reason, I slide my hand over his and interlock our fingers. He glances over to me in question, but I quickly turn my head from him and stare back out at the flowers.

I don't want to explain myself, or even utter a word. I feel like the sound of our voices will shatter this blanket of peace that has come over the both of us and I don't want that.

We stand, hand in hand, neither of us moving or speaking a word. Just the sound of our light breathing floating into the air. After a long while, Vincent uses his grip on my hand in his to pull me to him. I fall against his chest and he brings his hand to my neck where the cut is. He runs his finger over the raised edges before glancing up at me. The look in his eyes gives me pause and my heart stutters inside of my chest from the intensity of his gaze.

I mentally beg and plead with myself to look away, to move my hand from his, to do literally *anything*, but it doesn't work. I'm frozen in the magnetic pull of his gaze. His deep, chocolate brown eyes have me feeling like I'm fucking drowning the longer our eyes remain locked. He leans his head down, moving closer to my own.

Keeping his eyes open, he brushes his lips lightly against mine. My heart stutters painfully at the intimacy of such a feather light kiss, but it's enough to pull me from my daze.

I rip my eyes from his and take a step back, breaking the trance we had fallen in. My heart pounds against my ribs and my stomach twists into knots. The all too familiar feeling of guilt settles into the pit of my stomach and I suddenly feel queasy.

I attempt to wretch my hand from his, but he tightens his grip, refusing to let me go.

"I need to head back to the house, Vin. I don't feel so good." I peek up at him and see he's guarding me with an intense gaze.

"Why?" he questions warily.

"I don't know. Maybe because you wouldn't let me eat before we went traipsing through the woods and now I'm even more hungry than before." I shrug my shoulders, but I'm sure he can hear the sarcasm in my words.

Generally, my defense mechanism is to fight whenever I become uncomfortable or my self-loathing comes to the forefront of my mind, but I don't feel like fighting with him. My guilt is already bad enough and I don't want to add to it.

Vincent clears his throat before slowly pulling his hand from mine. "Yeah, okay." He mumbles before turning around and making his way to the house. I try to be annoyed with him and his sudden change in demeanor but I can't. I know his sudden mood shift is because of my abruptness to leave his patch of paradise, but I need to get out of here and away from him.

I'm fucking suffocating.

I can roll with a lot of shit life throws my way. In fact, I can take the fucking punches and even throw some back. But dealing with his kindness is one thing I can't handle. Hell and misery are all I have ever known and the fact he's now showing me kindness and a side to him I can guarantee not many have seen before—if any—it scares the hell out of me. I don't know how to deal or even process it.

Holley is the only one to ever show me love and kindness. She is all I have ever known. And now a different side of Vincent is coming out? A side which is the complete opposite of the one I've come to know?

Yeah. *I need to get the fuck out of here.*

CHAPTER TWENTY-FOUR
ESSA

Once we're back at the house, Vincent heads straight to his room and slams the door behind him, the sound reverberating through the house. Sighing, I pull my Converse from my feet and place them side by side next to the door. I pull my long sleeves up my arms before glancing down and then immediately covering them back up.

Some days I'm okay with my scars, and some I'm not. Today just happens to be a day where I'm not.

I make my way into the kitchen to find something to eat when my phone vibrates in my pocket, startling me. I reach my hand into my jeans to pull it out and freeze when I see the name on the screen. I look right to the stairs to see if Vincent has decided to come back down, but he's nowhere to be seen, so I flip the phone open and hit the answer key.

Pushing the phone to my ear, I whisper, "Give me a sec," as I dash to the front door and dart outside, closing it behind me as quietly as I can. I turn and face the house. I keep my gaze locked on the staircase I can thankfully see clearly through the glass walls that make the house. My heart pounds and the sound of blood rushes through my ears. A "Hello" sounds through my ear and it's enough for me to relax some. My shoulders lower slightly and I'm able to take a much needed deep breath before answering.

"Hey, sorry. I'm here," I whisper, just in case.

"It's okay, Ess, I understand you have to be careful. I know you said not to call, but I needed to let you know I'll be there in a few hours."

"What the fuck do you mean you'll be here in a few hours? I thought it would be a few days?" I trip over my own words as my brain kicks into overdrive. Anxiety creeps up my spine and my heart rate spikes. It's too fucking soon, I'm not ready.

"Yeah, well, I caught an earlier flight. I need to be there for you, Essa. But it's going to be okay. Once I land, I'm picking up a rental car and then I'll be headed your way. I'll wait until after dark so it will be easier for you to escape, okay? Just call me when he goes to bed and I'll be there."

I don't utter a word the entire time she talks about the plan.

I'm fucking panicking.

I can't do this.

I can't.

"Essa." That single word breaks my trance.

"Yes, I'm here." I spit out, my words labored with my heavy breathing.

"Calm down. You're okay. I'm here and we will get you out. We've been through worse, remember?"

Her comment about our childhood sobers me up enough for the fog to clear. Shaking my head, I clear my throat and stare forward. He's still upstairs, but I need to cut this call short.

"Yes, you're right. *Text* me when you've landed and we'll figure everything out from there." I emphasize for her to text me because I cannot handle the stress of another phone call while Vincent's awake.

"Yes, Essa. Oh, I've got to go, my plane is boarding. I'll see you soon. I love you."

"I love you too, bye." I hang up and shove my phone back in my pocket before going back inside. I'm not even hungry anymore after the phone call, my stomach too queasy, so I avoid the kitchen and head to the game room.

I find myself gravitating to the many books he has, so I randomly pull one from the shelf. I glance down at the title and it reads, *A Clockwork Orange*. The book itself is black with a mouth and flames above that, but the cover is interesting enough I keep it in my hand and move to the same chair Vin sat in as I danced for him.

I've never been much of a reader, but I'm hoping it might help to relax me and in turn, calm my nerves a bit. Besides, I *really* don't want to go upstairs to grab my iPod because Vincent's up there and I do not need to be around him right now. My poker face is shit unlike his and I can't fuck this up.

I open the book and skim through the first few pages, already bored but I decide to stick with it. I read for a little while before my stomach rumbles.

I guess reading relaxed me enough to become hungry again.

I jump up from the chair and return it to its rightful spot on the shelf before going to find something to satiate my hunger.

I shuffle around the kitchen, finishing the last few things before dinner and then set the table. On the table, there is a roasted chicken with vegetables and a side salad. Nothing fancy, but a meal, nonetheless.

With the last finishing touches in place, I drag myself up the stairs to Vincent's room. He played a "Me" today and locked himself in there. Once I reach his door, I lift my hand and get ready to knock when I hear the music he has playing through the speakers in his room.

"Crazy" by From Ashes To New is playing and I hesitate. I know this song by heart from having listened to it a million times, but the fact that this is the song he's listening to only intensifies the guilt I feel.

Taking a deep breath, I rasp my knuckles on the door three times and take a step back as I wait for him to answer. After a few seconds, I hear the music pause and then the door swings open. Vincent stands on the threshold with his hand still wrapped around the doorknob. I look to his hand and see his knuckles are white with the intensity of his grip and I take an involuntary step back.

"I—" I clear my throat and steel my spine. "I came to tell you I made dinner and it's done if you would like some." I put on the best fucking poker face of my life and hope it pays off. He remains impassive as he stares at me, his eyes completely blank, not giving anything away.

The fucking mask is back. Why the hell does it bother me so much?

We stare at each other before his eyes dip down my body. His gaze travels over me before moving back up to my face and my eyes do the same.

He's shirtless and his golden, tattooed abs glisten with sweat as if he was just working out. I don't remember seeing any exercise equipment in his room, but it doesn't mean he wasn't doing exercises without any, I guess. His athletic shorts hang low on his hips and his feet are bare. The man is a fucking sex god and damn me if my pussy doesn't know it.

I push my thighs together as subtly as I can before allowing my eyes to crawl back up to his face. He quirks his brow at me in silent questioning, but I ignore it.

"Are you coming down for dinner or...?" I ask, again.

"Yeah. Be down in a minute." He steps back and slams the door in my face. I roll my eyes and go downstairs to wait for him.

Dinner is silent and mostly awkward with Vincent not saying a word and my anxiety not allowing me to. The closer it gets to nightfall, the more anxious I become, and my body is beginning to exude that.

My leg jitters up and down under the table when all of a sudden, his hand shoots out to still my movements. My eyes fly to Vincent's as a meek smile graces my lips.

"Wanna tell me what the fuck's got you so jittery?" he asks, but I can tell it's a demand. I ponder my answer for a minute before deciding on giving him a half—truth so I'm not completely lying through my teeth.

"Just anxious."

"About?" He deadpans.

"You." I spit out before shoving a bite of chicken into my mouth before I blurt anything else out. His eyebrows draw together in confusion as he tries to figure out what I mean.

"Care to explain?"

"Not really. I'm sure you can guess," I quip before shoving more food in my mouth.

And that's the last of the conversation. We both finish our plates and work in tandem cleaning the kitchen up before moving up to our rooms for the night.

Not uttering a single word the entire time.

CHAPTER TWENTY-FIVE

ESSA

Buzz, buzz. Buzz, buzz.

My phone buzzes in the bed beside me and my heart leaps from my chest.

Fuck, fuck, fuck.

Okay, calm down. You can do this.

I sit up in bed and swing my legs over the edge as I flip open my phone to read the text.

On my way. The GPS says the ETA is in thirty minutes. See you soon.

My hands and legs shake as I stand and move to the chair in the corner of my room to grab my packed bag. I didn't pack much, only a few days' worth of clothes, but it's enough for now. I reach behind my headboard and grab the copied papers, shoving those inside of my bag along with my iPod and my phone. I don't have my fucking knife anymore. I don't know where Vincent ever put it after he took it away from me and I wish now more than ever I had it.

But it's too late now.

I swing my bag over my shoulder and walk to the glass, staring up at the moon and stars as they shine bright in the clear sky.

All right stars. I know I said I would never wish upon you again, but here I am, ten years later, fucking wishing.

I need this to work. I need to be free and I need your fucking help to do it.

Help me finally be free.

I take a deep breath and turn away, something like hope blossoming in my chest.

As I exit my room, I shut the door softly behind me, but then I move to Vincent's door and stop. My brain screams at me to keep going, to get the fuck out of here, but I don't listen. I fight my self-preservation as I carefully drop my bag next to me and pop open his door with a soft creak. I step inside and close it behind me.

He's sleeping on his back, and his left arm is curled up above his head and his right lies against his side. The black silky blanket rests low across his waist, leaving nothing to the imagination. His naked chest and abdomen are on full display as are his defined hips. I lick my lips and fight the urge to run my tongue along every fucking crevice of his body one last time.

I don't know what the actual fuck is wrong with me, but I move to the dresser that I know has handcuffs in it and slowly drag it open and, *thank god*, find two pairs right on top. I strip myself of the sweatpants I'm wearing so I'm in only my underwear from the waist down and move behind his head. As carefully as I can, I clasp the handcuff around his left wrist and then to the metal bar of the bed frame.

A deep breath leaves me when he doesn't wake from the sound and I move to put the other on his right when something catches my eye. I move closer to the nightstand closest to him and see the metal of a gun glint in the moonlight.

The very same fucking gun I tried to shoot him with.

Fuck, that was not a good night. I lost my damn mind.

I pick it up and turn it around in my hand. It feels heavier than it did last time and I wonder if it's because it's actually loaded this time. I set it down on the opposite end of the bed from Vincent and then crawl up to his right side.

I grab his arm and ever so slowly pull it up until it's above his head like his left. I close the cuff around his wrist and then the bed frame.

There. He's finally the one fucking trapped for once.

I haven't the slightest fucking clue as to what I'm doing. This was never part of the plan. But now he's trapped, I know what I want.

I want him one last time, but where I'm the one in control.

I drag the blanket off of him and crawl on top of him. I wiggle my hips a few times and his cock begins to harden beneath me. Though my pussy is still covered by my panties, I can still feel every ridge of his cock against me as I move on top of him. I fight a moan as I begin to rock my hips back and forth a few times, working us both up.

Though Vin's still asleep, he begins shifting his hips slightly with my movement and his cock throbs beneath me. It's not long before we're moving in tandem and my panties are soaked with my arousal. Vincent's eyes spring open and immediately land on me. He goes to move his arms, but when they clank with the sound of the cuffs on the bars, he jerks his head up to where the noise is coming from. He swings his face back over and gapes at me.

"Looks like I'm the one who has you trapped for once." I grin as I continue to rock my hips.

"Essa," he spits out through clenched teeth. "Let. Me. Go."

"No." I watch as he clenches his fists and yanks against the cuffs.

"You know that doesn't work, Vin," I say breathlessly as I rock my hips harder against him and he growls but keeps moving with me—almost like he can't help himself.

I know the feeling.

I can't take it anymore. I get up on my knees which rest on either side of him and push my underwear to the side. I grab a hold of his cock and line it up with my entrance.

My slickness makes it easy for him to slide inside of me as I sink down. A breathy moan escapes my lips once I'm fully seated on top of him. My eyes close from the pleasure but I force them open. Vin's eyes are locked on the junction of us. Hypnotized by his rapt stare, I swivel my hips and he groans while rocking his hips up. The force of his thrust is enough to bounce me up and I cry out when I come crashing back down.

Fuck, even when I'm on top and he's fucking bound to the bed, he still manages to fucking control me.

I grind on his dick as he moves with me. His stare never leaves my face and I have to close my eyes to avoid the intensity of it. His anger and arousal are so potent, I feel it radiating between the two of us. I place my palms on his chest to steady myself as I rock against him. It's not long before the need to come blasts through me and we both shout in unison as we reach our release at the same time. I pant as I slowly work us down before stopping all together. I rest my head against his chest and his arms clank as the handcuffs move against the metal.

"Let me go now, Essa." Vincent's cold words bring me down from the high I didn't even fucking get to enjoy.

"No," I refute as I climb off of him. His release slips from me and slides down my inner thighs, but I leave it as I pull my panties back into place and yank my sweats back on.

"Essa fucking Jaymes. Get the fuck over here and uncuff me, *now!*" he roars. His body visible shakes with his anger and sweat glistens across his skin from our fucking. His cock lays across his abs, still semi-hard. I lick my lips and move my gaze up his body, memorizing every fucking inch because I know this will be the last time I see it and as much as I want to be free of him—of everyone—I know some small, miniscule part of myself will miss this, *and him.*

My hand absently traces the wound on my neck as it begins to throb and the pain is like a punch in the fucking face, snapping me from my reverie. I don't need to miss him and I don't need to feel guilty for this.

He fucking hurt me.

He deserves to fucking hurt for once.

This needs to end.

My mind is consumed in a swirl of chaos as I move to the other side of the bed and pick up the gun I placed there. Once Vincent sees what is in my hands, he visibly pales. I have no clue what I'm doing as I round his side of the bed, gun in hand.

"Essa." He speaks in a low tone. "Put the fucking gun down."

"Now why the fuck would I do that, Vincent?" I shout as I wave the thing around.

I've really lost my fucking mind.

Nothing feels real.

Thousands upon thousands of memories race through my head, confusing me. I have no clue as to which way is up, down, left, or right. They fog over my vision and I feel like I'm spinning in circles, desperate to escape their hold.

Flashbacks of Ben raping me.

My mother ignoring me.

Always being fucking hungry.

Cutting myself to fucking survive, then attempting to end it all.

Holley leaving me.

Vincent butchering me like a fucking pig.

And the fucking worst of all.

Vincent pretending to care.

I let out a blood curdling scream and fall to the floor in a heap as they all devour me.

A sound rings out, blasting my eardrums and I scream.

CHAPTER TWENTY-SIX
VINCENT

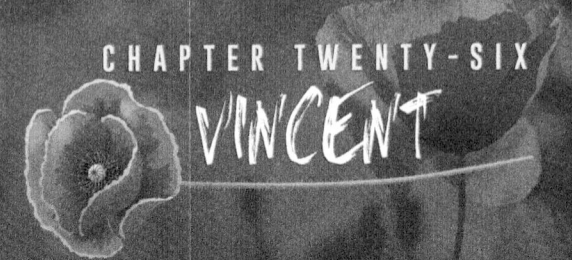

I cough a few times and as I bring my right hand to my mouth to wipe the spittle away, it comes back red.

Well fuck. That's not good.

I moan as I make an effort to sit up, but white hot fire shoots through my right shoulder. My left arm is still handcuffed to the bed, but Essa undid my right before she fucking *left*.

How the fuck did this happen? I search through my most recent memories, but nothing grabs at me. All I can remember is her screaming and the gun going off. Fire ripped through my shoulder and then when I looked to where Essa was, she was lying on the floor with the gun at her side.

She fucking passed out after *she* shot *me!*

I gritted my teeth as I lay there, waiting for her dumbass to wake up and come to her senses because although she fucking shot me, she was gonna get what was coming to her. Revenge already on my mind.

As I watched her breathing through the pain, her phone began buzzing in her pocket and after it buzzed off and on for a few minutes, she finally woke up and groggily took the call. But apparently whoever was on the other end said something to kick her ass in gear because she jumped up and began moving around but then started screaming when she saw I was shot.

The little bitch can shoot me but then have the audacity to freak the fuck out. How does that make sense?

I scoff, but the movement jostles me and I groan. After a few minutes, she steadied her breathing and grabbed the cuff key off of my dresser and then cautiously walked up to me and undid my right handcuff, letting my arm flop to my side. After a whispered I'm sorry and a kiss on my cheek, with tears in her eyes, she fled the room and out of the house.

Out of my fucking life.

I lean heavily on my left side to help relieve some of the pressure on my right. The pain coursing through me is enough to keep me alert, but every minute that passes by with no hope of getting myself free, the harder it becomes to stay awake.

Black dots distort my vision and my breathing becomes labored as blood slips from between my lips and down my chin. I lick my lips in a pitiful effort to clear the blood, but even more blood begins to spill out of my mouth. Coughs wrack through me as every breath becomes more and more strained. I struggle to breathe, and to even remain upright. My eyes sink closed in utter exhaustion as everything becomes too much.

I'll simply close my eyes for a minute as I think of a way to get out.

MARIE ANN

I hold on to every ounce of anger I have inside of me as everything finally goes agonizingly black.

CHAPTER TWENTY-SEVEN
ESSA

Holley and I are driving down the interstate and she remains quiet as I sit here trying to process everything that happened. My hands still shake even though we left a couple hours ago. Memories of his bloodied torso will haunt me for the rest of my life and I know I will forever feel this crippling amount of guilt.

I still can't believe I shot him. I didn't mean to, but I lost my damn mind and everything consuming me became too much and…

But I had to get out of there. I couldn't remain someone's prisoner for the rest of my life because it would've been forever.

I'm free.

I'm finally fucking free.

I can have a new life and start the fuck over, just me and Holley like I always dreamed of.

I repeat those words over and over again in my head like a mantra, hoping the more I repeat them, the better I'll feel. So far, it's not working.

"Wish You Were Here" by Pink Floyd begins to play on the radio and Holley reaches over to the volume knob and turns it all of the way up without saying a word. She knows me so fucking well sometimes.

Not being around her these last few months made me realize how much I miss her presence and how truly happy she makes me. Even though I feel like shit right now, I know I'll be okay as long as I have her by my side.

We've been through hell and back together. We fucking *lived* in hell.

We can survive Vincent fucking Anthony.

I twist my fingers in my lap as my leg bounces to the slow rhythm of the song. I close my eyes and lean my head against the window as I stare out into the dark night. I let the lyrics flow through me and tears trail down my face, but this time, I don't even try to wipe them away. I feel the music and let myself feel the pain.

All of it.

I fucking let it in.

And once the song is over, I bottle all of that shit back inside and wipe the tears from my face, attempting to pull myself together even though I know I'm a fucking mess. Holley turns the radio down and slightly turns her body to me, but keeps her eyes on the road.

"Essa. You don't need to pretend to be anything around me. You know that, right? I'm *here,* for you. I always have been and I always will be." She flicks her eyes over to mine quickly. I shrug and push her comment off. She has no idea how pathetic I am. How strong I'm really not.

"Don't fucking shrug at me, Essa Jaymes. I'm serious. I know you think I don't know anything, and that's probably mostly true, but I do know you have always had it worse off than me. I know father treated you differently and mom straight up acted like you didn't exist.

"I know you always put me first and struggled so damn much just to give me everything you could. I fucking love you and I appreciate everything you have done more than you could ever know. But now it's time for me to help take care of you. It's time for you to lean on me. It's time for me to be the strong one."

I glance over to her and the light from the dash allows me to see her tears that are running down her face. She sniffles, but somehow remains strong. *She has become much stronger since leaving home and I envy her so much for it.*

"I mean it. It's time for you to tell me everything. Tell me what the fuck all of that was."

I cringe, but I know it's time.

I dragged her into this and it's time she knows the truth.

The truth about *everything*.

Sitting up from my slouched position in the seat, I adjust my seatbelt and turn my body to the left until I'm sitting sideways in the seat, with my gaze directly on her.

She keeps driving, continuously flicking her gaze my way every so often as I spill my fucking guts.

I tell her everything.

Starting from the very first night.

The night Ben ruined me and crushed my fucking soul. The very same soul Vincent seemed to find again, but now it's gone forever. Left by his side when I stepped out of his room and in its place remains the creep.

All I've ever been is a goddamn creep. Useless, worthless, utterly fucking alone. Then Vincent came into my life and *fucked me up*. I was his slave in every sense of the word, but now I realize it was with not only my body, but to the way he makes me feel.

He irrevocably demolished my very existence and my heart will forever have a Vincent sized stain.

I take a deep breath to gather any ounce of remaining strength I might have deep down inside of me, and continue to tell Holley everything.

I tell her about wishing on the stars.

I tell her about the drugs and all of the things I witnessed.

I tell her about the things I endured almost every night for the last ten years.

But then it's time to talk about Vincent and I clam up. It's still so new, so fucking *raw*, that it physically hurts me to talk about him. I dig my nails into my palm, giving myself a little bit of pain to keep focused and tell her some things about him, but not everything. I can't tell her everything.

I can't tell her how badly he hurt me and I can't tell her how much I loved it. I made sure my entire body was covered in sweatpants and a hoodie with my long hair split down the middle to cover my neck. It's the one thing I refuse to tell her. I don't tell her I cut myself or anything related to it. I just can't. I think a part of me knows she'll be ashamed of me, or fuck, even fucking judge me and I can't risk it.

By the time it takes me to spill every bullshit thing I can think to tell her, it's been well over an hour into our trip. She didn't utter a single word the entire time. She remained quiet and let me say everything I needed to. I think she knew if she were to speak and interrupt me, it would snap me out of my reverie and the conversation would have ended.

Suddenly she pulls off on an exit ramp and pulls into a McDonald's drive thru, which is luckily open at three in the morning. She grins over at me and rolls up to the order screen, ordering every single one of our favorites—her attempt at making me feel better.

After devouring our food, we jump back onto the interstate, heading east. The sky is still dark, but I know it's nearing dawn.

"Hey Holl, I have to ask. How the hell were you even able to come to begin with? I know I was asking a lot of you to come get me, but if I'm being honest, I didn't think it was even possible."

"One, I will always do everything I can to help you. And two, I have a really amazing boss. Ugh, seriously, Ess. He's the freaking best." She gushes over him and how amazing he is for the next two minutes straight, but she pauses when she notices me staring at her with a smirk on my face.

"What?" She draws the word out as her face begins to turn red.

"Oh my fucking god! You like him!" I squeal and her face turns a brilliant shade of red.

"Yes, I like him. We're actually kind of… dating," she blurts out and I jump back in my seat, shock written all over my face. My sister, my big sister, has a boyfriend and she's happy.

Guilt threatens to consume me again because I dragged her into this mess. I took her away from her life and brought her right back. She was free and I've gone and fucked it up.

"Essa, stop." Her voice has me swinging my head over to hers.

"Stop feeling guilty. I came because I love you and I want to help you anyway I can. Liam understood and helped me out. Please don't worry, it will all be okay. And you'll love him! He's so sweet and kind."

She goes on and on and I rest back in the seat as I watch her speak. It's nice to simply listen to her talk and I appreciate more than she could ever know how she rolled over all of the bullshit I spilled and is—for the most part—pretending like it never happened because she knows I need time to process everything. And I fucking love her more for it.

She gets passionate talking about Liam and I can tell she's falling in love with him. Her eyes light up whenever she talks about something he did or said and it makes me smile a real fucking smile. It feels weird on my face, but also like it's supposed to be there.

A sort of weight leaves my chest and I take a deep breath as I glance out of the window again. I stare up at the stars and then close my eyes.

Thank you stars.

Thank you for finally saving me.

CHAPTER TWENTY-EIGHT
Essa

Tires screech as a loud crash rings loudly in my ears. My eyes fly open from my slumber and instantly land on Holley. The rising sun shining through the window is enough to blind me, but I fight the urge to blink when I see her. The moment I do, I notice how pale she is.

Her body gets wrenched to the side and we begin to spin around and around. Then suddenly, we're moving in a different direction. One second, we're upside down, and the next, we're not. It all happens so fast, but in slow motion. I can see everything and nothing all at once.

My head smacks around from side to side, even as my seat belt holds me in place as best it can. I try to keep my eyes on Holley, but the glass being smashed out all around us forces me to close them.

Holley's screams pierce my eardrums and I attempt to reach for her in my blind state, but the car rolls one last time and jerks to a stop. I peel my eyes open, blinking a few times to clear the haze. It doesn't work that well, but enough to where I can tell we're both suspended upside down but Holley isn't moving and I can see blood dripping from her lips.

I try to scream for her, for someone to come help us, but all that comes out is a raspy whisper and my throat feels like it's being crushed.

Something's wrong. Something is so very, very wrong.

My heart pounds in my chest as I yank on my seatbelt, trying to move closer to her, to fucking help her but the fucking thing won't move and it doesn't help my vision is still fucking fuzzy.

I hang there for what feels like an eternity when, suddenly, a pair of hands are wrapping around me, attempting to calm my flailing limbs.

"Hey, hey, try to calm down. It's okay. You're going to be okay." I don't know where the voice is coming from, but it's okay. It's okay. Someone's here. Someone's going to save Holley.

"Pl—plea—please sa—save my sis—sister," I manage to spit out as my body begins to go limp.

No please. Stay awake! Fight this! Save Holley!

"Okay, let me go check on her."

The hands that were around me disappear and they don't come back for a while it feels like, but everything is so heavy. My eyes close as the familiar feel of nothing overcomes me, but I force them to stay open and right as I do, that's when I feel the strangers' hands again.

"H—how's Hol—Holley?" I rasp. My head swims, but I focus my eyes and they land on a face. Now that I can somewhat finally see him, he begins to cut my seatbelt with some sort of pocketknife.

"An—answer me." I focus on his face, forcing myself to stay awake. I need to know Holley's okay. His eyes tighten and a grim look covers his face, but he doesn't answer me.

"What's your name?" he asks me instead while still cutting away at the belt pushing against my torso.

"Essa Mon—Monroe. Wha—what's wrong wi—with Ho—Holley?" I ask again, desperation leaking into my tone even more. I need to know how she is, that she's okay because the need to drift off to sleep is beginning to overwhelm me and it doesn't help that all of my blood is rushing to my head from being upside down for so long.

"My name is Dominik Reed and I'm going to help you. You're going to be okay." He continues to saw away at my seatbelt, but the black cloud swarms and I need my answer.

"Is Holley okay?!" I scream with all of my might. My throat and chest scream in pain from the force I use and tears fall down my face as dread fills my body. The look on his face is one I never wanted to see. Not in a thousand lifetimes.

"I'm so sorry, Essa, but she didn't make it. I just have to focus on saving you now. I'm so sorry." Tears run down his face as he jerks his arm harder, almost through the seatbelt.

No.

No!

No!

HOLLEY.

Come back to me Holley!

Stars, bring her back to me! Bring her back to me! Bring her back to me!

This is the worst fucking nightmare of my life. I have never wanted to be awake so desperately.

MARIE ANN

I sob as I repeat those words over and over in my head like a mantra.

This is a nightmare, a horrific nightmare.

The stars will bring her back to me and everything will be okay.

My body hits metal as I drop from where my seatbelt had me trapped. My head smacks against something hard and then… nothing.

CREEP

ACKNOWLEDGEMENTS

    The first two people I have to thank are my husband and my son. Ray, you're my constant fucking savior. Through all of the bs I've put myself through writing this book, you've had my back and have talked me off of countless ledges. I will forever be grateful for you, baby. Creep wouldn't exist if it weren't for you always saving me. Then… and now. E, you may not know it, but you have given me insurmountable strength and you continue to inspire me to be the best version of myself—for you. I love you both, always and forever.

    Second, I want to thank all of you, my readers, for picking up this book and giving a new author a chance. I wouldn't be able to do this author thing if it wasn't for y'all and your support means the world to me!

    I want to thank my beta's; Rae and Vanessa. Y'all were lifesavers helping me last minute and your constant comments while reading through hyped me up and made me feel so damn confident in this story. I love you both.

My Creepers street team, I appreciate every single one of you and your continuous support! I met most of you when I was a bookstagrammer myself, so for y'all to support me while I make this author journey means more than you could ever know! Hopefully there will be a day when we can all meet, and if that day comes, drinks are on me ;)

Thank you from the bottom of my cold heart, Haley, for this amazing cover and stunning formatting. You swooped in and saved the day with your offer to do it for me, and let me just say—I will forever be obsessed. You made my vision come to life.

Amy, my bombass editor, thank you for taking a chance on me and dealing with the constant shenanigans—aka the "slight" time crunch. I was so nervous about putting this book out into the world, but through the editing process, you helped me realize my book isn't a huge pile of trash and for that, I will be forever grateful. You rock.

K, you were the first person to introduce me to the dark romance world with These Monstrous Ties and you blew my perception of romance the fuck up with the Unsainted world by making me fall irrevocably in love with utterly dark, twisted, and bloody romance. But not only that, you became such a close friend. You're honest and fucking real, something someone like me appreciates more than anything. You supporting me is what initially gave me the confidence to spit out my thoughts and put them to paper (metaphorically) and you taught me that it's okay to love what you love and I have nothing to be ashamed of. I love you, and I make it my life's mission to meet

CREEP

your beautiful ass one day and hug the hell out of you—and that means something 'cause I am definitely not a hugger haha.

Chelsea, Jess, Ramzi, Nyla, T. Bishop, Liza, V. Domino, RuNyx and all of the authors I met through this community. I feel like I have finally found my people and each and every one of you have made me feel so welcome. Just know y'all are phenomenal writers and you continue to inspire me every day.

Roxy, you are the first friend I ever made in this community and our friendship is what got me here. I flove you.

Last, but definitely not least, my pickle heads, my fucking soulmates. My Ghost face Smedium Pickle Goldfish Bitch and My Sweet and Spicy MF Pickle OnBrand Bitch—that was a damn mouthful haha. Y'all are the calm to my crazy and the crazy to my calm. I've never had friends that I felt this deep soul connection with and what better people to be the first to read my book baby. You gave me the confidence I needed to put Creep out into the world and I will forever be indebted to you both. You're continuously pushing me to be my best self with your support and honesty—even when I don't want to hear it. I love you both endlessly and ridiculously.

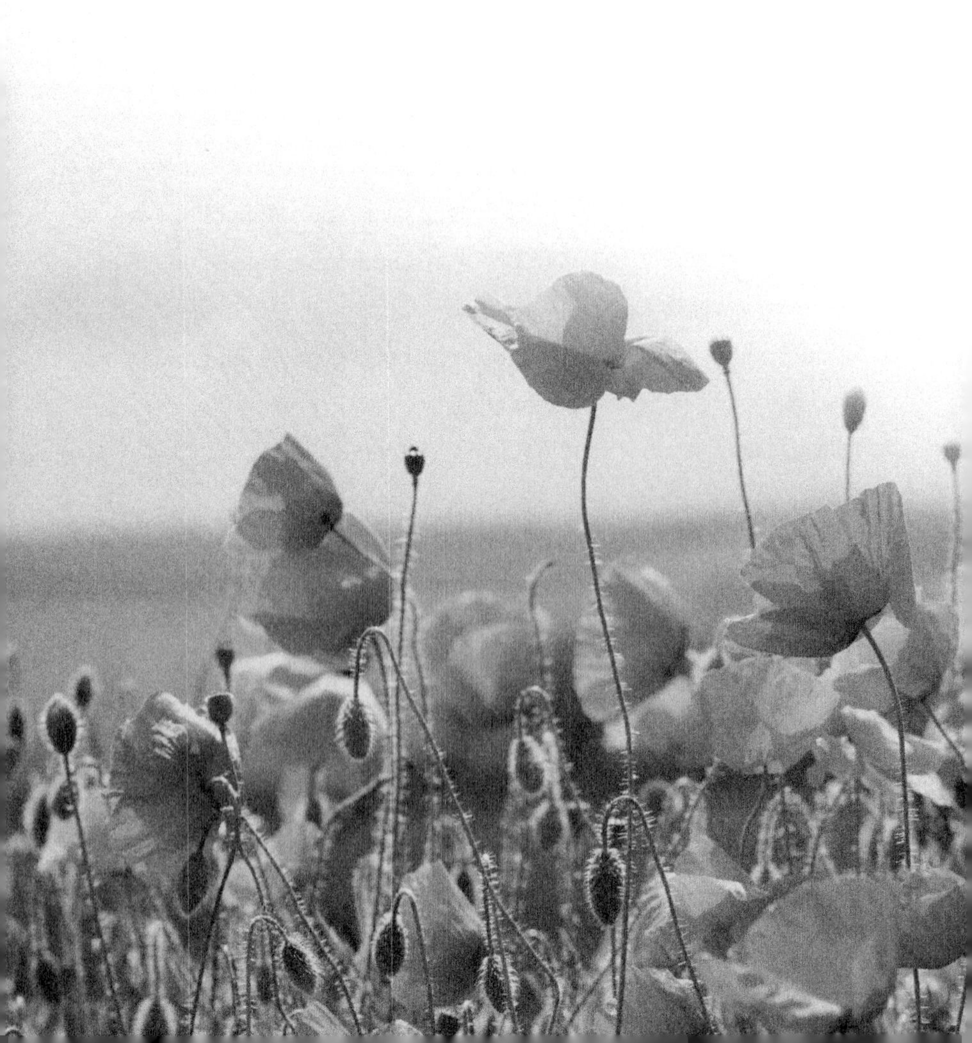

ABOUT THE AUTHOR

Marie Ann

Marie Ann is a dark romance author who has a weakness for writing toxic and damaged characters. She survives on astronomical amounts of coffee and sarcasm. She loves all things deemed creepy and odd-the more twisted and taboo, the better!

Creep is her debut novel.

MARIE ANN

Afterword

I know this story was, at times, difficult to read, but I'm glad you stuck through and made it to the end. Essa and Vin have a special place in my heart but their story is a disastrous one, to say the least.

I put my heart and soul into this book and even though this is a work of fiction, I put much of myself in Essa's character as a way to exercise my demons. This story is painful and utterly fucking brutal, but it's raw and honest because things like this—addiction, abuse, and self-harm are real life issues that we shouldn't shy away from just because they're painful. I am in no way romanticizing those things, but I am simply trying to make aware that romance—and life in general—is not always rainbows and butterflies. It's the hard parts too—especially the parts that make us uncomfortable.

With that said, I hope you got lost in the swirl of chaos that is this story.

I know I did.

MARIE ANN

Printed in Great Britain
by Amazon